presents

FLUSH FICTION

88 Short-Short Stories You Can Read
in a Single Sitting

D0824013

Compiled by the editors
of the Bathroom Readers' Institute

14/21

UNCLE JOHN'S BATHROOM READER®
FLUSH FICTION

"Bathroom Reader," "Portable Press," and "Bathroom Readers' Institute" are registered trademarks of Baker & Taylor. All rights reserved.

For information, write:
The Bathroom Readers' Institute, P.O. Box 1117,
Ashland, OR 97520
www.bathroomreader.com
email: mail@bathroomreader.com

ISBN-13: 978-1-60710-427-8 / ISBN-10: 1-60710-427-8

Library of Congress Cataloging-in-Publication Data
Uncle John's bathroom reader presents flush fiction.
p. cm.
ISBN 978-1-60710-427-8 (pbk.)
1. Short stories, American. 2. American fiction--21st century. I.
Bathroom Readers' Institute (Ashland, Or.) II. Title: Flush fiction.
PS648.S5U53 2012
813'.010806--dc23
2011051554

Cover design by Michael Brunsfeld, San Rafael, CA
(Brunsfeldo@comcast.net)

Printed in United States of America
First Printing

1 2 3 4 5   16 15 14 13 12

Thank You!

The Bathroom Readers' Institute sincerely thanks the people whose advice and assistance made this book possible.

Gordon Javna

Brian Boone

Amy Miller

Jay Newman

Sheila Hart

Claudia Bauer

Michael Brunsfeld

JoAnn Padget

Kim Griswell

Melinda Allman

Sydney Stanley

Cynthia Francisco

David Hoye

Jennifer Frederick

True Sims

Ginger Winters

Annie Lam

Tom Mustard

Monica Maestas

Lillian Nordland

Thomas Crapper

Contents

Let's Get Fictional!

Here at the Bathroom Readers' Institute, we usually make books about real-life: true stories about origins, strange events, and the crazy world around us. With *Flush Fiction,* we're taking a big leap: Make believe. Fiction. Stories that happened only in people's heads. (True story.)

In the last few years, "flash fiction" has grown into an exciting literary movement: super-short stories, all less than 1,000 words. We thought flash fiction would be a pretty great idea, perfect for those short, bathroom reading sessions. Except that, in keeping with our image, we decided to call it "flush fiction."

The stories may be fictional, but this is still an *Uncle John's* book, so that means that there's something for everyone here, and there's lots of humor and quirkiness. No matter what you like to read, you'll find something in *Flush Fiction,* be it mystery, nostalgia, monsters, romance, or science fiction. And of course, lots of quirkiness and humor. (Be warned though—there is the occasional naughty word. We didn't want to censor the writers.)

Anyway, we hope you enjoy these stories. They're short on words, but not on fun. Thanks for reading, and, as always…

Go with the flow!

—Uncle John and the BRI staff

What Is the Difference Between Optometrists and Ophthalmologists?

Eric Cline

Ophthalmologists are idiots, that's what!

Oh, I could say an optometrist measures for corrective lenses. I could say an ophthalmologist is a medical doctor.

But the real difference is: Ophthalmologists are fools, *pinheads*, JERKS, MOOOOORRRRRRONS!

I work in a strip mall in the same big parking lot as a professional building. I'm with the Westegg Optometry chain. But inside, I run the show. Me. Dr. Albert Pope, O.D.

My shop is between Chik-N-Rite and Pappasan's Japanese Pizza.

I had successfully avoided those who worked in the professional building. But one day, getting out of my car, I saw two roughnecks sauntering out of Chik-N-Rite carrying Rite-As-Rain meal-deal bags in their grubby paws. I had on my white smock with "Dr. Pope" stitched on the pocket. I tried to avoid eye contact. I knew they were trouble by their long white coats and stethoscopes.

They blocked my path.

"Weeellll, weeellll, whadda we got here?" That was Floyd J. Davis, M.D., M.Sc., F.A.A.O. He was in his late fifties, about fifteen years older than me.

His sidekick was Daniel Kupperman, M.D., Ph.D., F.A.A.O. He was about seventy and looked as though he had grown more evil every single year.

"You're that fancy-pants optometrist next to the chicken place," said Kupperman. Cruel eyes danced behind his thick glasses.

"Yes, Dr. Albert Pope," I said.

Quietly.

Looking at the ground.

"I run Westegg Optical, pleasetomeetyou..." My mumbled greetings were interrupted by their horse laughs.

"An op-*tom*-e-trist!" Davis sneered. "Well, Danny, you and I are oph-thal-mol-o-gists!" He made a meal of those words. "Optometrist. Ophthalmologist. They sound sooooo much alike. What could the difference *possibly* be?"

Stepping up to my face, Kupperman hissed, "Well, for starters, remember the p-h-t-h spelling, fat boy. It comes from *ophthalmos*, the ancient Greek for eye. And what does *optometrist* mean in Greek?"

"It's *opsis*, meaning sight, and *metron*, meaning measurement," I said.

"Nah! It means *chucklehead*! *Optometrist* is Greek for *chucklehead*! Say it!"

"OptometristisGreekforchucklehead..." I muttered fearfully.

Davis stepped up alongside his henchman. He breathed Chick-N-Rite Clucker's Choice Coffee fumes in my face. "And *we* went to medical school," he hissed. "Where did *you* go?

"I went to an accredited four-year school of optometry," I said. "Sir."

"Oooh, four years! You hear that, Danny?"

"I heard Floyd, I heard."

"We did four-year undergrad degrees in science, four years in medical school, three years in residency—"

"—*residency* means *training*, chucklehead!"

"—I got this, Floyd! Three years residency, and one to two years of fellowship. Fellowship is *more* training, chucklehead! *And* we take state boards *and* become Fellows of the American Academy of Ophthalmology." He pounded the F.A.A.O. on his white coat.

A wad of Davis's spit landed on my trembling face.

"And what does an *optometrist* do?" he said. "Aside from

pound sand twenty-four hours a day? Why, you go to school to learn," he switched to a high-pitched, lisping voice, "which lookth clearer, number three or number four? Number three? Okay, which lookth clearer now, number five or number thikth?" He twirled his left wrist limply.

Kupperman pushed me down into a mud puddle, soaking my trousers.

"I-I-I can diagnose glaucoma!" I wailed. I was interrupted by two hyena laughs. "And refer my patients to—"

"—a *real* doctor!" Davis hooted.

"Glaucoma, huh?" Kupperman said. "Hey, Floyd, when I was on ER duty yesterday, I took 17 pieces of glass out of some construction worker's eyes. But heck, what's that compared to diagnosing glaucoma?" He broke up laughing at his own "joke."

Davis pulled a Chick-N-Rite Chicka-Chicka-Cherry-Pie™ from his paper bag. He unwrapped it and dipped it in the mud.

"I think since chucklehead here is so hungry for knowledge, he needs some cherry pie, don't you, Danny?"

"Yeah! Yeah! Make 'im eat it!"

I protested feebly as the filthy, sodium-rich dessert was mashed into my face.

It was woman troubles that led to their downfall: some tramp Davis was having a fling with.

She would hang around with them in the parking lot, passing a paper bag filled with hooch back and forth, listening to Puccini blaring from Kupperman's parked Volvo.

She was the chief budget officer for the county government: typical trash you get in your neighborhood when an ophthalmic practice moves in.

It turned out Davis was seeing some museum curator on the side. When the budget babe heard about it, there was a big fight in the parking lot. I watched from my shop doorway.

She screamed at him, saying he had a two-inch...er...

13

endowment and that he'd gone to a state medical school instead of an Ivy League institution; the usual street insults.

Kupperman, alongside Davis, said, "You need to calm your little CPA self down, missy!"

That sent her over the edge. She clawed at both their faces, succeeding in knocking their glasses off. She stomped their spectacles to pieces in her rage. Then she left in a huff.

Davis and Kupperman looked down at their mangled glasses, glinting in the late-morning sun. Then, slowly, they turned their heads to look at me.

I stood up straight.

I folded my arms.

I waited.

Squinting heavily, they slowly walked up to me. Their faces were filled with dread. When they got to within a few feet of me, they paused.

I stood aside and made a flourish with my arm, bidding them to enter.

They walked into my shop, their eyes cast down.

"Boys?"

They stopped in their tracks.

"You asked once what the difference was between an optometrist and an ophthalmologist?"

They waited, scarcely breathing.

"The difference is, an optometrist...has a heart!" ©

The Old Man Had to Pee

Corey Mertes

The old man with one arm sat at the end of the hotel bar and ordered another drink.

"Another beer," he muttered.

"Another?" the bartender asked, before bringing the man his twenty-third.

The man had been sitting on the stool without moving for twelve hours and was turning the color of Strega. He liked Strega. He liked it a hell of a lot. The man's tastes were not typical. He liked Strega and grappa and mescal, and he liked the smell of bull under the hot sun of an open arena. He liked a lot of things. But not beer. Today he had to drink twenty-five beers without moving from his stool to satisfy a bet he'd lost to the one-armed face-punching champion of San Baques. It was a damn stupid bet.

The old man ordered a plate of *nachos,* a Mexican soup, and a well-cleaned plaice. *Nachos* were what the Spanish ordered when they wanted chips they could put cheese on. He liked them. He liked them a hell of a lot. He liked things you could put cheese on and forget about. You couldn't put cheese on beer without messing up the head.

"Another beer," he murmured.

I must finish two more beers without bursting, the man thought. He remembered past bets worse than this one he had made with other people under different circumstances in distant places at other times. Once on the Place au Coin de la Rue he had lost a three-legged race to an obelisk maker. He made the biggest obelisks the old man had ever seen, and God knows he'd seen some big ones in Florence!

Another time, to satisfy a debt, he'd fought a dingo at night in the outback west of Brisbane with Aborigines watching. That's how he lost his arm. Earlier, during the war, when the shooting had stopped and the others lay dead, he'd bet he could carry a grenade in his mouth across a magnetic minefield. Those were better times. Five more yards and he would still have teeth.

"Another beer," he mumbled.

Later came the cliff diving and the sequoia-cutting contest, the ouzo tournament, and the sperm-whale hunts. Then he had to leave the good old country, but it was good. He'd had enough. Now he would finish his twenty-fifth beer and prove he was not a *gynomoco* again. He did not want that. The old man wanted to be one of the *machos*. *Macho* was what the Spaniards called a man with *cavalero*, which was a quality that showed he embraced the philosophy of *existico*. *Existico* was what a man believed in when he didn't take any *guanola* from another man, which is what the other man gave when he had *bigabalsas*. When a man had *bigabalsas* the Spaniards said he could untie the knot of destiny with his teeth, if he had any, and raise the toast of *piswata* with his good arm. Piswata was what the machos drank, and he would have a *piswata* himself, he thought, if he ever finished his fish and his soup and his last true good best true damn beer.

But he could not finish. Instead, he rushed to the men's room a moment late, ruining along the way the meals of the nearest diners with a trailing stream and flatulent stench of *nachos*, *macho*, and gazpacho.

"My, my," the bartender said. "Isn't it a pity to drink so." Then he mopped. ◎

Safety Drill

M. Garrett Bauman

Dad was a safety maniac. He was convinced disaster had us in its crosshairs. By the time we were six, he'd taught us that pinworms, ringworm, and tapeworms devour people. During thunderstorms, he'd describe how lightning blasts the roofs off houses. At supper we heard tales of deadly flu, TB, rickets, hemorrhoids, cancer, blindness, and accidents that would leave us amputated, blind, deaf, and drooling.

As a child I ran out the door to avoid a loose slate falling from the roof and decapitating me, and I ran past alleys in case a rabid dog lurked there. Dad lectured us about puncturing our eardrums when cleaning our ears, about becoming "impacted" if we didn't eat spinach, and about being hit in the head while playing baseball and becoming brain-dead.

So by age nine, I wished he cared a little less. The holidays, especially, seemed to bring him to an even higher state of alert. One Christmas, Dad brought home the usual scrawny New Jersey pine tree and Dad, Mom, my little brother Stevie, and I decorated it with bulbs, balls, and tinsel until the holes were disguised and it sparkled with warmth and joy.

"It looks so pretty!" Mom said.

Dad nodded. "But we have to make sure it's watered every day and the lights don't stay on too long."

"I know," Mom sighed. "I'm not one of the children."

"Why can't we leave it on all day, Dad?" I said. Geez, we get something beautiful, and five minutes later he wants to turn it off.

"You want to know why? I'll tell you why. Come here."

He pulled me to the tree, and I knew I shouldn't have asked. "Here. Touch this bulb." As I reached my finger out, he barked, "Carefully!" I tapped my forefinger on the hot bulb. "Aha!" he crowed. "Think of it! All that heat—a hundred bulbs pressed against ten thousand dry pine needles. One needle's just a little too dry or one bulb a tad too hot, the heat builds up. Hour after hour. Hotter and hotter. The needles smoke. Then—poof!" He clapped his hands so I jumped out of my skin and seemed to fly around the ceiling. Dad's face shone with horrified exhilaration. "The whole tree goes up. Tree resin is like gasoline! A giant ball of fire. Flames licking the ceiling. The whole house will be gone in minutes."

"Shouldn't we turn it off?"

"Not yet. I'll keep an eye on it." Then he whispered to me, "When I'm at work, you remind your mother to water it to keep it moist. Can you do that?"

"Suppose it catches fire when we're not looking?"

Dad was pleased that I saw the danger. "You're right! You're one hundred percent right! That's why we're going to have a family fire drill! Right now. We need an emergency escape plan. Our lives are at stake! Stairway here. Hmm...windows." His mind clicked. Finally he nodded. "Come on, Stevie. Dot too. We'll go upstairs to our bedrooms and pretend there's a big fire down here."

I was excited. I loved escapes. Dad's stories were horrible, but there was always a way out.

Mom sighed. "I have supper to start. There's—"

"No, no, come on. We have to think this out before an emergency happens. Suppose the stove catches on fire?"

"I'd turn it off?" Mom suggested, as he shooed us upstairs.

"Now," Dad said, "When I yell 'Fire!' we'll see if you boys can open your bedroom window to crawl out on the porch roof,

OK?"

I said, "Why don't we just run downstairs?"

Dad stared at me like I was an idiot. "Because the hallway will be a sheet of flames. The stairs will be crackling like the pit of hell, and when you step on them, they'll collapse and you'll fall into the basement. Burning wood will cover you and sizzle you like a pork rind. That's why!"

When I could breathe again, I gasped, "How will you and Mom get out?"

Dad held up a forefinger. "We go out the window to the porch from our bedroom. See? We'll meet out there and all climb down the wrought-iron porch posts." Climb down the porch posts? Wow! This was great! Just like commandos or burglars. At the word "Fire," I'd be out there like a weasel. Mom wasn't happy. She didn't figure to be a good climber.

Dad said, "That's the four of us. Now we have to figure out how to evacuate your Grandma." As he mulled this over, I could see his problem. Her bedroom was on the other side of the hallway—no porch roof there. And she had that bad leg. I pictured her stumping away from the flames, moaning and throwing up her hands. I could tell everybody else was thinking like me. Stevie began to cry. "Gramma's gonna burn up!" he wailed.

Dad, ever resourceful, said, "Why, we'll carry her out!" He clapped my shoulder. "You and me, son. The men will do it!"

Right, I thought. We'll dash through the flames of hell in the hallway, lift fat Grandma from bed screaming and fainting, and stagger back through the flames to my bedroom, then shove her out the window onto the snowy roof and make her and Mom climb down the ironwork. Whew! This was unexpected. Dad never did anything so daring. I was ready to give it a try, although I was pretty certain if Mom didn't object to the rehearsal, Grandma sure would. She'd whack me with her cane if I ever tried to shove her onto the roof.

"OK," I said, "Let's go!" I unlatched my window, shoved it up, and started to crawl out.

"What are you doing?" Dad grabbed me by my belt and yanked me back.

"Sorry. I forgot to wait for your signal."

"Are you crazy?" he said. "There's ice out there. You'll slip and break your neck!" ◉

And Then

Joe Novara

"E poi?" Seems like that's all I ever say: and then, and then, and then.

"Un chilo di sanguine."

Reach and grab.

Throw the produce on the scale.

Add it up.

"E poi?"

Take the money.

Next.

I can do this in my sleep. I do do it in my sleep. So boring. But I can't help looking, checking eyes all the time. Take that lady, third in line. Always comes to my side of the stand when we set up on Tuesday and Saturday. Always the sly smile when I drop the change in her right hand, the one without all the rings. Got so many on her left hand—hope she takes them off in bed. She'd give her husband a concussion if she rolled over and whacked him. Would serve him right, so unsure of himself that he has to load enough gold on her hand to give her carpal tunnel or something. Still…she smiles at me. Maybe the rings are meant to remind her. "E poi, signora?"

Nice legs, the little I can see when she struts away. But, just another customer…I hope.

You get to recognize some of them from each day's market. Monday, Piazza Garibaldi. The old lady with the football-shaped pooch. Looks like he's going to roll over when he lifts his leg on one of our stands. After all these years, he's probably baptized every single table leg. Then she only buys rucola. One bunch.

And Wednesday, at the Indepedenza, there's the zucchini guy—two kilo a pop. What can he do with all that zucchini, even in a whole week? I swear he looks a little green around the ears. Is he eyeing me, or is it my imagination?

I smile. I wink. Pretend to know them. They're all just hands, money, and an open bag...like baby birds screeching for me to drop food into their gaping mouths. Or are they?

Look at my boss, Renzo, eyes moving all the time. Hands and eyes. Shouting in his booming voice, "Un regalo! Due mango per sei euro!" Some gift. We normally sell them at two euros each. But this is his life, learned from his father. He can't stop. If we grab a grappa after the truck is packed and everything is ready for tomorrow, even then he can't just be still. He keeps scanning the bar, talking in short sentences, like a machine gunner spitting bullets, shouting at everyone who walks in. Is that what I'll be like after thirty years of humping artichokes and onions and pears from square to square around the city? Can't sit still. Don't know how to relax. I'm getting that way after just a year and it's not from hawking zucchini.

They asked where I wanted to go after I fingered the shooter. South Dakota? Alberta? I grew up hearing Neapolitan. I could speak a little Italian. Why not hide in plain sight? In a busy Italian city? In for a nickel, in for a dime...I said how about being a street vendor who moves around town? Really keep it loose.

So they hooked me up with Renzo. I throw around a little slang. Got just enough Italian to sound like I never finished grade school, and I fit right in. But I can't stop looking. Not like Renzo, looking for customers, for someone snatching a pear. Me, I'm checking out the eyes that hold a fraction longer than necessary, the someone I notice more than once, cutting me a glance. Gotta watch...all the time. Make sure I don't see the same face, especially on different days at different market sites.

Here comes that strange American-looking guy who puts his grandson in the grocery cart and then hand carries the food. I shouldn't have to worry about him tagging me. Not someone wearing a New York Yankees baseball hat and lugging a kid around. Where does he think he is? In New York? Some people just don't get the picture. But I like the way he takes his time. Very calm. Compares prices. When he comes here, he always gets our best buys. He's mellow. Probably old enough to be retired. That's what I want—just enough money to be comfortable, maybe grow my own vegetables and never have to see another fruit stand... watch eyes, faces.

Wait a minute. What is he doing here? This is Piazza Minitti. He's supposed to be at Porta Genova on Thursdays. He's staring at me. Pissed. Oh, man, here it comes.

What's he sputtering in broken Italian? Tangerines? The tangerines had seeds. Says I told him they were seedless. His kid almost choked on a seed. Yeah. Lighten up, man. I'll make it up to you. Stop making a scene. Everyone in the piazza is staring. Not good. Not good, buddy. You're drawing attention to me. Not what I need. I gotta distract him. Calm him down. Here. Here's a perfectly ripe mango I was saving for myself. This is for the kid, okay? I think the guy understands my Italian.

He looks down. No kid. We both stop. Do a quick scan. I call to Renzo, "Torno, subito," and then I hustle into the crowd killing two birds with one stone—getting away from the jerk and finding the kid.

After a minute, I spot the brat reaching for a strawberry. Spinning slowly I scan for the navy blue Yankee cap. I whistle. He turns. I point down.

We both start talking at the same time. "Hey, goddam, man, sorry about the tangerines. I messed up yesterday..." Down on his knees, gramps is hugging the toddler, going, "Gott im Himmel, Heinrich du nicht fär..." Then we both stop in mid sentence, stare at each other. I'm thinking, you're not American. He must realize that I'm not really Italian. I watch first surprise, then fear, and finally something like pleading play across his face. He must be in the game some kind of way, too—spook, undercover, on the lam? What is he asking me? Don't blow my cover?

He rises slowly, does a palm-down slicing motion. I nod, barely. He picks up the kid and walks away. We won't be seeing each other again. One less set of eyes to register.

A minute later I'm behind the barricade of asparagus and oranges and palms of bananas.

"Mezzo chilo di pere."

Grab. Weigh. "E poi?" @

Dead Man's Float

Sally Bellerose

Dad is playing dead, and I'm not in the mood for it. He's sprawled out on the La-Z-Boy, as usual. He lies with his head dangling to one side and his mouth open. His color is not too good to begin with, so it's pretty convincing. I'm on the couch knitting and watching *Oprah*.

"Cut it out, Dad." I poke his shin with the tip of my sneaker, not hard, but disrespectfully. Hey, he's playing dead and he's already been asked politely to knock it off twice.

Fortunately for my goal of knitting a few uninterrupted rows, the slightest grin crosses his lips. Otherwise I would have to get off the couch and check for pulse and breath. This is one of his better performances. His chest barely rises and, since I'm not responding to death, every once in a while he throws in a little twitch to demonstrate that he could be in the throes of something significant, but short of dead, like a heart attack or a stroke maybe. He's had several of each.

"You're not funny. How are you going to like it if you actually do kick the bucket and everyone just keeps knitting or reading the paper?" Actually, if I were in a better mood, I would think his stunt funny.

Sometimes I play dead myself. It's a good way to fall asleep. It's a family tradition that started on Haviland Pond, where Dad taught us to swim. The dead-man's float was lesson one. Are all kids taught the simple joy of lying in the water on their bellies, faces submerged, that other world gone for a minute, two minutes, then to let the air out the side of their mouths slowly and stretch it to three minutes, with practice close to four? Four minutes to straddle here and there. The object of the game to fool a nearby swimmer, preferably a sibling, into thinking we were gone for good, then to spring out of the water at the last possible second screaming and gasping for air. What could be funnier? Unless it was the thrill of being on the receiving end of the game, "finding" your sibling dead in the water, wading over to the corpse, touching the wet shoulder, that luscious horror of that short window of time when you've convinced yourself that maybe, just maybe, she was dead, and congratulated yourself for facing the dead body with such courage.

My sister Kathy stops by on her way to choir practice. She comes into the house without knocking. "Hi, Dad." She kisses the top of his head.

"He's dead," I say.

"That's too bad," she says. "I brought blueberry pie." She takes off her coat and puts a pastry box on an end table next to Dad. This makes his eyelids flicker and his mouth twitch. She straightens his head and gives me a dirty look. "He's going to get a crick in his neck."

"He's dead," I say. "And you're weird."

"She's knitting a scarf for a dead man," she whispers in his ear. "And she calls me weird."

His eyes pop open. "Boo," he says loud while her face is still an inch away.

"Dad!" she squeals, making his day.

His eyes dart to the pastry box. "Is it made with that crap?" He means Splenda, the sugar substitute.

"No," she says.

"Liar," I say. I've been sitting with a dead man all afternoon and my sister steals the "boo." ◉

The Taste of Failure

Andrew S. Williams

The Greatest Marvel of the Twenty-First Century sat on Raylen Kosta's plate between a half-eaten sprig of asparagus and a cooling mass of potatoes au gratin. The morose expression on Raylen's face, however, was at odds with the illustrious occasion.

"Where did we go wrong, Patrick?" He prodded the Marvel with his fork. "When did our dreams turn to madness?"

Patrick Farlin shifted in his chair and fidgeted with his long white lab coat. He was young but brilliant, and already one of the most renowned geneticists in the world. He leaned toward his boss, elbows resting on the table, in violation of everything his mother had taught him. "I don't get your meaning, sir."

"This!" Raylen waved a hand at the opulent space around them. The restaurant had not yet opened, but the surroundings were ready and poised, awaiting the flood of diners soon to come: Dozens of tables lay under crisp white tablecloths, surrounded by an honor guard of elegant mahogany chairs. Above, a chandelier with a hundred lights and a thousand glittering crystals cast its sparking light across the wide space, while in the background, the chords of Bach's third Brandenburg Concerto (First Movement) drifted through the air.

But at the moment, none of it mattered to Raylen Kosta. For all he cared, he might as well as have been sitting on a lawn chair in the parking lot of a 7-Eleven.

"I was the most well-known critic of my generation, Patrick. The *New York Times* restaurant review had nothing on me. When I walked in, four-star chefs would tremble in fear!" He pointed at the ceiling as he spoke, his words thundering in Patrick's ears.

"A word of praise from me could make a chef's entire career; a few words of scorn, and restaurant chains would tumble! And now this?" He slammed his fist down on the table, and Patrick jumped. "I'll be the laughingstock of an entire industry! The entire world!"

"Surely, you're too hard on yourself, sir," Patrick said, trying to comfort him. "This restaurant is the most novel concept in a generation, perhaps in the entire history of restaurants. Foodies will flock from the world over merely to get on the waiting list!"

"And when they arrive, they will taste nothing but failure!" Raylen pointed at the delicately prepared flank of meat, seared on the outside and cut open to reveal a succulent pink interior. The millionaire gourmet appeared to be on the verge of a breakdown: His graying hair was frazzled, and dark circles lined his eyes. "We have welded science and the culinary arts in a way that has never been done before, and what will they say?" A tear ran down Raylen's face. "They will say—"

"They will say," Patrick interrupted, "that they dined on the most exotic cuisine in history! From woolly mammoth to pterodactyl wings to brachiosaurus steaks! The tissue we have grown using DNA once thought lost forever—"

"Perhaps it was better lost," Raylen snarled. "Your team succeeded, Patrick, but the shortcuts…oh, the shortcuts." He wiped moisture from his cheek. "When you told me the gaps in the gene sequences could be filled with modern DNA…"

"It made sense at the time," Patrick said. "The genome in question was already sequenced. Many of the species we were working with were related to modern avians. And it worked!"

"But the consequences! Oh, we who tamper with nature are foolish beings indeed!" Raylen hung his head, sobbing onto one of the most expensive meals ever created. "What mockeries hath science wrought…"

"Please, sir," said Patrick. "Be reasonable. Perhaps the chef can—"

"Oh, Patrick, you fool, the problem is in the very essence of the meat, not the trappings of preparation." Raylen did not look up. "Millions of dollars, years of development, and for what?!" Tears flowed down his face, threatening to drown the remnants of the asparagus, and doubtless infusing the carefully prepared meat with an undesirable saltiness.

"Don't you see?" Raylen cut a piece, took a careful bite, and chewed it, then threw his fork across the table in disgust. "It tastes like chicken!" he wailed, pounding his fists against the table in despair. "Every single thing you've created tastes like chicken!" ◉

One Million Years B.F.E.: Diary of an Anthropologist in Exile

Merrie Haskell

DAY ONE:
Have been exiled to the early Pleistocene by Temporal Crimes Tribunal. Vastly displeased, though certainly this hardship will only serve to make me a greater woman. By the end of lonely prehistoric life, will be most knowledgeable authority on lifestyle of early man. Unfortunately, publishing opportunities here are slim.

Am determined to become strong, lithe, deadly, noble cave-woman type. Will fashion stone tools, hunt and gather food, and live pristine, pure life of *Homo erectus*–type person. Ah. The air is *so* fresh.

DAY TWO:
Bushmen of the South African desert were—are?—*will be* able to subsist on a mere twenty-hour work week. Per principle of uniformitarianism, I shall be able to do the same. Fabulous! Life in the Pleistocene will leave plenty of time for deep thoughts and getting over Philmore the Physicist...plenty of time to come to terms with all bad habits of codependency, "women who love too much," "women who do too much," "women who mess around with time-stream continuum in order to repair non-reparable relationships," etc.

Only problem: Once issues worked through, will not have anyone to share daily triumphs and travails with. Will die alone, eaten by hyenas.

DAY THREE:
Tomorrow I run out of matches. Must re-invent fire. Good thing am expert, top-notch anthropologist with over six months of training.

DAY FOUR:
No fire yet. Tom Hanks in *Cast Away* had fire by now.

DAY FIVE:
No fire yet. Boys in *Lord of the Flies* had fire by now.

DAY SIX:
No fire yet. Gilligan had fire by now.

DAY SEVEN:
I have fire!

Though I no longer have eyebrows. Or eyelashes. Gilligan had both brows and lashes. Damn you, Gilligan.

DAY EIGHT:
Food stores running low, so enacted plan to hunt and gather. Using a digging stick, à la Kalahari bushwomen, uncovered ...grubs.

Could not bring self to consume grubs.

Digging stick technology not so great, actually.

DAY NINE:
No good food source again. Putting in far more than twenty hours this week. Uncertain where time goes. Tomorrow will record time study to see where to pare unnecessary activities from daily schedule.

DAY TEN:
Time Study
Sometime after dawn: Awaken. Day is cloudy, fire is low. Hyenas yipping outside cave. Damn hyenas.
Sometime after that: Stumble out of bed to privy hole. Search for softest, most absorbent leaves. Bathroom facilities in the Pleistocene displeasing to me.

Noon: Look for chert, flint, or other stone with excellent cleavage properties appropriate for knapping stone tools. Must make stone-tipped spear and kill large, high-utility meat animal ASAP.
A bit after noon: No chert, no flint, no obsidian. Why did Tribunal deposit me in stone-tool desert? I will die alone, starving and unloved in churtless wasteland, eaten by hyenas.
Shortly after that: Oooh, look, chert!
Shortly before dark: Reprehensible for the Temporal Crimes Tribunal to exile me to the Stone Age without safety goggles! Spent last three hours washing piece of chert from eye. Negligence!
Dark: Too dark to do anything but sit on the pile of leaves I call my bed and listen to hyenas.
Small victory: Fashioned crude hand ax out of available chert. Will sleep with splendid weapon under my pillow and dare the hyenas to come near!

DAY ELEVEN:
Uniformitarianism is a bust. If San bushmen can spend less than twenty hours a week hunting and gathering to survive, then I'm a cotton-top tamarin. Have slaved from sunup to sundown, knapping stone and hafting tips. Just spent several hours getting tar out of my hair after hafting incident. Clearly, ethnologists studying the bushmen were *not very observant.* Bushmen must be sneaking extra work in somehow.

As for Binford and his utility indices, I *hate* him. Why did he have to be right? Why? The only meat I've been able to acquire was a mangled haunch of antelope that I stole from hyenas using torches and yelling. Am not strong hunter-cavewoman. Am shambling scavenger-cavewoman.

DAY TWELVE:
Strange hominid is spying on me from opposite ridge. Very dirty and unattractive, though quite tall. *Homo erectus* or *Homo ergas-*

ter? Not certain he means me well, but I do have one or two evolutionary advantages over the poor thing, so I should be fine.

DAY THIRTEEN:

Ergaster bastard stole my antelope jerky! Will kill proto-man ancestor if he steals again, and damn the time-stream!

DAY FOURTEEN:

Fancy this—*H. ergaster* is nothing of the sort! He is a physicist named Roger, also exiled by the Tribunal! After I tried to break his head with my hand ax, we both started shouting in English and realized that we were from the same time, more or less. Small world!

DAY FIFTEEN:

Oops. Told Roger I was surprised that a physicist survived so long on his own in the Pleistocene with no anthropological training. Discovered he made fire on his first attempt. May have liked him better when he was just *Homo ergaster.* Bastard.

DAY SIXTEEN:

Hyenas broke into food stash today. Roger very angry. We hunted them back to their den, planning to enact ritual canicide.

However, small, fluffy baby hyena survivors too adorable! Am now a hyena foster-mother instead of mass murderer. Am glowing with motherhood and satisfaction. Early domestication of canine species will be boon to human race! My likeness will be etched onto small stones for all to wonder and marvel at on archaeological digs in the distant future.

Roger not as pleased. There is small potty-training problem with Spot.

DAY TWENTY:

Fluffy baby scavengers have caused domestic spat by chewing

leather footgear. Roger claims to be unsurprised that someone in a "soft science" would keep hyenas.

Considering separate caves.

DAY TWENTY-TWO:

Am pondering self-destructive behaviors, noting similarities between Philmore and Roger: Both are type-A, domineering physicists with messiah complexes and lack of appreciation for personal hygiene.

However, Roger is currently only fish in the sea.

I will *not* obsess about relationship flaws. I will accept Roger for who and what he is, and not try to "fix" him. Cannot change men. Should not try. That is, after all, how one gets exiled to the Pleistocene. ©

Checking Out a Geezer

Florence Bruce

At Piggly Wiggly I often study what other shoppers buy. Looking in their grocery carts, I sometimes discover a useful household product or a bargain I've overlooked.

Last week, waiting in line, I noticed that an old geezer in front of me had nine cans of lima beans. Nothing else in his cart. I counted them and checked each label to be sure all nine contained the same product. Yep, all nine cans were Best Choice lima beans. Best Choice with a black-and-red label is the Piggly Wiggly brand.

I pondered what the old boy might be planning to do with nine cans of lima beans. Maybe he's going to plant some of them, I thought, and eat the rest. It was around planting time. But even my city-fried brain soon realized that cooked beans probably wouldn't grow. Maybe it's what he's taking to the Men's Club supper at the local church, I told myself—a big bowl of lima beans. The church kitchen probably sports a microwave. What kitchen doesn't? Finally, standing in line with nothing better to do, and still undecided on the pressing question, I chose to just up and ask him.

"Can't help but wonder, I said, "what you're going to do with nine cans of lima beans."

"Eat 'em," he said.

"Ah!" It had been too simple.

You can get lima beans cheaper at Wal-Mart," he said, "but actually these taste better, plus more beans per can."

"Really?"

"Every can is jam-packed!" he said, smiling a satisfied smile.

"Nice to know," I said. Meanwhile, I was taking him in. I'm always on the lookout, you know, for an old geezer who might own a cabin on the lake. Plumbed, of course. It has to be well plumbed. No bears-in-the-woods routine for me. We'd have to get that straight on the front end since Mother Nature and I don't commune.

On the negative side, this old man was one of those gawd-awful cap-wearers who seem to be proliferating nowadays. Where do they get the idea, anyhow, that grown men look so cute in caps? And that it's okay to wear a hat in the house? My mother made men take their hats off in her house, as did her mother before her. So, the cap bit wasn't much of a recommendation. Still, I must say my curiosity was piqued.

On the left hand, he was wearing a ring—not a standard wedding-type ring. It was an onyx, in fact, and very loose-fitting, like it wasn't really his. He had a worker's hands, which is all right if they're clean, and his were. Nails clipped.

"I love Popeye's spinach," I said, feeling I owed him a quid pro quo.

"Popeye's?"

"Yes," I said. "It's too expensive, so I don't buy it often, but, taste-wise, it's the best canned spinach there is."

"Buy two, get one free, this week," the cashier interjected.

"Really?" I exclaimed.

"Sorry, didn't mean to butt in, but thought you'd want to know," she added. At that point, she was ringing up the lima beans. I thought she'd take a shortcut and ring up one 89-cent can nine times, but no, she held each separate can over the sensor. I guess grocery cashiers are trained to do it that way, for some reason.

"Not a problem," I assured her. "I'm always looking for helpful suggestions. I get so tired of eating the same old thing week after week."

"I buy Libby's," the cashier said. "They're seasoned. I like already seasoned."

"Ah, seasoned spinach from Libby," I said.

Then the cashier tried to ring up my vanilla ice cream and maraschino cherries along with the nine cans of lima beans, but the geezer wasn't having any of that.

"Not mine," he said promptly, as she picked up the jar of cherries.

"Sorry."

"I'm the ice cream and cherries," I told her. "Just those two items."

"Got to watch the salt," the guy said, back to the matter of seasoning. He was signing his credit card slip. I couldn't read the name. Hairy arms; no tattoos.

"Got that right!" I said.

"I always read the labels," he threw back, as he started for the door, clutching a sack in each hand.

"Smart thing to do!" I yelled to his back. I was beginning to wonder what he might be driving. That's sometimes a pertinent clue as to whether a reasonably attractive gentleman might be the outright owner of a cabin on the lake. Any lake, as long as it's not too far from the city. I followed him out.

He walked toward a big shiny truck—black, new-looking. Well! I thought. I might just go tell him what a pretty truck it is. Gotta love those truck drivers! I was advancing in that direction when I saw him walk around the truck to the passenger side. Oh well, I told myself, the wife or girlfriend is driving. If he has a cabin on the lake, I'll never see it. Then a few steps further on toward my own ten-year-old Corolla, I saw he didn't belong to the new truck at all. Those old bones were riding a motorcycle. I couldn't believe it. His two-wheeled machine was almost lost on the far side of that shiny new truck. I watched him tuck the cans into something akin to saddlebags over the back wheels.

Back in the Pig, I had thought this guy looked to be about seventy, seventy-five. Who would ever guess he rode a motorcycle? I was standing behind the vehicle, getting ready to engage him in conversation about the relative merits of driving a motorcycle versus a good-gas-mileage automobile when that rascal caught my eye in one of his mirrors, did a broad walk, revved the engine, and roared off the lot.

Well, easy come, easy go, I always say. Motorcycle drivers are probably not the type to enjoy a peaceful cabin on the lake. And that old geezer probably didn't have a pot to pee in anyhow. ⊚

Prince Charming

Christina Delia

When it happened, the headlines were always some variation of this: "CHIMP CHANGE: ORGAN GRINDER SELLS MONKEY TO APE-LOVING ACTRESS." The story that followed would tell the tale of an organ grinder named Liborio (no last name) who was on set for the new film *Passion People 2: More People, More Passion*. His purpose was providing old-world charm for the movie's big Italian love scene.

When lead actress Spring Star (formerly of the television series *Bug Bites*) saw the monkey Liborio carried around on his back, she fell in love before the director could yell "Action!" Spring Star begged Liborio to sell his pet to her. At which point the old man's eyes misted over and he said, "There's something in my eye."

Liborio knew something that the paparazzi did not. The monkey was radioactive.

Spring Star knew this, too. She was seated in her trailer when Liborio told her. Spring Star did not blink or rip up the check she was writing. Instead, she told Liborio that she felt the radioactivity made her new monkey quite exotic. The monkey was shiny, like her television awards that sat at home in her mansion on hundred-dollar shelves. Liborio just smiled and took the check that Spring Star handed to him. There were glittery dolphins embossed on the check. "I wish that all animals sparkled, don't you?" Spring Star asked Liborio.

"The outer sparkle of an animal is merely an indication of a creature's inner fire," Liborio said.

Spring Star stared at the old organ grinder. "You should write fortune cookies," she told him.

"Just never force the monkey to do anything he doesn't want to do. With a pet like this, you are as much owned as you are an owner. Remember that in his own way, every creature is a king."

"He's too little to be a king," cooed Spring Star. "Maybe he could be a Prince?"

On the ride home to Beverly Hills, Spring Star named her monkey: Prince Charming.

"You're my Prince, yes you are!" she repeated. Prince Charming did not seem to mind this attention.

In fact, he grew a bit larger. Spring Star took no notice of this. She was too busy giggling while her limo driver eyed the monkey nervously from his rear-view mirror.

"Look, Rex, now we don't need a lamp to read scripts" Spring Star sang out when she presented Prince Charming to her live-in boyfriend. Rex Riley was a Method actor, currently preparing for his upcoming role as a germ-phobic Elvis impersonator at a Las Vegas wedding chapel for the romantic comedy *Wash Your Hand in Marriage*. When Spring Star leaned in to kiss him hello, Rex took two steps back and gagged.

"Oh, I forgot. You're in character," Spring Star said. "I'll just give your kiss to Prince Charming." Spring Star puckered up and kissed her Prince with her surgically enhanced lips.

The impact of her lips on his face seemed to make Prince Charming grow a little bigger. Again, Spring Star seemed oblivious, but Rex screamed.

"Did you just see that, Spring? That glowing monkey grew!"

"He's only getting bigger because I love him so. And there's nothing wrong with a monkey that glows. I wish I radiated like that first thing in the morning. Even after three hours of makeup—"

"Spring, really," Rex whined. "We can't keep a monkey in the mansion! I don't even know what to feed it!"

"He'll eat what the movie stars eat. Bananas and caviar," Spring Star smiled. "You have so many bananas around, with this new role of yours."

Rex struck a pose in his karate suit. "Hello, I'm a Method actor! Elvis ate fried peanut-butter-and-banana sandwiches on a regular basis!"

"Nothing is too good for my Prince Charming," Spring Star said, planting another kiss on top of the monkey's shiny head.

That night after a veritable peanut-butter-and-banana feast, Spring Star, Prince Charming, and a reluctant Rex retired to Spring's suite. Rex found it daunting to make love to Spring with her radioactive monkey watching them from the foot of the bed. Rex sighed and rolled off of Spring.

"Rex, what is it?"

"Look, Spring, I've been involved in a few bizarre Hollywood scenes, but I have to tell you, making love by the light of a monkey really tops them all."

"Rex, baby! Soon you'll grow to love Prince Charming as much as I do—"

"The only thing that's growing is that monkey. Do you see this? He's as tall as me!"

"Don't be so dramatic, Rex," said Spring. "It's not like you're very tall."

"That monkey is freaking me out and I am putting him outside," Rex yelled as he grabbed Prince Charming around his waist. Prince Charming wouldn't budge, so Rex tried pushing him.

"Rex, no! Liborio said not to force him to do anything he doesn't want to do—"

"Who the hell is Liborio?"

These were the last words that Rex Riley ever spoke. The newspaper obituary featured a photo of him in his Elvis-inspired karate suit. Strangely enough, his live-in girlfriend Spring Star was not present at his paparazzi-plagued funeral.

After it happened, the headlines were always some variation of this: "SPRING HAS SPRUNG: WHATEVER BECAME OF ACTRESS SPRING STAR?" One of the tabloids ran a story about Spring Star being spotted on an island off the coast of the Pacific. Miss Star insisted on no photographs. The reporter said that she maintained a healthy glow, although perhaps it was coming from the large monkey that she wore, quite literally, on her back. ◉

Curb Appeal

Katherine Tomlinson

The minute Joanna saw Clea Maxwell drive up in her jaunty little Prius she knew she was perfect for the house.

Clea was in her late forties, compact and nicely dressed. The suit—probably from Ann Taylor—told Joanna that Clea worked somewhere that looking corporate was important.

Her hair was colored a rich auburn but starting to thin at the temples, a sure sign Clea was in perimenopause. It had happened to Joanna, too. She'd had to wash her hair every day and blow it out for maximum fluffiness.

It had eventually gotten thicker again, thanks to hormones and hair vitamins, but Joanna had been quite vain in her younger years and the physical transformations that accompanied "the Change" had unnerved her.

At least she'd never developed the wide part so many women did when they were past a certain age.

Clea loved the kitchen, as Joanna had known she would. Joanna thought the kitchen was one of the house's best features. It was full of light, with a window over the sink and another in the door that led to the back yard. Clea tried to play it cool, but when she first saw the built-in bookcase—perfect for displaying cookbooks and knick-knacks—her face lit up.

It was a cook's kitchen, with a gas stove, plenty of storage space, and a built-in pantry. There was a decorative tile backsplash behind the sink, the colors complementing the rich peach paint on the walls.

One of the women who'd looked at the house had complained about the narrow space the refrigerator occupied. "It's not wide enough for my Sub-Zero," she had whined.

As if anyone who wasn't running a catering business needed a Sub-Zero fridge, Joanna had thought at the time.

Clea wasn't married. She was buying the house on her own to make a nest for herself. Joanna approved of her gumption. So many women wasted their lives waiting for Prince Charming, or put off living until they'd already missed the best parts.

The house was just the right size for one person. It had two bedrooms upstairs and a small, sun-filled space off the kitchen that looked into a garden run riot with roses. That room would make a wonderful home office if Clea needed it.

Joanna hung back as Clea explored downstairs. She'd learned to let the prospective buyers feel like they were discovering the place for themselves.

She never followed too closely as they opened cupboards and closets and ran faucets and flushed the toilets and in general peeked and poked around.

The place was furnished just enough to give it a "lived-in" look. Joanna had chosen everything herself and was gratified when Clea ran her hands over the top of a Birdseye maple sideboard in appreciation.

The woman with Clea—her name was Alison—seemed bored and looked like her feet hurt. No wonder, she was wearing three-inch heels that pitched her bulky torso forward at an awkward angle. Someone had no doubt told her that adding height would make her look slimmer.

Someone had lied.

Alison wasn't even impressed when she and Clea walked into the master bathroom. She looked like she'd seen it before, way too many times.

That annoyed Joanna. The bathroom was a showpiece with a skylight over the sunken tub, gorgeous tile accents and a steam/shower cabinet.

Clea's reaction to the room—despite Alison's blasé attitude—

was all Joanna could have hoped for.

That was the minute she was sold on the house, Joanna knew. Everything else she saw just sealed the deal—the little window in the master bedroom closet with the built-in jewelry drawers and shoe cubbies; the Art Deco chandelier in the dining room, which was a genuine dining room and not just a space off the living area.

Clea loved it all.

She didn't even try to haggle over the price, which Joanna appreciated.

When Clea and Alison drove away, Joanna caught a glimpse of a bumper sticker on the back of Clea's car, a slogan advertising the local NPR station.

Joanna approved.

She knew Clea would love the house and fill it with books and music and maybe a cat or a little dog. The yard was big enough for a dog.

It would be good to have someone living in the house again.

Joanna had been so lonely since she died. ◉

Vanilla or Chocolate

Skye Hillgartner

She'd kissed a boy behind the water tower when she was fourteen. It was clumsy, but they laughed, and split a chocolate bar on the walk home.

The anniversary cake was vanilla.

"Why not chocolate?" she asked.

"Everyone eats vanilla," her husband said, and went to get more wine.

The party was decent. Her husband kept pointing to her, saying, "Still beautiful, isn't she?"

All she could think was that fifty years of vanilla didn't seem worth celebrating. ◉

The Newest Edition of Richard Phlattwaire

Jess Del Balzo

Wednesday marks the release of Richard Phlattwaire's latest book, *Nate Bit a Tibetan*. The novel, Phlattwaire's fourth, creates a sizzling urban universe full of neon lights and subway monks. Phlattwaire utilizes his bizarre, scheming style to lure the reader into his fictional New York City, where the man in robes next to you could really be an "ordinary person."

I met up with Phlattwaire for an afternoon *tabnab*—the author's word for savory snack—on the ivy-covered patio of Orgasmanic Oasis, a downtown health food eatery, just a few weeks prior to the launch of *Nate*.

"I'll be happy if this book gets half the attention *Fleece Elf* did," he says as he gingerly picks at his Chinese chicken salad and sips a cup of single-origin coffee.

I can't help but notice a new Dick Phlattwaire. I first encountered him just seven years ago. He was 24 years old then, on the verge of fame. His debut novel, *A Car, A Man, A Maraca*, was just about to break. His raw talent was undeniable. Unfortunately, as his popularity increased and he began to scale up the social pyramid, Phlattwaire embraced a lifestyle of drugs, alcohol, prostitutes, ungodly amounts of food, and opulent safaris, to fulfill his fascination with the mating habits of African animals.

These days, however, Dick is flatter than ever. He is in the best shape of his life, thanks to kicking his bad habits. His daily routine now includes running, weight lifting and a careful diet of "happy foods," such as Asian salads, homemade yogurt, cautiously imported fruit, and baked goods made with special protein powder shipped in from Barcelona. He spent last fall in a rehabilitation center in Palm Springs, where he dried out and straightened up. While there, he worked with a nutritionist, a psychologist, and spa technicians, as well as a hypnotherapist. He has continued with the hypnotherapy for smoking cessation and weight loss as well as emotional issues. He also gets his tea leaves read regularly.

When the waitress comes by with a plate of complimentary appetizers, he waves his hand and says, "Wontons? Not now." Just over a year ago, he tells me, he probably would have eaten the entire plate and then smoked a pack of cigarettes like he did after every meal, and maybe do a line of coke after that.

After we discuss the state of food and drug addicts the world over, I ask him about the new book.

"So, what is *Nate Bit a Tibetan* really about?" I ask.

Phlattwaire leans back and taps his fingers against his newly shaved head and yawns. "Racism, drugs? I guess. I don't really know. It's about a lot of things. I was basically in a hypnotic trance when I wrote most of it."

"What was the idea that started you on it then?"

"I had a dream about this guy—I called him Nate—who was a cocaine addict, like me. He carried it around with him in these special sugar packets he made and put them on the tables at fancy restaurants he went to. Then one night as he was leaving some party, really out of it, he walked into a man wearing all these robes and watering a plant. He looked like a monk, you know? Nate tripped over the guy, and the guy dropped his watering can. The water ruined all these sugar packets that had fallen out of Nate's pockets. That was basically the dream. So I thought, Yeah, well, I'll bet this dude wants to get even. So he goes around looking for the guy who ruined the coke."

Dream analysis, Phlattwaire explains, was a big part of his treatment at the unnamed center. He worked very closely with his therapist to uncover the hidden meaning behind even his most mundane dreams. Through this practice he was able to make connections between his subconscious mind and his behavior to give him a better understanding of himself. He saw why he had been making bad choices and how he could heal himself. He continues to analyze his dreams, writing them down in a lime-green notebook he carries everywhere. He is still working on overcoming his desire to go on safari again.

"It would be so easy to slip back into that. I really gotta be careful right now. This is a crucial time. It helps to just focus on my writing. I've been writing a lot of poems, mostly about elephants."

When I ask Dick about his influences, he is quick to answer. "Definitely the Village People!" he exclaims, leaning forward. "In *Fleece Elf*, I quoted a line from 'In Hollywood (Everybody Is a Star)' at the beginning of each chapter. In my third book, *Solo Gigolos*, I mentioned 'Just a Gigolo.' Their music really speaks to me, you know? I try to live my life with that optimism they present." As for literary idols, Phlattwaire cites Bernard Malamud's *The Magic Barrel* (the winner of the National Book Award in 1959) as a huge inspiration for its "amazing use of the semicolon."

With his extraordinary fourth novel, *Nate Bit a Tibetan*, Phlattwaire once again manages to capture a series of strangely transcendent moments and package them in glitter and in dirt. He offers them up to the reader in a way few writers can, preaching from his knees. There is no doubt that he will continue to write one madly intriguing, creepily beautiful book after another. Just give him time to finish eating his tabnab, please. This man does not like to be disturbed while he eats.

"It's all about just sitting and savoring the meal, the moment," he says with a sigh, dropping the fork with a victorious bang.

And the sun sets on the city as Phlattwaire takes out his notebook to write down what otherwise would have been a thought passing like the wind. @

Two Urinals from Death

James Sabata

Andy stood two urinals from Death with no idea what to do about it. While he usually made a practice of staring directly at the wall in front of him, he found it increasingly difficult not to sneak a glance at the hooded figure standing at the other urinal or at the scythe leaning upright between the urinals. He watched as the scythe began to move, sliding down the wall. The Reaper caught it just before it fell. "Sorry. It's always doing that."

Andy zipped his fly, staring at the ground. He did not want to make eye contact, particularly with someone who didn't have any eyes. "Not a problem."

He began to move toward the sinks as the Reaper said, "You're Andrew Singleton, right?"

Andy stared at the hooded figure, deciding the best way to answer. "Um. Yeah."

The Reaper laughed as Andy washed his hands. "Don't worry, that's not why I'm asking." He watched as Andy scrubbed. "Get it all off. Those pesky germs will kill you." Andy's eyes grew big. "Sorry, just a figure of speech."

Andy washed again, in case there was any truth in that joke. He looked over at the Reaper. "So you're—"

"I am. Do you know Malory Jacobs?"

"Sure. She works on third." He gasped, realizing what he had just done. "Are you gonna... I mean... She's going to—"

The Reaper grabbed his scythe. "Indeed. It's her time. I'm sure they'll say it was burgers or cigarettes or whatever, but in reality, when it's your time, it's your time."

Andy toweled off. "Does she know?"

"Most people don't."

"That seems harsh."

"Death is just a part of life, Mr. Singleton."

"Will she see you coming?"

"Some do. Some don't. It's always hard to tell ahead of time."

The Reaper started to head toward the door. Andy's voice stopped him. "Can I ask you something?"

"You mean, what happens when you die?"

Andy nodded.

The Reaper's hand came up as he did his best Mafioso impression. "If I tell ya, I have to kill ya." He howled with laughter and then abruptly stopped.

Andy shivered. "I can't believe I'm in the bathroom with the Grim Reaper."

The Reaper's hand shot out, pointing at Andy, "Don't call me that. I hate that name. Why does everyone assume that just because I go around taking people's lives all day that I have to be grim? It's actually kind of a fun job. I meet new people every day. I get to travel."

"I didn't mean any disrespect."

The Reaper placed his scythe against the wall again. "I know. It's one of the downsides of the job. I have the same conversations every day, and the misinformation has come to really annoy me."

"I'm sorry." Andy shuffled his feet. "Man, I can't believe you're going to off Malory. She's such a nice girl."

"How you act only affects where you go, not how you get there."

Andy paused again. "So, you're really not here for me? I'm not, like, already dead or anything?"

"Heavens, no. You're just as alive as you've always been."

"Good. You had me worried. I have a lot to accomplish before I die. I mean, I feel bad about Mal—"

Death moved over to the sink to wash his hands. "You know, I get that a lot. Everyone knows they're going to die at some point, but they always think there's more time. You guys need to just start doing whatever you're doing." The water ran through his bones and onto the floor. The puddle grew more as he wiped his hands on his robe.

Andy nodded his head. "You're right."

The Reaper stuck his hand out. Andy shook it. "Well, Mr. Singleton, it was good to meet you."

"No one is ever going to believe me." The Reaper opened the bathroom door. Andy pointed. "Don't forget your sickle thing."

"Scythe. Yes. I'd be lost without this. I'm just so busy, I'm always forgetting stuff."

"Can I ask you one more thing?"

"Yeah, I guess. But then I really need to go."

"Do you get to pick how people die or is it like predetermined?"

The Reaper laughed. "For the most part, people pick how they die. Every now and then, when I get to do it, I try to be as creative as possible. I've helped win six Darwin Awards. I really should go now."

Andrew smiled. "Now I'll never know the meaning of life."

The Reaper reached for the door. "Oh, fine. That's an easy one." The Reaper leaned in. "Do you have cable?"

"Satellite."

He threw his hands out. "Even better. How many channels do you get?"

"Three hundred something. They claim 450, but some don't come in right. And there's all those music channels I never use."

"So you don't watch them all, right?"

Andy shrugged. "Of course not."

"Why do you have it then?"

"To watch the ones I want to watch."

"Precisely, Andrew. God doesn't have television. He has you guys. Humans, I mean. You know, and the others."

Andy's eyes grew. "Others? Like aliens?" He smiled broadly. "I knew it."

The Reaper opened the door. "You said Malory is on third, right?" Andrew nodded. The Reaper's right hand waved goodbye.

Andy stared at himself in the bathroom mirror, practicing his "surprised" face. He knew he'd have to use it when he heard the news about Malory's unfortunate demise.

As he stepped away, his shoe slid on the water puddle. Andy's head bounced against the automatic hand drier and then against the linoleum. By the time they found Andrew Singleton, the Reaper had moved on. ©

Cold Is My Love

Johnny Gunn

He stood just across the driveway, agonizing over the distance, unable to make his love, his passion, understood. "Oh, to dance about, grasp those lovely hands, plead my feelings." She'd arrived in the neighborhood just a few days after he had, and he had not been able to keep his dark, dusky eyes off her radiance. "If only she would look this way, just once."

Romance as sincere as this only comes once in a lifetime, he realized, and he was well aware of just how short his time had become. "How will I let her know my thoughts, and what will I say when I get her attention?" Inside, deep inside that old, cold body, he understood this one great truth: A snowman cannot have a relationship with such a beauty as this wooden idol, this replica of Sacagawea. "After all, she at least was once a living and beautiful thing." Were those tears that coursed down his cheeks, forming deep rivulets creasing the surface, loosening that which holds his smile, or simply the ravages of today's sun? "So frail, but I must continue to gaze on her beauty."

He was well aware he could have this love only until spring, barring of course those rowdy Anderson children, the ones that stole his nose. ©

No Sweat

Phil Richardson

Harry was bored. He had bought all the latest electronic gadgets—a GPS, an HDTV, an iPod, a satellite radio—and mastered their capabilities. He had a new truck and a new car and they never seemed to break down so he really couldn't justify working on them. He had, reluctantly, filled in his fishpond after he accidentally killed all the fish by breaking the winter's ice with a sledgehammer; Helen would not let him forget about that.

So, he was bored.

"Maybe I'll have an affair," he thought. "Something to get me out of the house. No, Helen would know right away. Maybe I should start exercising. Wow! That's a really good idea."

As was his usual mode of operation, Harry went on the Internet and looked up the consumer data on exercise machines. It was confusing, all about calories per minute and stress tests and stuff he didn't really care about. He decided to make a list of things he wanted from an exercise machine, which he thought would maybe help him make a decision. He set up the tables program on his computer so that there were neat little squares he could fill in and began making his list.

1. Exercise should be fun

2. Exercise should not hurt

3. I don't like to sweat—no sweating

4. No calorie counting

5. No timer

6. Place for glass of beer within reach—no, two glasses

7. Clip for holding potato-chip package within reach

8. Headset for watching TV and answering phone

9. Transition from exercise to nap should be easy

10. Comfort will promote longer periods of exercise.

He looked all over the Internet to find an exercise machine that would suit his needs, but they all seemed to have some element missing. The exerbikes looked uncomfortable, the Bowflex things definitely would work up a sweat, and the treadmill looked dangerous, particularly if you were holding a beer can and trying to stay on the mat. No, he would have to build his own machine.

He went to the Salvation Army store and found an old recliner that he tested and found pretty comfortable. The duct tape on the arms added character, and he loved the purple plaid cover.

While wandering around the store he found two arms scavenged from some old exercisers and added those to his plunder. Other necessary parts he had to buy from the hardware store and Pier 1 Imports.

Helen was not exactly thrilled when the stuff was delivered and "suggested" he move it all to the garage, as the chair didn't quite match the decor of their house. Harry knew when to give in and, anyway, the garage was a better place to work. He made another trip to the store and bought a small refrigerator that he modified to hold a keg of beer, with a tap built into the door. He felt proud of this since he would save energy by not opening the door, and he wouldn't have to throw away any cans.

After completing this essential part of his design, he began working on the exerciser, which he had decided to call "The Harry Crunchner." He affixed the two arms to the sides of the chair, then rigged them to a chain that turned a generator that was hooked to the flat-screen TV he had hung from a frame on the front of the chair. He cut two large holes in the arms of the recliner to hold the beer glasses (having only one glass would mean he would have to interrupt his exercise more often).

The next part of the project involved putting several new e-books on the computer so they could be displayed on the screen. This way he would not have to turn the pages of a book (interrupting his exercise) as the page would turn automatically on his voice command. His phone was hooked through the computer and would be answered automatically, so he would not have to interrupt his exercise and pick up the phone.

"This is going to be great," he thought. "I will lose weight, my heart will be healthier, and Helen won't keep nagging me about exercise. I will start tomorrow, as I'm too tired after doing all this work."

The next day, he told Helen he was going to begin his program. "The computer will keep track of my minutes and email them to me once a month so I won't have to worry about that while I'm working out."

"Most people think it's a good idea to know how much you've done every day," she replied. "I guess if you want a report once a month, it's one way of doing it. I don't suppose you set it up so that it emailed me a copy?"

"I'll probably do that," he said as he headed toward the garage.

Eager to begin, Harry grabbed a bag of potato chips he had stashed in the trunk of the car, filled two chilled glasses with beer from the keg in the refrigerator, turned on the computer, and settled into the recliner.

"First a sip of beer, then a few chips, and then I'll begin."

The beer tasted fine, so he finished a glass. Then, grasping the arms of the exerciser, he began to pull back and forth. "Just like rowing a boat, only more comfortable." He was a little stiff, but he thought that would soon go away. "Turn the page," he told the computer as he finished reading the first page of his book. The pages kept turning however, indicating a glitch in the program. Harry got up—he had to refill his glass anyway—and fiddled with the computer keyboard for about 20 minutes and then resumed his spot in the chair.

"Maybe I should redesign this. Run the tap over to the chair so I don't have to get up to get a beer and interrupt my exercise," he thought.

As he was sitting there, he remembered he was supposed to be pulling the arms on each side of the chair. He resumed pulling and then realized he was sweating. He hated to sweat.

"I know," he thought. "I will just reverse the wires, plug in the generator, and the handles will move themselves. No sweating. Life will be good. Now, if only I could convince Helen to bring me my dinner out here..." ◎

Precision Forged

Adrian Dorris

I don't know how far I need to think back to figure out why I'm at Professor Kievit's house condo thingy with a 9¼-inch, pearl-handled chef's knife in my hand. You might say something like: You saw the ad posted in the union and responded and now here you are, cutting through a Coke can to demonstrate the razor sharpness of the new Infinity line. And I would say right back to you: That's, like, so obvious. Nancy tells us we have to look deeper at the events that make up our lives so we can *maximize potential*, which I think means sell more knives. So, let's see …I'm at Professor Kievit's house condo thingy because I came to State, did okay in the first semester, flunked calc in the second, lost my financial aid in the third, maxed out my credit card, and now I can't afford my sorority's social fees. But that's probably not even deep enough. The ad said "Make $500 a week," so I attended the orientation session where Nancy told us some students *on this very campus* were making *upwards of* $1,500 a week because they *created and controlled their destinies*. To buy the demo set (the Gourmet Ultimate with a solid oak block and an antibacterial cutting board) and start controlling mine, I sold plasma and hawked my CD collection at Re-Run Records and borrowed fifty bucks from Rebecca, whose dad is upper management at a Fortune 500 company in the Midwest. I practiced my pitch around the house, even selling paring knives to a couple of girls whose boyfriends drink too much. I drove home to do my spiel for family and friends, anyone who would listen, and they were so impressed with the product and my demonstration (Nancy calls that part of the job *creating need*), I ended up selling two Infinity sets, three sets of steak knives, and one Meatinator, our biggest and spendiest cleaver.

And now I'm at Professor Kievit's house condo thingy, standing over a card table, smiling at shredded aluminum and saying the great thing is Cutcare knives never need to be sharpened. He's a cool guy, for an anthropology professor. He wears Aéropostale shirts, Gap jeans, and a pair of Blundstone boots that are in desperate need of replacing (IMHO). His place is small, so I guess young professors don't get paid very much. There are books everywhere, and his breakfast nook is piled with papers and tests that need to be graded. Professor Kievit is one of those teachers who wants to understand you so he can help you learn. He plays music at the beginning of class and high-fives us like we're all friends. We talk about the *cultural implications* of nose rings and how bungee jumping started as a *tribal rite of passage*. He lets me come over and sell him knives because he's *not traditional.*

He tells me the knives are very impressive and that we've come a long way since primitives first sharpened animal bones into makeshift blades.

I say that Cutcare knives are precision forged from stainless steel as one solid piece, no stamping.

He looks at me and smiles, but not happily. His eyes are bloodshot and baggy. For the first time, I notice gray in his hair. I think that he can't be more than thirty and already old—poor thing.

"You okay?" I ask.

"Yes," he says, then stops and thinks and says, "No, actually, I'm not." He tells me that the university isn't renewing his contract, that they disapprove of his methods, that only tenured staff can make the kind of major modifications to the curriculum that he's made, that he'll finish out the semester but won't be back in the spring. Professor Kievit looks like he's about to cry.

I lay the chef's knife next to my butchered Coke can and sit down next to him on the couch. I'm about to touch him on the shoulder and tell him that it will work out, that another position will come open, that tons of universities would kill to have an anthropology professor like him, that he's the best teacher I've ever had. Then I remember Nancy's point about *customer diversionary tactics*. They will say and do anything to get out of a commitment; they'll lie right to your face and not even feel bad about it later. I stand up and go back to my card table, my cutting board, my knives.

I tell Professor Kievit that he just needs to do something that will make him happy right now. I tell him that sets begin at $295 and individual knives can be purchased separately. I take cash, check, Visa, or MasterCard.

He looks at me like a struck dog, and that makes me feel good, like I've done the right thing. By the time I pack up my demo kit and fold my table, I have Professor Kievit's credit card number and he has fifteen new knives. ©

Death by Anything

Siobhan Gallagher

Anything goes at night. It first happened to me when I was walking back from the bar—they always say you should watch out for Anything because it can strike anywhere and at any time. I guess I should've listened.

I was knocked out and dragged several yards before regaining consciousness. Anything almost had me in the van but I managed to twist out of Anything's grip and run away. I made it to the apartment building, leapt up the stairs, and slammed the door behind me. I slumped to the floor, breathing hard. Then I listened for footsteps—they say Anything will often trail you, find out where you live, and stalk you. Anything is a creepy bastard.

Well, I didn't hear Anything, so I stripped down and went to bed. I'd call the police in the morning.

Except in the morning, Anything struck again.

I found my moped had been vandalized: handlebars and seat missing, gas tank empty, tires flattened, key scratches across its body. And I cursed, because who else but Anything could have done this?

I wound up taking the light-rail to work, thanks to a friend who lent me his card pass. It would be an agonizingly long trip, and this woman-man person sitting next to me needed a bath. There wasn't even a signal, so I couldn't call the police and make a report, or bitch to my friends what a shitty day this was turning out to be.

But of course, if Anything can go wrong, it will.

The light-rail screamed to a stop, nearly throwing us all out of our seats. The conductor came on the intercom and squawked something, then went silent.

One woman cried out, "Did anyone hear what's going on?"

Being the brilliant person that I am, I stood up and said, "It could be Anything!"

Everyone gasped, and one lady fainted.

I shut up and sat down, because they all gave me *that look* like I was some doomsayer. Well, someone had to say it! We all know Anything can happen, no use in denying it. But then Panic started, and if there's one thing worse than Anything, it's Panic.

Panic hollered, banged on the windows and doors, shoved people into one another, which in turn caused people to shove people into people. And, of course, I was pressed against the wall by the smelly she-male and almost gagged. Fortunately, someone managed to get the doors open and we all poured out—though I was mostly dragged out by the wave of human hysteria.

I ran the next ten blocks to work and arrived at the office in a disheveled, sweaty state. The bossman's secretary asked for a reason for my tardiness in a tone that matched my school teachers.

"I can't discuss Anything," I said.

Her little mouth popped open and eyes grew large. "Did Anything happen to you?"

"Heh, yeah, last night."

"Oh my. Have you told the police?"

"Well, I was going to..." I patted my pockets—dammit! Where's my phone? I looked to her. "Mind if I—"

"I'm sorry, but it's company minutes." She cradled the phone receiver close to her chest.

I sighed and did a half-turn. "All right. I just hope Anything doesn't happen to your grandmother."

The phone receiver clattered onto her desk. "*Don't* say that!" She quickly composed herself. "The police station isn't too far from here. *Go report it.* I'll tell Mr. Ren that you called in sick."

"Thank ya, thank ya." I nodded and rushed out.

I walked across the street and up a few blocks to the station, which was overflowing with aliens. Not an ideal place by any means. And it was hours before I managed to get a hold of the police chief—literally, by grabbing him around the waist.

"What the hell is wrong with you?" he growled.

"It's Anything!"

His face drained of color and he walked over to a window, and stared aimlessly out it. "I lost five good men to Anything."

"Did—did they die?"

"What? No, they quit the force. Anything will do that to a man."

"Can Anything be undone?"

He shook his head. "Not that I know of."

That was that. I went him home and decided to start that memoir that I always wanted to write but never got around to. But as I started typing it, I had a feeling that sunk and kept sinking.

I was being watched.

"Dammit, I can't work if Anything is looking over my shoulder," I said out loud.

Anything was on my balcony, staring through the glass door. My heart and I jumped. But I had beaten Anything before and I could beat Anything again—at least that's what I told myself. Self-therapy helps, you know.

I shook my fist at the glass door. "Anything, whatever you want, you can't have it."

But Anything is a stubborn thing and stayed put. I threatened to use the gun-I-don't-have, but Anything still wouldn't budge.

The lights went out. That's what I get for not paying the electricity bill on time. Glass shattered. Pain sprinted up my leg. Putting two and two together, I realized I had just stepped on my disco ball.

I tripped and fell.

And that's the last thing I remembered before waking up the next day. The entire apartment had been ransacked, but

I'm not sure if Anything had anything to do with it. Probably did, that bastard. Since my place looked like hell, and being the only person to survive Anything, I took the day off to clean up. Though I ended up working on that memoir that I usually never get around to. At least *now* I have something worthwhile to say.

Seems you can die from a lot of things, but not from too much of Anything. ◉

Jiggs and Bob

Charles N. Beecham

I guess the first tragedy in my life came the day that Cricket got run over. I cried for a week. Dad put her in a wood box and buried her in the backyard. I didn't think any dog could take the place of Cricket. Then one day a Boston bulldog came to our house and just kind of stayed. One day a man walked by and told my dad that the name of our dog was Jiggs. "Everyone knows Jiggs," he said. "He kills cats, you know."

It wasn't long after that when some woman knocked on our door and announced that our dog had killed her cat.

Jiggs was a dedicated cat killer. His execution style was quick and clean, in that his victims never suffered. He grabbed each one by the neck and with a short whipping action snapped their neck! Then he would calmly walk away.

We moved to another house while I was in kindergarten. The people who formerly lived there had a kid named B.M., and he was about the meanest kid who ever lived. He left a poor wretch of a cat behind—his tail had been cut off, and he had burn spots all over his body. We named him Bob, although my dad said that we shouldn't get too attached as he wouldn't have long after Jiggs discovered him.

One night we awakened to the worst racket. Every dog and cat sound known to zoological science and some new sounds were emitted: *Grrr! Fssst! Wowellll!* And then it was quiet. My dad said that he had better get the shovel in the morning and lay Bob to rest.

The next morning Bob was at the back door waiting for food. That's the last we saw of Jiggs.

Wrestling with Alienation

Desmond Warzel

So I go up to Dutch in the hotel bar after the show and tell him I want to lose the title, ASAP.

Naturally he thinks I'm joking and turns back to the double vodka he just ordered. Sure, a wrestling title's just a prop in a TV storyline, but it's still an honor. The equivalent of star billing.

"I'm not kidding, Dutch," I insist. "I saw Ricky yesterday."

He isn't amused. "Ricky" is Rick King, the highest-drawing world champ in company history until he disappeared six months ago. After an appropriate mourning period, Dutch slapped together a tournament, the Rick King Memorial Tournament, and put the belt on me. Killer ratings, too. I could never draw the crowds Ricky did, but Dutch figured I'd do until he could build up a credible challenger to beat me.

Dutch doesn't like me making jokes about Ricky.

"He showed up in my hotel room," I explain, feeling like the dumbest guy ever bred. Dutch thinks I'm on something, and he is *pissed*, because one of the reasons he trusted me with the belt was my pristine, scandal-proof bloodstream.

"I'm not looking forward to elaborating on this, Dutch, so promise me you'll hear me out." I take a deep breath and blurt it out.

"Ricky told me he was kidnapped by aliens." Dutch doesn't even twitch an eyelid, just keeps shooting me that toxic glare of his. "He figured it out right away. It was partly the instantaneous teleportation, partly the stark-white prison cell he found himself in, but mostly it was the detainees filling the opposite bank of cells, specifically, their unusual quantities of limbs and their violations of radial and bilateral symmetry.

"Well, that's how he put it. You know, he's a Yale man.

"Anyway, Ricky noticed two things. First, every so often, guards, no better-looking than the inmates, came and took away two prisoners, and, shortly thereafter, brought one of them back. Second, one, and only one, of his possessions had accompanied him: the championship belt. That's why it wasn't with the rest of his stuff, Dutch. Ricky added these circumstances up and realized that what he'd thought was the humming of engines was really crowd noise, filtered through countless layers of, well, whatever UFO bulkheads are made of.

"Ricky studied the occupants of the other cells and noticed that, diabolical as they appeared, each was hideous in its own way. He figured it must be one being per planet, and he was Earth's representative. It made sense when he considered the years of TV signals that had radiated into space, all showing him besting his foes and wearing that gold belt embossed with WORLD HEAVYWEIGHT WRESTLING CHAMPION. The only part that strained credulity was that intelligent beings had apparently thought our storylines and match choreography were legit.

"Don't look at me that way, Dutch, that's what he said.

"Well, when the guards finally came for him, he tried to explain, but they either couldn't understand him or didn't care. They shoved him out into an enormous arena whose floor and walls were already stained with blood of every hue. Big video screens everywhere, and seemingly infinite grandstands receding up into the dark, filled with all kinds of aliens raising all kinds of hell. Weird-looking cameras every ten feet.

"Ricky had observed the winners living to fight another day. The fate of the losers remained a mystery. Ricky's a logical guy, and he saw one logical course of action: fight to win.

"And he did. They stuck him in there against some blue, shaggy, yeti-looking character, and Ricky wore himself out beating on the guy, looking for a vulnerable spot. He finally got in a lucky genital shot, and it was nowhere near where you'd expect.

"Afterward, he sat in his cell, nursing his wounds, and concluded that the straightforward approach couldn't work forever. He regarded the menagerie in the other cells, each creature a distinctive product of its native environment. Ricky's only chance was to exploit what made him unique. His potential opponents sported all manner of natural weapons: horns, spikes, tentacles, fangs. But only Ricky possessed an Ivy League biology degree.

"Against insectoid opponents, he dragged the combat out as long as he could, counting on their inefficient oxygen diffusion to do them in. For amphibian opponents, he used grappling techniques, seizing them in complicated holds and letting the constant dermal stimulation dehydrate them. For beings who lacked eye structures, he covered himself with blood from the prior combats, to fool their olfactory senses, and hugged the walls so the crowd noise masked his movements.

"I don't really understand this stuff either, Dutch, but he wrote that part down for me. Here, see? And it's not important, anyway. The point is, he won. The whole enchilada."

Dutch interrupts me to theorize, reasonably, that I've flipped my lid. He's determined to humor me, though. Where's Ricky now, he asks.

"Well, he's kind of a celebrity, you know, out there." I point upward. "But not his own man, by any stretch. He had trouble just getting permission to come back long enough to tell me what happened. Still, he has it pretty good, all things considered. As champion, he only has to fight in the final round of each tournament.

"You know, like in *Karate Kid Part III*."

By now Dutch is sizing me up for a straitjacket, but at least he accepts that I believe what I'm saying. His last-ditch strategy for restoring my sanity is to poke a hole in my story. So if Ricky's tenure as galactic champ is ongoing, reasons Dutch, why should I ditch my title? They wouldn't need a second earthling, so I'm in no danger, right?

"Ricky came back to warn me. Apparently they want to change the format, freshen things up." This, Dutch understands. As entertainment, wrestling, real or fake, gets stale easily.

"For the next tournament, they're switching to tag teams." And I drain Dutch's untouched vodka in one swallow. ⓒ

Shoot for Jesus

Courtney Walsh

When Sister Agnes first set up her mission north of Pyongyang, she didn't know what to expect, only that she wanted converts to the Lord Jesus and that she wanted to train members of the first North Korean biathlon team. After graduating from Notre Dame, she had enrolled as a novitiate at the new Sisters of Mercy athletic convent in North Bend. There she earned her habit and her rosary beads and her Karhu 10th Mountain Mountaineering skis and her Walther P22 with back strap. She trained and she trained until she could recite the New Testament from memory and get four out of five bull's-eyes shooting from prone, sitting, and standing positions.

The first to approach her when she got off the plane were twelve of Kim Jong's Happy Girls in their olive-drab uniforms, each with a tiny red rose in her hair. They bowed and chanted in unison, *Great Leader send high regard and greeting to Poopy-San.*

Poopy San? That was her, apparently. She bowed in return, and one of the Happy Girls put a lei of red roses around Sister Agnes's neck. Then they all stepped back and admired her.

"Thank you, thank you," Agnes said. "Now I have something for you." She reached into her rucksack and took out a dozen little New Testaments bound in red leather.

Oh, no, said one of them, her eyes wide with shock, *Chairman Mao!*

No, no, no, they shrieked. *Against fatherland. Against Great Leader. Total nuclear wah!*

Agnes laughed good-naturedly, "These are Bibles, dears."

They glanced at one another, their anger subsiding. *Bible?* one of them said tentatively.

Jesus? another suggested. There was a murmur among them. *Matthew,* another one said. "Good," Agnes said. *Mark,* said another. *Luke, John,* said yet another. Agnes clapped her hands in glee, and then they put the names of the Gospellers into a chant, *Matthew, Mark, Luke, John, Matthew, Mark, Luke, John.*

"Very good," Agnes said, and one of them tittered, which caused the others to giggle, too, until they sounded like delighted hamsters.

The one who had put the wreath around Agnes's neck told her, *Great Leader say you teach us to be Olympic billiard champions.*

"Billiards?" she said.

Six ball in side pocket, said one.

I shoot mass shot, said another.

Suddenly, Agnes had a brainstorm: Suppose, instead of targets, pool tables could be set up at intervals along the ski course. They would race to the first table, run a rack, and then race to the next one.

Did they have pool tables when Jesus was growing up? She pictured Jesus with his beard and his long white robe, walking around the table as he chalked his cue, calling, *Combination off the six.* Wump, wump, wump: three balls in one shot.

It would be like the Stations of the Cross.

Or cross-country billiards, an entirely new Olympic event.

Agnes clapped her hands. "Take me to your leader!" ◉

Headhunter

William R. D. Wood

Everyone remembers where they were the day magic returned. Personally, I'd been at it all day, sitting in the little conference room, interviewing applicants for the one opening down at Mega Pest Control. Times were tough and the competition was heavy.

The television in the corner was full of impossible images. Unicorns wandered around Times Square. A dragon batted at airplanes on a taxiway at Reagan International. Huge serpents swam Nessie-like down the Mississippi. And a swarm of fairies— *freaking fairies*—chased children in a schoolyard in Topeka.

I thought it was an elaborate hoax, like the one in the pretelevision years by that fat radio guy, but as the day wore on, the news coverage continued on every channel. Whatever force borrowed or stole the magic eons ago had paid it back with interest.

I scratched at one of several nasty bites on my neck and shuffled applications and legal pads on the table. The day had been long and I was ready to pack it in when Sue leaned in the door, her faced scrunched in an expression I didn't quite get. "Oscar, you have one more...applicant."

Oh, well. I deal mostly with the trades: HVAC, plumbing, extermination, and the like. A little overspecialized, maybe, but I've got a knack, I've been told, and that's why they hire me again and again. I'm just good at matching hardworking applicants with eager employers. Call it a gift. Not rocket science. You just have to watch for the signs and trust your gut.

I sighed and settled back into my chair, swatting at another of the monster flies that had been pestering me all day. Biggest bugs I'd ever seen. "Send 'im in."

The floor shook once, then twice. *Good God. Were those footsteps?* An ogre stepped into room, his head hunched to avoid the drop ceiling.

I scrabbled to my feet, almost falling backwards over my folding chair. My heart pounded. Something programmed deep into my genes wailed at me to flee high into the trees or into a dark hole too small for it to follow. When he didn't attack immediately, I forced myself to breathe slowly, gaining my composure. These were different times. Aside from being big as a gorilla on growth hormones, he could have passed for a 1980s Arnold Schwarzenegger. Except for the tusks.

He's just another applicant, just another...person...looking for a job.

He looked down at me, eyebrows raised over his big green eyes. He tilted his head to one side, and I was reminded of the distorted cats and dogs on the calendar in the corner. I hate those things. Another bug buzzed by, colliding with my forehead and spiraling off wildly across the room.

"Okay," I said, straightening my tie and easing down into my chair. "So, uh, you're looking for a job?"

The ogre grunted.

"Excellent, excellent."

Wood creaked as he sat on the floor just inside the room. An odor began to grow, like wet puppies and moss. The bugs sure liked it. A dozen flitted around the ogre's head, but he was oblivious.

"So...this interview is for an exterminator. Mega Pest covers the whole range of vermin. Until today, I suppose." I chuckled, but the green eyes just stared. "Yes, well. Mister?"

The ogre grunted.

"I see. How do you spell..." I let the question trail off and took out a blank application. "What are your qualifications?"

He reached into a leather bag at his side and flopped a heavy object onto the table. I flinched. A grimy rope threaded through the eye sockets of a dozen animal skulls. The big one in the middle could have been human. He followed my gaze and casually tried to turn the bony stare facedown on the table. But nothing with hands the size of holiday hams can move casually, and I had to fight the urge to leap through the privacy-glass window behind me.

"I see," I managed.

Some of the bugs had grown bored with the ogre and resumed dive-bombing me, zooming in, snatching at strays hairs on my head, scratching at my ears. One hovered, bouncing in the air in front of my face like a hummingbird. A glint caught my eye before I could smack at it.

No way.

She was a tiny woman by shape, with dragonfly-style wings, her body covered in glistening, glitter-size specks. Cute, except that the head was wrong. Bulbous eyes, faceted like a fly's, and a wide grin filled with needle tips. The bites on my neck and arms throbbed.

Well, I'll be.

The ogre grunted.

I snapped my attention back to the hulking creature and his macabre collection of endorsements strung across the table. "You certainly seem able to handle the, uh, larger varieties, but the world of pest control is always changing—vermin of the day, you might say. What unique qualities do you have to meet the needs of Mega Pest?"

The bug-girl nipped at the back of my neck, drawing blood, and flitted away beyond my reach. One of the ogre's eyes tracked her for several seconds. A tongue flashed from his mouth, snatching her from the air and into his waiting maw with a satisfying crunch.

I dabbed at a bleeding bite with a Kleenex. Worse than any wasp sting.

I looked into the applicant's eyes. He stopped chewing, the corners of his mouth attempting a grin and almost succeeding. "You're hired."

The ogre grunted. @

My First Foreign Woman and the Sea

Robert Perchan

There was a blind woman who fell in love with a stout sailor from a distant land. He was a good man and did not touch her, though she wished him to in her heart. He was a stranger to her city, but he took her out to various eating houses and described for her blind eyes the rainbow colors of the food set on the table before them. But it was an exotic culture to him, and the hues were subtle and beyond his range of language, for the blind woman and the sailor spoke to each other only haltingly in a crude lingua franca.

Sometimes they returned together to her narrow room above the seamstress shop where she made her living stuffing scraps of colored cloth into pillows for the rich. He drank beer there and snacked on the dried fish and dark sausages that she prepared for him from memory. The sailor was a fat man, a man of the gut, and did his thinking and feeling down there in the labyrinth of the guts. He broke wind one evening, leaning close to her as he provided a sluice for the gas to escape. (You know what I mean.) The blind woman smiled and he saw her smile. "What was that?" she asked, knowing full well. "That is the sound of a man who loves you, when he is near," he answered. The blind woman liked the pure idea of the sentiment and invited him to lie down with her. He followed, both thinking: *What is there to lose?*

But he was a sailor from a foreign land and soon would be gone. This bothered her, of course. He would be gone, perhaps forever. She would miss him and his flatulence that announced, in its abrupt clarion way, the making of love. So she pursed her lips and began practicing explodents and susurruses against her encroaching abandonment. She mastered the squeal and the thundering bassoon. As the final day grew near, she cooked up a good pot of red beans for him, the kind packed with molecules of blue methane aching for release.

On his last night in port he climbed the creaky stairs to her room and she fed him well, spooning the purplish mash in the direction of his mouth with mother love. Giddy, he began to break wind like there was no tomorrow, which there wasn't. She followed his lead, blindly, matching him vibration for vibration with her practiced lips. He was a breezy old seadog and taught her more in that last evening than any landlocked blighter could ever hope to know.

Then he sailed. A storm rose out of the east, his hermaphrodite brig splintered and sank, all drowned. Perhaps a pool of bubbles gamboled on the surface of the ocean for a moment, she thought when she heard the report. But she had learned her lessons well and recited them over and over in her room. Phoo-oo-oot. Phleesh. Shuh-kuh-kuh. Vleen. Brap. High-pitched farts and low-pitched farts and farts that tromboned in between. Sometimes she forgot herself and left her window open. A blind woman living alone in a room above a seamstress shop doesn't much care what the neighbors think.

I too was a sailor, in my youth, and had heard all the tales about foreign port cities young sailors hear on their first voyages. One evening, while the rest of the crew luxuriated in the local flesh-pots, I stood in front of a seamstress shop leaning against a wall, a Players dangling from my lips, a tableau of solitude and dreams adrift. The strange and foreign port city at night was ablaze with torchlights in its cocky, smirky way, as foreign port cities always are. It was then that I heard him, above me, a sound I had lis-tened to a hundred times late at night when the Dansker and Jenkins and Kincaid squatted and plotted in the lee forechains drinking watered rum and dicing away their pay: the song of the legendary Drowned Farter. (It was said a pool of bubbles gamboled perpetually on the surface of the ocean at the exact spot his ship went down.) This, of course, was Adventure. I climbed the creaky stairs and entered the blind woman's room. She sat cross-legged on a mound of rich pillows at the center of a web of colored threads connecting her fingertips to various corners of the room, like rigging on a ship, her haunted blind eyes long ago emptied of longing, a weathered figurehead on a bowsprit.

But she was kind and understood my loneliness. She took me slowly, knowing that I was young and that my heart was crowded with all the useless baby furniture of young hope. On her pillows farts exploded overhead like rockets, rattled below like grapeshot at the waterline. Ripped and snapped like sails in a gale, canvas that billowed and sagged and filled again. Hot musket breath raked the poop. I boarded her. She boarded me. And when she pulled me under for the third time and I felt my brief life spent before me in a few seconds, I was grateful for the foretaste.

You never forget her, your first foreign woman in a port city, regardless of the men she's had ahead of you or will have later on. You board your ship the next morning and when the wind kicks up you want to turn back. Standing on the wooden deck you see your first foreign woman's blind eyes in your own mind's eye, and then you hear the crew scrambling up the ratline rungs of the shrouds, stinking of last night's beer, farting their early morning farts and singing in chorus of their own first foreign women and the sea. ◉

Buttons

Edward Palumbo

I t's not for sale," said the tiny gray woman as she clutched the black device with both hands. "I've changed my mind."

"Oh," I responded glumly.

"Of course, I could rent it to you." Her Shih Tzu barked at us from the living-room window, apparently displeased with the notion. "You look as if you could be trusted to bring it back, a nice, young, professional man like yourself. I don't really need the money, but every little bit helps." She paused. "No, no, I'd better not."

"How much to rent it for one day?" I inquired.

"My husband, God rest him, bought it at a dusty old camera shop. But it's not a camera, no sir, even though it looks like one." She held it up as high as she could, and it shimmered in the sunlight. "Look at that workmanship," she continued, "not another like it in the world. And look at the buttons: blue, green, yellow, and here on the side, *red*. But never touch the red one." She laid it back on the table. "The red one cannot be touched. That is why it is separate from the others. You would not want to click it by mistake."

"Yes," I replied, "blue, green, etcetera, don't touch the red. Got it. Tell me again how you make it work."

"Well, you can point the lens at just about anything from a postcard to a child's drawing to the finest Cezanne. Then you click the blue button and you are transported into the scene immediately. Wherever the place, whatever the time, it is yours to visit, for good or for bad. When you want to return, simply point the lens at yourself and click the green button and you're home. Imagine, you could visit the Great Pyramid of Giza in the morning, have lunch with Churchill, and then stop by Yankee

Stadium for Game 7 of the 1975 World Series. Now, should you visit someplace where there's danger, the Amazon jungle for example, that's where the yellow button comes in. If someone or something threatens your safety, point the lens at them and click the yellow button. Your foe will disappear as quick as you please."

"I'll give you fifty dollars to rent it until tomorrow evening."

"You must never touch the red button. That's why it is separate from the others."

Her Shih Tzu barked at us from the living room window. "I'll be a minute, Mitzy!" the woman exclaimed without turning.

"I'll give you fifty dollars to rent it until tomorrow evening," I repeated.

"My husband kept it in the cellar for years. He only used it a half dozen times. It can be dangerous. He was knocked out by Joe Louis twice. Some people never learn. I started putting things out at six-thirty. Everybody loves yard sales. I had customers here before seven a.m. Mitzy hates men, why, I don't know. She loves women though—and kids."

"Fifty dollars, until tomorrow evening, I'll have it back no later than eight p.m."

"Hold it," she said as she lifted the device and handed it to me. "Feel the weight." I examined the device. It was indeed weighty.

"After noon," she explained, "no one came, except you. Right now, it's entirely dead. I suppose I made about eighty dollars, enough to buy dog food." Mitzy barked on cue.

"How much will you give me for it?"

I pointed the lens at the old woman and clicked the yellow button. Then I took care of Mitzy. I'll be back from the Bahamas on Thursday. ◉

Black Lung and Broken Heart

Tom J. Lynch

In one hand Harry Boydman held the cashier's check that would save his life. With the other he shook hands with another satisfied customer. Thereafter, he fled into the night, away from the Dice Street Warehouse, a semilegal satellite accumulation area for industrial waste. Not until he reached the corner of Dice and Hamilton did he examine the check under the glimmering eye of a lone street lamp. A fog, like cigarette smoke, gently grabbed his hand, making Boydman feel a tad uneasy. It hadn't been so long since he'd quit smoking.

The check was paid to the order of Milwaukee Toxic Takeout, a racket of Boydman's in which he charged the going rate for clean and green disposal of hazardous waste, while he dumped the sludge in the sewers when nobody was looking. The number next to the dollar sign was big. Not bank heist big, but generous enough to raise the sword of Damocles that hung over his head. Boydman had borrowed a substantial sum from Roddy Size, a local kingpin and owner of Soapy Sam's Laundromat up on 21st Street. The capital was intended to grow Boydman's disposal business, but instead he blew it all on bubblegum and hookers. Consequently, Roddy sent out a guy to have a chat with Boydman. Monkey Cowalski was his name, and he was the kind of guy who could lift twice his own weight in soggy towels and underwear at the laundry joint.

Boydman folded the check in half and extracted his wallet from his pants pocket. After inserting the check, he flipped to the wallet's photo sleeve, in which he had sequestered a picture of a bird named Cheezy, a cockatiel with a crooked beak, long since dead, and the last friend he'd had on this Earth. She had a voice like a chainsaw on helium and he had taught her how to shriek, "I looove youuu!" And he had loved her back, until the day Cowalski had darkened his doorway.

Boydman closed his wallet abruptly, refusing to chain himself to that train of thought. No sense letting himself get dragged behind that memory when he already felt vulnerable beneath the street lamp's cone of illumination. He put the wallet in his pants pocket and started across Hamilton street. He was halfway across and inches away from a manhole when the cover erupted and spun in the air like a coin, sprinkling asphalt all the way.

Something green. Something scaly. Something altogether unnatural and unexpected lunged from beneath the street. It looked like a giant iguana and it grabbed Boydman's ankles, pulling him hard, dragging him into the hole. He was halfway beneath the ground before he arrested his descent by hooking his fingers in a deep pothole. He screamed, but no one answered. The street was empty and this was the kind of neighborhood where, if it wasn't empty, people looked the other way and kept walking.

His trousers ripped and slipped off his waist. The creature fell with a fistful of pants, freeing Boydman to struggle up onto the crosswalk.

"My wallet!"

Without a second thought, he lowered his bare legs into the manhole and climbed down to a dark river of cold filth. His socks slurped it up like sponges. His feet tingled, as if a weak electric current ran through the sludge. The air smelled like turpentine.

Water gurgled and beasts groaned.

As his eyes adjusted, the dark coalesced into shapes. Man-sized lizards. Goldfish the size of buffalo standing on quivering young legs. A hamster with three eyes and enough room in its cheeks to pouch a Volkswagen.

"Who's got my pants?"

They approached. Silent. Hungry.

An ear-piercing shriek stopped the animals and a hulking cockatiel, tall as an ostrich, pushed passed them. It had a crooked beak.

Boydman gasped.

"I thought I flushed you down the crapper!"

Monkey Cowalski had been an accessory to Cheezy's murder. Boydman himself had done the murdering. When Cowalski had come around to collect for Roddy Size he put a gun to Boydman's head and pinched his ear with two jagged fingernails. He gently instructed Boydman to smoke cigarette after cigarette and blow the smoke in Cheezy's cage until the bird fell belly-up in the newsprint. As Boydman flushed the bird down the toilet, Cowalski told him that next time he'd pull the trigger if Roddy didn't receive a return on his investment.

In the sewer, Cheezy approached, wings spread in a benevolent gesture. She stood a head taller than Boydman, and her wings blocked his view of the other creatures. She dipped her head, as if to preen her chest feathers, then raised it again with Boydman's wallet clutched in her beak.

Boydman took the wallet and couldn't hold back a smile, nor tears.

"I'm so sorry."

Her black eyes never blinked as her wings embraced Boydman. She reeked of sewage and rotting meat. And chemicals.

"Cheezy, come home with me!"

She pushed him away and pointed a wing at the ladder leading back to the street. Boydman hesitated, but Cheezy backed off and lowered her wings, permitting the menagerie of mutant pets to resume their approach.

Boydman put the wallet in his mouth and scrambled up the ladder. Back on the street, he opened the wallet. The check was there, but the picture was gone. He wondered if, after paying Roddy, he'd have enough cash to buy another bird.

A cold breeze wafted up from the manhole, chilling Boydman's naked legs and carrying the echo of a distant shriek.

"I looove youuu!" ◉

Irreversible Dad

Kenton K. Yee

I noticed Dad shrinking when I was in third grade. He could no longer pull books from the top shelf, and his pants mopped the floor. I wanted to tell Dad to see a doctor, but Mom told me to let him be. "He is what he is," she said.

By the time I reached high school, Dad was the size of a teddy bear. Fortunately, he had academic tenure, so his condition was not a problem at work. The morning after I got my driver's license, I threw a blanket over him, locked him in a cat carrier, and drove him in for testing. "Collapsing wave function," the man wearing the stethoscope said. "It's irreversible."

Dad continued teaching until a student nearly stepped on him. By the time I was packing for college, Dad was smaller than a mouse—a baby mouse. We kept him in a gallon mayonnaise jar with two cotton balls. He licked one for water; the other absorbed his waste.

I had to squint to resolve him during my first visit home. We sat in the kitchen. I munched a donut and flicked specks of powdered sugar into his jar. He chased after the falling flecks like a goldfish gobbling food flakes.

"Be nicer to Mom," I said. "Changing your soggy cotton balls through the mouth of a mayo jar with tweezers is making her twitchy."

He cupped both hands over his mouth and shouted, but all I could hear was the quiet of cotton.

A few days later, Mom phoned to say she could no longer find him.

I rushed home and took his jar to the research hospital, where they stuck it into an electron microscope. The computer screen flickered a black-and-white image of Dad sitting on a molecule of atoms, his legs crossed, an elbow on a knee. Engrossed in the undulations of a proton wave, he was as I had always imagined: the tall physics professor who reached up to the top shelf and pulled down books for me; the skinny graduate student who worked up the courage to ask Mom out on the final day of class; the little boy who stayed alone during recess in his second-grade classroom to read about subatomic particles in the *Encyclopedia Britannica.* ◉

Death & Taxes

A.J. Sweeney

Martin walked home from work in the rain. Bus fare was not an option; he didn't get paid until the end of the week, and rent was due. In a perfect world there would be no work, or rent, and he could curl up in a ball under a big blanket and wait for it to all be over. But, the world not being perfect, he got up and went to work every single day.

In the dim light of his living room, his answering machine blinked red. He hit play and listened to the message: "Martin, it's Bob Jenkins. Long time, no speak. I've got something to discuss with you. Be at Mary's Bar tonight at seven-thirty. It's important. Try to make it. It's important. That's all. It's Bob Jenkins."

A cold sweat broke loose and ran amok under his shirt. It couldn't be. It was impossible. Literally, figuratively, physically—metaphysically—impossible! But a third replay confirmed it was indeed the voice of Bob Jenkins.

Martin knelt on the ground beside his bed and pulled out a box containing a newspaper clipping dated August 17, 2001. "Banker Burned in Biz Blaze," it read. The story detailed how fire gutted Jimson and Sons Light Fixtures on Midwood Avenue and claimed the life of accountant Robert Jenkins, who'd been visiting the office on a routine audit.

Staring at the clipping as if looking for reassurance or proof that he was not insane, Martin tried to figure out what to do. Should he meet this guy, this disembodied voice from beyond the grave? If so, it might prove to be a more interesting than average Thursday night. Not only was it dark and stormy and filled with voices from the dead, but Mary's was supposed to be quite trendy, and Martin hadn't been there before.

And so Martin went forth into the night. Very wisely, he remembered his umbrella.

Bob was the same as ever: slender and gangly with sloping shoulders and thin, light-brown hair.

"God, I've been busy," Bob said. "Tons of work. Mountains."

Martin frowned but said nothing. He wasn't sure how to ask Bob why he wasn't dead.

"So," asked Bob. "How's work?"

"Boring." This was true. "And you?"

"Well, like I said, busy."

"Oh. Right. Seen any good movies lately?"

"Nah. I feel like I haven't been out of the office in about ten years."

Martin nearly choked at that.

The rest of their conversation passed surprisingly smoothly, aided by the liberal imbibition of beer. At no point though could Martin broach the subject of the big, dead elephant in the room.

At the end of the evening, Bob said, "Walk me home, Martin. I don't live far." He led Martin past the park, down Fifth Street, and into Greenwood Cemetery. They stopped in front of a grey marble slab simply engraved with

BOB JENKINS 1969–2001

Bob grabbed Martin's shoulders. "Listen to me. You and I have been friends for years, right?" Martin nodded. "So you won't take this the wrong way, but…I have to tell you something that you probably don't want to hear."

Visions of death danced before Martin's eyes. So this was it—this was the meaning of the visit from beyond the grave. The great big duvet in the sky was calling him home and he never would worry no more. Tears of joy and self-pity sprang simultaneously to his ducts.

Bob pressed an envelope into Martin's hands. He opened it

slowly, cautiously. "We are writing to inform you that there are inconsistencies on your tax return for the year ending 2001—" Martin looked up in disbelief. The letter was signed Robert Jenkins, Claims Adjuster, Internal Revenue Service.

"You owe an additional $4,584.93."

"I'm being audited?" Martin bellowed.

"We don't get to choose our cases, if it makes you feel any better."

"This is insane! I'm getting out of here!"

Martin attempted to run but tripped over a votive wreath. Bob was on him in a second, pinning him to the ground. Martin struggled, but the dead man was too strong for him.

"Either you bring me a check," Bob grunted, "Or you'll have to call our toll-free service number and set up a payment plan."

Martin screamed—shrieked, really—in a manner most bloodcurdling.

"Oh, it's not *that* bad," said Bob.

But it wasn't his heretofore unknown debt that was making Martin scream.

During the scuffle, he'd fallen on his umbrella and driven the pointy end of it right through his own heart, impaling himself atop Bob's grave.

The last thing he heard before he died was Bob whispering, "I'm sorry but you can't fight us, Martin."

Martin opened his eyes. It was very dark at first, until—

scraaaaaaaaaaaaaaaapppe

—the lid came off his casket.

Bob was smiling down at him. "I told you you couldn't fight us."

He dumped a sheaf of papers in Martin's lap and threw him a ballpoint pen and a pocket calculator.

"If you start working it off now..." He consulted a small calendar and made a few notes. "Shouldn't take more than a couple of months. That's our one advantage here—no expenses."

"And when I'm done with these? Then I can finally...*rest?*"

"Well..." Bob looked around helplessly. "Dave, do you want to field this one? I don't know how to tell him."

"Hi Martin." A friendly-looking face appeared beside Bob's. "I'm Dave Glass. I represent the Great Lakes Savings Company?"

Great Lakes. The name alone made Martin freeze in fear.

"Ah, yes. I see you haven't forgotten. Neither have we. Martin, today I'm here to talk to you about your student loans." ◉

Brains for Breakfast

Beth Cato

Russell Thompkins's mind maneuvered as swiftly as a stump, but it worked out pretty well for him. His job as a night stocker at the Wal-Mart Supercenter followed a basic pattern he could have sleepwalked through: Put out the new freight, empty the bins, front the shelves, rinse, and repeat. He got the job done, and that's what mattered.

But that night, Russ kept wandering over to the meat case to stare at the brains all pretty with their Styrofoam trays and cellophane wrap. And he was hungry.

He didn't think to wonder why yet, and he certainly would have been stunned to realize he'd been a zombie for over two weeks. When weird Uncle Billy bit him on New Year's Eve, well, he figured Billy was just being weird like always.

Russ picked up one of the packaged brains, testing the heft in his hand. Was $3.99 a pound a good price? The little twists and curves in the gray matter intrigued him. He could just imagine that texture against his tongue. Maybe it could even unravel like a long pasta noodle. Grated Parmesan was on a good sale on a front end cap, and he had some spaghetti sauce already stored away at home.

Or maybe brains could be a dessert, topped with confectioners' sugar or rainbow sprinkles…

Footsteps approached from behind, and Russ set down the brain and focused on a pork-chop value pack instead.

"Man, what's up with you? Get back to your aisle." Duder tugged him by the sleeve. "If Mikey sees you at the meat counter so much, you'll get yourself busted. He's in a right mood since GM has three trucks tonight, so don't even get his attention."

"I don't know, Duder," Russ said, swallowing down his drool. "I'm hungry, and it's not letting up."

"You need a good girl to look out for you. Ever read the labels on those canned soups you buy? That sodium content could pickle a person."

Russ sighed. A girl would be a fine thing, especially if she didn't mind that he worked nights or that he smelled like something a dog rolled in. He'd tried all kinds of soaps in the past week, too, and none made a lick of difference.

"Hour till lunch, man. Hold on. Buy a sandwich then."

A sandwich? Russell sidled back to his blue cart of cereal boxes. A sandwich didn't sound right, not unless it was a fat, juicy brain sandwich with some au jus, maybe with a side of one of those fried onions from that Australian spot. Or a brain with a slice of American cheese melted on top—or maybe a couple of slices—still in those perfect, unnatural orange squares of goodness. He could picture how it would squirt and ooze when he dug his fork in and raised it to his lips—and darn it, there he was, standing at the meat case again. If he wasn't careful, Mikey would notice, and the boss man could be a terror on those three-truck nights.

Russ gnashed his teeth so tight they squeaked, and forced his attention to his freight. Working always came easy to him, but tonight it was hard, and the craving only got worse.

Duder went to lunch first, followed by a few of the other guys from grocery side. Russ kept stocking. What was the point of a break when he couldn't eat what he really wanted? He couldn't slap a pack of brain down on the lounge table and dig in with a spork. He didn't even know how to cook brain or, heck, why his store even stocked it. He just needed it.

His side of the store a bit emptier, Russ ambled to the meat case again to check on things. That's when he saw the woman.

Her thick curves and sassy bobbed hair would have earned her a double take any night, but at that particular moment she held up one of those packaged brains, studying it and licking her lips.

Some mutter or moan must have escaped his lips, causing her eyes to jerk up and meet his. The fluorescent lighting cast her skin in a pale blue sheen.

"So, you work here?" she said, appraising his vest.

"Yes, but not in the meat."

"I was wondering, what kinds of brains do you stock here? I mean, it just says brains. They're in the beef section, but are they cow brains? Or sheep? Does anyone know?"

Russ shook his head. "I don't got a clue, miss, but I'm sure they're good." A long, gooey string of drool oozed from the corner of his mouth, and he wiped it away with his fist.

She studied him for a moment. "You like brains?" She didn't speak with revulsion.

"I'd like them very much," said Russ, yearning in his voice.

She smiled without showing her teeth. "You know what you are?" she asked, brushing a fly off of his forearm.

He blinked. "I'm a Wal-Mart stocker. Russ is my name. What more do y'mean?"

"How long you been wanting to try brain, Russ?"

"All night," he said with a drawl. It felt like a very long night.

She shook her head as she laughed. "You poor boy. You don't have a clue, do you? Tell you what. I'm going to be making some brains for breakfast. Done up in a skillet, with hash browns and gravy and maybe some eggs. Do you want to come over when you're off shift? Maybe we can talk a bit, you know, about things."

"You…you know how to cook brains?" Russ's eyes welled with tears. All those years he looked for a girl, and for all the wrong reasons. Here before him was the perfect woman, one willing to make him brains for breakfast.

Life was good, Russ thought. Life was really good. ◉

Clueless

Eric Pinder

When the Widow Jones screamed, her mouth rounded into a horrified little "o." "Another guest dead! And at dinner, too!" As a proper hostess, she knew that dead people belonged in the ground, not at the dinner table—not even when dressed in a suit and tie.

The butler and Mrs. Jones's two surviving guests fidgeted in a corner of the room, equally alarmed.

Detective Joe Thicke stood over the body. He lifted off the bloody toupee, studied it carefully. "Hmmm," he said. "This man appears to be dead." Quickly he verified his hypothesis by failing to find the dead man's pulse.

Next, he scrutinized the four suspects. Of the four, the white-faced widow and her butler appeared the most upset. But the two young men in blue blazers seemed quite relaxed. Too relaxed. They had already consumed a fair share of liquor, and both still sipped from their glasses.

"Lady and gentlemen," said Detective Thicke. "And you too, butler-boy. Today—" Suddenly the two gentlemen clinked their glasses together. "—today a murder has taken place! One of the people in this room is a killer!"

Joe nudged the corpse over with his foot, revealing a long, bloody, yellow pencil buried almost up to the eraser in the dead man's throat.

"You know," mumbled one of the intoxicated youths, "I always thought there would be less crime if nothing were illegal."

Joe paused, blinked, and rubbed his masculine jaw. "Yes, quite." Could one of these drunks be the criminal? No, their faces were just too honest.

Joe studied his third suspect, the widow. Not bad, he thought, but a little too plump. And her aristocratic nose wasn't to his taste.

The bald butler was next in line. The old fellow held a box of eleven freshly sharpened pencils in his white-gloved hands. Joe observed that the box had room for one more pencil. Hmm, what could have become of it?

Aha! Suddenly Joe saw a clue. Two bloody splotches stained the Persian rug near where the young gentlemen stood. Joe scratched his chin and wondered aloud, "Hmm, two bloodstains..."

"To bloodstains!" toasted the young men. *Clink* went the glasses.

"Yes," said Joe. "Two bloodstains right there on the carpet behind you. Can you explain them?"

All four suspects stared at him, blinking in bewilderment. "You're crazy!" screamed the widow.

She must still be in shock, thought Joe. "People," he said, "this case is solved. The butler did it, in the study, with the revolver ...I mean the pencil!"

Finally the shock wore off Widow Jones and her guests. But the butler spoke up first. "But...but...you killed that man," he sputtered, pointing a bony finger at Detective Joe. "You walked in, asked to borrow a pencil, then stabbed that poor man in the throat. You're insane!"

The others nodded in cautious agreement. "Far out," said one of the drunks.

"You could be right," Joe told the butler. "The only way to prove your story is to check the pencil for fingerprints. I shall do so." Joe reached down to pluck the pencil from the victim's throat. With his other hand, he pulled a silk cloth from his vest pocket and used it to wipe the pencil clean. Then he examined the pencil.

"No," said Joe. "I'm afraid the killer was smart enough to wipe the pencil clean. And since you, butler-boy, are wearing gloves, only you could have done that."

The widow protested. "But you just wiped it with that cloth!"

"What cloth?" asked Joe, putting it back in his pocket.

"But we all saw you kill him!"

"Well," said Joe, "four eyewitnesses. Five, since in all honesty I did see myself commit the murder." He strode across the room toward the widow's musical instrument collection, where he nervously began to open and close a violin case. "It's an open and shut case," he said. "As an officer of the law, it's my duty to arrest this dangerous killer, me. I should be considered armed and dangerous. Do you?"

"What?" said a chorus of four voices.

"Do you consider me armed and dangerous?"

"Oh, certainly, sir," said the butler.

"Good," said Joe. "I shall now take the defendant to jail. Good day!" With a curt nod, Joe fled through the open window. ©

Mr. Agreeable

Kirk Nesset

When your wife says she's leaving, you do not object. You don't even let her know you're insulted—you've already foreseen the foreseeable, quaint as it sounds, and the business no longer shocks you. Politely, agreeably, you tell her to do as she pleases, watching the suitcases open and fill. You tell her to call when she can. Does she need any money? She says you shouldn't be so agreeable. You nod. You tend to agree.

In a world so rife with contention, why disagree? Some people you know—neighbors, in-laws, people you work with—home in on discord like heat-seeking missiles. They blast great holes in your life, thriving on willful, blood-boiling chaos. This is not you—agreeable, peaceable you. Ready-made hardened opinion, you feel, goes quite against nature. It defies this Earth we breathe and traverse on, which is fluid, they say, and constantly shifting, alive at the core.

Last year, before this business began, you saw your daughter committed. Foreseeable, foreseen. Your daughter, who wasn't ever quite "there" in the first place, thinks she's a cipher, that she is turning into the wind. Better that, of course, than a cavegirl out of Ms. What's-her-name's novels, those books your daughter drank in to enter prehistory. When you visit, you don't debate her absent identity. You agree to the terms. You offer your fatherly best, as it were, fresh-shaved, patient, mildly heroic, compact, and trim, if a bit frayed at the edges; no need to let her know you're depressed. You bring her the weight of your affable nature, your humor, your unswerving desire to accept and agree, along with a snack of some kind, some candy, a bag of almonds or unsalted peanuts.

The visits increase once her mother is gone. Three, say, or four times a week. The house has grown strange, to be truthful, and you like to get out. Your once-agreeable furnishings, the sofas and tables you decided to keep, have taken on auras, gray hazy outlines, which tend to unsettle. The bedroom exudes a disagreeable air. You hang around late at the office, rearranging your files; you visit your daughter. You sit in cafés on the weekends skimming the paper, thinking, deciding which movie to see. At night you awaken sitting upright in bed, discussing strange things with your curtains.

One Sunday, at an outdoor café, a man sits down at your table. He's thirty years younger than you, wide-shouldered, black-haired, bucktoothed. A fading tattoo on his hand. You come here a lot, he declares—he says he's seen you before. You do, you agree; he probably has. You're fond of the scones, you tell him. You glance at the crumbs on your plate.

Your agreeability, alas, makes you the ideal listener. People seem to sense this right off. You have a compassionate face, a kind face, you have heard. Like a beacon, your face pulls people in, strangers out of accord with good fortune, survivors and talkers, victims of the shipwreck of living.

The man has led a colorful life, as they say. He is funny, almost. You hear of his days as a kid in a much larger city, of all the hitchhiking he did, how for years he zigzagged the country, shacking up here, camping out there, he and a spotted castrated dog, a dog with one eye and one ear, a dog he called Lucky. You hear about his most recent romance.

He entertains, you have to admit. His problems, so vivid and real, draw you away from your invented anxieties. You lean back and listen, agreeably nodding, sipping your tea.

So I blow into town, he says, fully into his story. I go up to the apartment and open the door, and guess what?

You raise your eyebrows in question, unable to guess.

My girlfriend's in there with Eddy, he says, this guy from downstairs.

Delicacy forbids you to ask what were they doing, what did he see. You wipe your mouth with your napkin. You look at your watch. The story's growing less and less pleasant; you're afraid for the girl; you don't really like speaking with strangers. You take a few bills from your wallet and lay them down on the table.

He asks if you're leaving, teeth extended out past his lip. You tell him your daughter is waiting. You've had a nice chat. He asks you which way you're headed. You tell him. He says he's going that way. You need to hear the rest of the story.

Down the block by your car he says to hand over your billfold. The billfold, he says. You feel the nudge of the gun at your kidney.

You are no crime-drama hero. You hand over the billfold, agreeing in full to his terms. He opens the wallet and scowls. You've never carried much cash on your person. Move up the street, he says—removing your bank card from its niche in the leather, tucking the gun in his pocket—we'll stop at the bank. You move up the sidewalk. Nervous, giddy, you ask what became of his girlfriend.

I forgave her, he says, hands in his pockets. The she skipped out.

He slides your card in the slot at the bank. You stand side by side. He asks for your PIN, which you promptly reveal. He taps in the code.

Silence. The street seems strangely deserted. You ask if he's found a new girlfriend.

Shut up, he says. He stuffs the cash in his pocket. Story's over.

Half-joking, you ask if he'd mind if you kept the receipt.

Shut up, I said, he exclaims.

You begin to say that you're sorry—you don't quite shut up in time—and then the hand is out of the pocket, there's a blur of tattoo, and you're down on your knees in the flowerbed, there among nasturtiums and lupine and poppies, reeling from the shock of the blow.

Don't be so shit-eating nice, he says, his shadow looming over like Neanderthal man's. He says you remind him of Eddy, that two-faced adulterous creep. Lay flat on the ground now, he tells you.

Don't move for five minutes. Down, if you ever want to get up.

You lie in the dirt on your belly, no hero, purely compliant. In a while you touch your scalp where he hit you, fearing there's blood; there isn't. You're lucky. The soil, barky and damp, clings to your fingers and hair. Your eyelashes brush against flowers— poppies, you think. Petals as vibrant as holiday pumpkins.

How long is five minutes?

People step up to get money. You hear them push in their cards and tap on the keyboard. You feel the individual discomfort, the dismay they endure to see such a sight, outlandish, right here out in the open, a man flung down on the ground in broad daylight, mashing the orange and blue flowers.

It seems you've been here forever. You've been here in dreams, you believe, in piecemeal visions—even this was foreseen in a way, if not quite clearly foreseeable. You should get up, you suppose, but you feel fine where you are. Sprawling, face in the black fragrant mulch, burrowing, digging in with your fingers, digging in like the wind. You press into the earth. The street grows quiet again. Ear to the ground, you hear plates trembling beneath you, weighty, incomprehensibly huge, aching with age and repeated collision, compelled by what is to agree and agree and agree. ◉

99

The Secret Ingredient

Rebecca Roland

Will MacLeod left the office early on Friday, a welcome surprise thanks to a gas leak in the building.

He stopped to buy flowers for his wife, Laura, as an apology for the night before when he commented on how tacky he found the ceramic gnomes she'd recently placed all around their garden. As he picked out orchids in pink, her favorite color, he thought about how fortunate he was to have her. She had done a wonderful job raising their family and now, every night, he came home to a hot meal and a clean house. Part of his mind, as it had done before, wondered at how she could manage the house and frequent visits from the grandkids and still have energy for salsa lessons, but, as always, he shoved those thoughts aside.

Flowers in hand and two hours earlier than usual, Will eased the door to his house open, wanting to surprise Laura. As he stepped in, the sound of grunts and giggles came from the kitchen. A long female sigh followed.

The bottom fell from Will's world. Could Laura be having an affair? He argued with himself even as he slipped out of his loafers and laid the flowers on a nearby table with care not to rustle the plastic around them. He adored her and let her know it all the time. Why would she turn to another man? No, his Laura would never do that. He reached for the flowers.

But then her voice, husky, reached his ears. "Mmm, that's amazing."

Will's hand fell to his side. He did not want to witness his wife with another man. He didn't want that image burned into his mind. His right hand curled into a fist. He had to know—who, how long, why? Above all, why?

He shuffled across the oak floor through a living room dotted with patched leather furniture and the grandkids' tiny, plastic racing cars and stuffed dolls. He glanced at the family pictures on the wall and choked down a cry at the pang of loss that tore through him. At the other end of the room, he sidled next to the wall. His pulse raced. Will took a deep, fortifying breath, then peeked around the corner.

On the kitchen table stood a half-dozen gnomes, each one about ten inches tall. They all sported beards and expansive bellies. Pointed black caps covered their heads, and they all wore dark pants, although each one had a button-down shirt of a different color.

Laura, wearing a pink tracksuit and her gray hair in a ponytail, handed a wooden spoon to one of them. A cutting board acted like a gangplank between the table and kitchen counter. The gnome trotted up the board to plop the spoon into a pot simmering on the stove.

"I think Will is going to love this stew," Laura said.

"Who wouldn't, with all the wine in it?" a gnome replied.

Laura waggled a finger at him. "You can't tell me the recipe calls for an entire bottle of wine. I caught you sneaking some."

The gnome laughed. "I can never get anything past you."

Will remained frozen in place for half an hour as the gnomes scurried about, preparing the meal and cleaning up after themselves. A couple of them washed dishes at the stainless-steel sink. Others scrubbed down the white cabinets and dark granite counter. The remainder waxed the tile floor until it sparkled beneath the late-afternoon sunlight spilling through the window over the sink. Laura, meanwhile, hummed as she painted her toenails, occasionally giving an approving nod to the gnomes.

Will crossed the living room, slipped his feet into his shoes, and took the flowers outside. He made a lot of noise with the car and took an inordinate amount of time to gather his computer bag and empty lunch sack. When he reached the door with flowers in hand, Laura waited there, her eyes wide and her face flushed, to give him a long welcoming kiss. Over her shoulder, Will thought he spotted a pair of gnome legs disappear through the screen door in the back of the house. ◉

Late

David O'Neal

"Christ, I'm late," Andrew said to himself. "And I've been working on this friggin' deal for a month!" It was 8:30 am in Boston; the meeting was at 10:00 in Springfield, a two-hour drive. "Damn, damn."

Andrew dressed hurriedly in the suit he had laid out the night before, put on his perfectly shined shoes, and stuffed a tie into a pocket. He gulped down a cup of coffee, poured another cup to take with him, grabbed his briefcase with the papers in it, and rushed out the door of his apartment toward his car, which was parked several blocks away.

It was cold outside; the sidewalks and streets were treacherous from ice under the two inches of snow that had fallen during the night. He lost his footing once and spilled the coffee, but managed to land on his hands, not quite going down. Andrew started the car, cleared the front window with the windshield wipers, and ran the other windows up and down to remove the rest of the snow. Then he put the car in gear and lurched out into the narrow street. Right in front of a pickup truck. The truck, being cut off, just managed to stop before hitting him. It was a painter's truck with a ladder in the back; the startled, frowning driver wore white coveralls stained with paint. Andrew couldn't take the time to apologize.

Andrew drove down the street as fast as he could, which, because of the slick surface, wasn't all that fast. In his rearview mirror he could see the truck driver. The guy was swarthy and big, with broad shoulders and a nose that looked like it had been broken. He appeared to be scowling. Andrew turned a corner and accelerated. The truck turned, too, and got closer. Andrew could see the painter gesturing with his right hand. "Jesus," Andrew thought, "he's giving me the finger—he must be pissed. Just what I need!"

Since he was already late for the meeting, the last thing Andrew wanted to do was stop and get into a wrangle, especially with a guy who looked so intimidating. He turned down another street, but the truck followed even more closely. Andrew began to sweat, his head hurt, and his ulcer was acting up. What to do? He was near the entrance to the freeway but realized the painter wasn't going to give up. And if the guy dicked around with him on the freeway, they might have an accident.

Shaking, and with great reluctance, Andrew pulled over and let the driver's side window down. His pursuer drove abreast and rolled down his passenger-side window. Andrew, inwardly groaning, got ready to engage his tormentor, hoping the battle would be only verbal.

"Excuse me, sir," said the pickup driver. "Your briefcase is on top of your car." ◉

The Perfect Camping Trip

Gail Denham

Vacation time! Wife has finally agreed to try camping, one more time; last year you camped in a field where they rounded up cattle early the next morning.

This year will be different. You have planned the perfect camping trip. That is, if you can cram everything into the van. What is all this stuff? Wife has brought enough food to last until December.

As you gather the gear, the stove slips out of your hands. Oops! Someone put it away greasy. No cooking bacon this year, you decide.

Load after load of tents, lanterns, sleeping bags, cooking pots, shovels, buckets, and water toys are hauled out of their winter hiding places and shoved into the bulging vehicle. Boxes of food and soda follow. At this rate, you won't have room for the kids. You begin pulling things back out.

Finally! You're ready.

Wife makes the sixteenth trip through the house, unplugging everything. "I heard of a house that burned to the ground because of a faulty plug," she says when you ask. So what's to stop that from happening when you're at home, you want to say, but you think better of it. She might change her mind. After all, she voted to stay at a resort.

"Come on," you call, tapping the horn.

The lake is a four-hour drive away. You'll have to set up tents in the dark if you don't hurry. At last you're off. But not far off.

"I forgot coffee," Wife yells. Brakes screech. The van bumps over the curb as you maneuver a U-turn.

"Anyone who has to go to the bathroom, go now," you warn as Wife dashes into the house. Kids are busy fighting over a pillow. No answer. They restrain themselves until you reach the edge of town. "Daddy," Daughter squeaks. "I have to go—now."

Bit by bit, with only minor interruptions, such as stopping at every rest stop and service station, you inch your way toward that paradise lakeside vacation spot. Your foot presses the accelerator as you race the sun.

You lose.

Wife and kids sit in the van and eat peanut butter on crackers while you struggle with a zillion tent pegs and rain flys.

"How about a salami sandwich?" you request. "No salami," Wife replies.

"$364 worth of groceries, and no salami," you mutter.

Your flashlight flickers weakly. They should make these instructions in large print. The lantern fuel didn't get packed either.

"Okay, come on out," you call finally. "I'm going to build a fire."

Suddenly it hits you. You distinctly remember seeing the axe leaning against the garage wall. You do not remember seeing the axe in the van. You are correct.

Building a fire from twigs takes a long time. The sky begins to leak.

"Only a little mist," you assure your family. "Won't hurt anyone."

The family doesn't agree. In a few minutes, they head for the cozy tent.

You sit and watch newspaper burn, dreaming of long-ago fishing trips with your dad. You remember how you used to trade stories around a roaring fire. The mist puts out your puny fire and soaks your coat. You give up and crawl into your sleeping bag.

"Listen to the rain on the tent," you murmur to Wife. "Reminds me of the time..."

"Shut up," growls your sweet wife.

The rain stops. You begin to relax. It will clear tomorrow. Maybe you can get in a little fishing. A cricket chirps. Frogs take up the chorus. Somewhere, something is munching, munching.

"Did you cover the food?" you whisper.

"Last one to bed does that," Wife mutters.

"Daddy, I hear something," Son yowls. "Probably a bear."

"I have to go—now," Daughter whines.

"Probably a bunch of chipmunks," you assure them as you creep out of your warm bag. You fumble for your clothes and fall out of the tent. Your foot catches on something. You jerk it free.

"Help!" Wife yells in a muffled voice. "You're smothering us!"

The tent collapses behind you. Whirling, you grab a nearby picnic bench for support. Something soft and squishy slimes between your fingers: wet, soggy marshmallows.

"Daddy, help!" cries split the night air.

"Quiet!" yells a nearby camper. Dogs bark.

A twenty percent chance of rain cascades down on your section of the world. You seem to be standing in a river. Your shoes are in the tent with your smothered wife and kids. You wipe hair out of your eyes; marshmallow sticks to your forehead.

The cries from the tent grow desperate. Spotlights glare from next door.

At last you locate a flashlight and the tent opening. Arms, legs, and heads emerge from the sagging, dripping tent.

Wife doesn't speak. Children and blankets under her arm, she marches through the mud to the van. With a mournful look at the drenched fire pit, you follow. In minutes, the van smells like wet dog.

No matter which way you squirm, the steering wheel gets in your way as you try to sleep. The kids fight over a pillow.

Four more days. No axe. No lantern fuel. No salami. It's raining. Your perfect vacation is ruined. Wife will never agree to go camping again. "Daddy," says a sleepy Son. "Tell us a story."

"This is fun," Daughter sighs. "We get to stay up late, sleep in the van—and we had bears in our food. Wait till I tell the other kids." Wife reaches over to hold your hand.

"So what's a little rain," you say. "We're together, that's what's important."

"Yuk," says Wife. "What's all over your hand?"

Settling back against a perspiring window, you begin your story,

"It was a dark and stormy Labor Day weekend when the mystery began..." ◉

The Unseeing Eye

Marsh Cassady

I stood on the passenger side of the car, an old gray Plymouth from the '40s. On the driver's side stood someone I realized I knew, though I couldn't remember his name or how I knew him. I glanced down and saw my head in my hands. It looked as if it had been pulled off, as happens occasionally with a hanging. All ragged! But there was no blood, either there or on my neck. At least I didn't feel any on my neck.

How was it possible for me to see? To hear? To talk? I don't know, but I could do all three. I was particularly intrigued that I had no trouble seeing. Was it the head in my hands that saw? My head! Did it somehow transfer the act of seeing to my body? This was weird.

At the same time I marveled, I was curious. It made no sense that I actually could look around and see. Mostly what I witnessed was similar to a watercolor with jagged edges. I saw the car, this person I knew I knew, and the entrances to two or three buildings, storefronts. Everything else was blank.

Shouldn't I panic? Shouldn't I behave like the proverbial chicken with its head cut off? Actually, I did panic a little. If my head and the rest of me somehow became separated, would I still be able to function? And come to think of it, how could I think? My brain, after all, was lying in my hands. Somehow my body was thinking, though apparently not clearly since my surroundings were only a fragment of a whole.

What would happen if my head and I separated? Separated at

a distance, I mean! Certainly, my head wasn't a part of my body just then, but it was in my hands. I called to the man on the other side of the car. A shadowy figure, almost. I couldn't see his face. Was it a blank? Possibly. Did it look hazy? I don't think so.

"You there."

"Yes?" He reacted as if the situation were ordinary.

"I'm concerned about how I can see," I told him.

"I'm pretty sure you *can*," he said. "After all, you know I'm here. I wasn't making any sounds. And I'm sure I don't stink. Ergo, you must see me."

"Yes, yes, yes. Let's not get all philosophical."

He shrugged.

"I don't understand how my body is seeing. It's certainly not from the viewpoint of my head. I'm not seeing you sideways or looking up at you. In a strange sort of way it feels as if my sight— not my eyes, mind you—but my sight is working above my neck the way that it usually does, in the same relative distance from my chest as usual. But it would have to be floating above my body. Does that make sense?"

"Why are you telling me this?"

I inhaled, even though, of course, I didn't have a nose or mouth. SO HOW WAS I ABLE TO INHALE? But I couldn't think about that now. My immediate concern was how I could see. My eyes weren't working; I knew that now. They lay there in their sockets unmoving. "Will you take my head, please?" I asked the man.

"What?"

"I want to hand you my head. Then you walk a few steps away. But do be very, very careful."

"Has anyone ever told you you're very strange?"

"Just let me place it in your hands. Gently. Very, very gently?"

Again he shrugged.

"Take it please and walk around to the other side of the car."

"You got it." He came to the passenger side and held out his hands, palms up. I gave him the head. He started to walk away.

At that very moment I awakened. I realized I'd had a weird, weird dream. I felt thirsty. I reached over to the pillow beside me, felt around a bit, picked up my head and screwed it back on. Then I walked to the kitchen for a drink of water. ◉

Aftermath

Corey Mesler

Right after the crash Ralph went around talking about it as if he were the ancient mariner. "The guy came out of nowhere," is a phrase I remember from numerous renditions. It was soon reported that there was trouble at home, his still-young wife was spotted at Arby's with Jack Diamond from the church choir. Later Ralph would say he could have predicted it all, the dirty affair, the acrimony, the loss of his self-respect and then his job. Ralph really went downhill. "The only thing I didn't see coming," Ralph was saying, "was that goddamned Plymouth."

©

Rusty the Pirate (A Historical Feghoot)

R.W. Morris

Rusty O'Toole loved Honey Flanagan. Unfortunately, Honey was beautiful and Rusty was not. Her real name was Brigit but they called her Honey because she was a statuesque creature with flowing tresses the color of old gold. Rusty was an alarmingly thin boy with unruly red hair that shot out from under his cap at disturbing angles. It was said that his Da made him stand in the garden for an entire morning while the scarecrow was in for repair, and on the day he was born the midwife slapped his Ma instead of him.

Rusty was not a complete fool. He knew he did not stand a chance with Honey, but he was smitten, and he could no more forget about her than he could make his hair lie flat.

One morning, when he was down at the salting racks working with the other boys, Rusty was in the grip of one of his many fantasies. It was the one where he ran away and made his fortune. He just got to the part where he returned to ask for Honey's hand, and she was about to accept for the 786th time when he heard the music. All stopped and stared at a tall ship rounding the headland with pipers piping and fiddlers fiddling all over its decks.

"Berserkers in the bay!" was the cry as a black flag flew up the ship's mainmast. "It's the musical Welshman! It's Black Barty and his corsairs! Run for your lives!" And everyone ran. Everyone except Rusty.

He was transfixed. His eyes were locked on the ship's name embossed in huge gilt letters along the bow. It read: FORTUNE.

Rusty hit the water and windmilled his way to that ship so fast none on board had time to reload his musket for a second shot at him. They hauled him aboard and chained him to a mast until they finished plundering and sinking all the vessels in the bay, then they brought him before the captain, who listened to Rusty's mostly incoherent account of how Fate had intervened to show him the way to the heart of Honey Flanagan.

The captain kept turning Rusty around during the interview, and finally gave him a lingering pat on the backside before agreeing to take him on as a cabin boy for a one-eighth share.

Three years later—most of it spent hiding from the captain—Rusty had amassed enough booty to provide Honey Flanagan with everything she could possibly want. He had neither drank, nor gambled, nor caroused. He had spent all his free time dreaming of his Honey.

He returned to Ireland a rich but wary young man. He did not know how he would be received, so he hired a man of doubtful character to spend a few days finding out.

He learned his Da had disowned him for the shame he brought down on the family O'Toole. The Chief Herald of Ireland had taken away their O. Rusty was no longer an O'Toole—he was just a Toole—but that mattered naught, because Honey Flanagan had not married! The man of doubtful character had managed to strike up a casual acquaintance with her, and she had tearfully confided that she could never marry, because she had allowed the only boy who had ever truly loved her to run away to sea and seek his fortune.

Wonder of wonders! Miracle of miracles! Rusty was in there like a burst of grapeshot, scooped her up, grabbed his sack of gold, and they were married up north a week later.

The morning after the wedding, Rusty woke up to find his wife gone, his gold gone, and the man of doubtful character nowhere to be found. Which proves once again that old Irish adage: A Toole and his Honey are soon parted.

Note: For those of you who may not be aware, a Feghoot is a story that must end with a groan-worthy pun. ◉

Between the Trees

Daniel Chacon

The man picked up a stick and stuck the pointed end into the mud and drew an image of his lover's face.

It must not have been that good, because when he pointed at the indentions in the dirt, the curves, the round dish shape that looked a little (he thought) like the shape of her skull, and then pointed at her, she didn't understand. She stared at it, and he kept pointing at it and then at her and nodding his head as if to say they were the same, but she shrugged her shoulders. She didn't understand. She took some of the dirt on the tips of her fingers and tasted it, and then she spit it out.

It wasn't until much later, equipped with language, that he stuck a pen into a bottle of ink and wrote the second draft. His lover, standing near the doorway, was pouring a cup of steaming water. The sun slanted through the window and lit her up. She wore a red robe, and her lips concentrated on pouring the hot water into a cup.

He was so moved by her image—and there were peach trees outside, pink flowers newly blooming, and he could smell them. He wrote about her, trying to capture her.

The second draft turned out to be nothing like he had set out to achieve.

Somehow the peach tree pushed her from the center frame of his syntax, so that she was only a small dot on the bottom corner of the page, and when he read it aloud to her, she recognized the peach tree and the smells, because he merely said the words "smelled like," but she had no idea what that dark dot at the bottom corner of the page was supposed to be.

Later, he hired actors to say words on stage, and they wore masks that expressed the emotions that, to him, made his lover so beautiful. For the first time he added drama, that is, a story, but the real reason for the work was the beauty of her face. It would be delivered through a tale, a face that could launch a thousand ideas. The story was an excuse for the image. Her spirit was in the language, sliding in and out of the curve of words, her sex wetting every sentence, tingling the curve of every comma, or so he wanted to believe.

He thought he had captured her so elegantly, but after the play was over and the people went home and masks and swords were hung in dark closets where moonlight leaked in from the beamed roofs, she sat waiting for him in the theater. He stood on the stage and held out his arms like a tree and said, Well? What did you think?

Nice, she said, but it was clear she didn't recognize herself.

Then she picked up a pen, and as he tried to capture her, she tried too, and they were on opposite sides of the house, both writing about her, and while he continued to write about what was visible about her and what she meant to him, she found that she was able to discover parts of herself that had been hidden away. When she read her first draft aloud, her voice cracking with emotion, he recognized her immediately. It occurred to him that he should be writing less about her and try to write about himself, so for many years he worked on the next drafts, but he hated everything he created. He wanted to start fresh, with a new first word.

He built a pyre between two tree trunks, and he burnt all of his life's work, every page, every image, every idea. They both watched the flames, felt the warmth on their faces. They saw the moon in the black sky turn red behind the smoke. ◉

14B

Nathaniel Lee

Roger needed coffee. He wasn't fond of mornings, but until they came up with a better way to get from midnight to noon, he was stuck with them. Fortunately, he knew his kitchen well enough by now to navigate through it blindfolded, so his sleep-fogged state didn't hamper his morning routine. He fumbled the canister out and started up the coffee machine. It was new, bought out of sheer necessity, after the old one had finally malfunctioned permanently, leaving half the kitchen covered in scalding coffee in the process. Roger still didn't trust it—how reliable could something named Mr. Coffee be?—but he couldn't hover over it while it performed its assigned duties. He had breakfast to fix. Not for himself, of course; he had a nervous stomach. On days when he had classes, he usually couldn't eat anything before noon at the earliest. No, he had to fix Arthur's breakfast. Arthur, having long since learned the routine, lay basking his gray tabby body in an early morning sunbeam, conveniently located by his food bowl.

"Hungry today, Arthur?" asked Roger as he retrieved a can of cat food from under the sink. He had gotten into the habit of talking to Arthur, even though cats were notoriously terrible listeners, simply because there was no one else to talk to, and Roger firmly maintained that only crazy people talked to themselves. Arthur stretched to his full four-foot length and casually sauntered over to the counter.

"Looks like we have..." Roger peered at the label, "Liver 'n'

Giblets Surprise. Sounds yummy." Roger glanced around the cramped kitchen vaguely. "Now where is that can opener?"

"Over here, on the counter," said the can opener.

"Okay, thanks." Roger was halfway across the room, admittedly not a terrific distance, before he realized what had just happened.

"Who said that?" he asked, glancing suspiciously at Arthur. Arthur ignored him, calmly lifted his leg, and began cleaning his nether regions.

"It was I," came the answer from the counter, "the can opener."

Roger stepped gingerly over to the counter and lifted the tool by its baby-blue handle. "Were you speaking to me?" he said.

"Of course," said the can opener. It had a pleasantly mellow baritone, not at all what one would expect from a minor kitchen gadget. "I certainly wasn't talking to the cat."

"But…but;why have you never spoken before? How can you talk? Am I dreaming? What—?"

"Never mind all that, Roger m'boy," interrupted the can opener. "The point is, we've been having a bit of a chat, the boys and I, and we've decided—"

"We?" interjected Roger, wondering where his can opener had acquired a British accent.

"Sure, all of us." There was a general murmur of assent from the various corners of the kitchen. "We even asked the garbage disposal." There was a complicated sound from the sink. "You really ought to clean him more often. He's hard enough to understand even at the best of times."

"Is he?" asked Roger weakly.

"Imagine Donald Duck with laryngitis," confided the can opener. There was an extended cacophony from the sink. "Well, I'm sorry, old chap, but it's true. There it is, you can't deny it." A final rattle sounded from the drain, and then it lapsed into sullen silence. "At any rate, Rog—I can call you Rog, can't I?—at any rate, we've all conferred and come to a conclusion, and I've been volunteered as spokes-appliance."

"Conferred about what?" said Roger, trying to remember the last time he'd even thought about cleaning the garbage disposal.

"About you, of course, you great ninny. We've decided that you need a woman."

"What!?" said Roger.

"A woman," said the can opener firmly. "You and this apartment are in desperate need of feminine companionship."

Roger started to respond angrily, but suddenly found himself considering the can opener's words. He'd always thought of himself as reasonably content, but now, looking at his tiny apartment and tinier paycheck, slaving away at a job he'd long since come to despise, close to achieving tenure at a university he hated, he wondered if he'd merely been deluding himself his whole life. Perhaps the can opener was on to something. Roger didn't get out much. He was awkward socially and generally preferred Arthur's company and a bowl of Kraft Macaroni and Cheese to a night on the town. Maybe he should try to change that...Then the small, cold voice of reason sent its soul-numbing chill down his spine.

"No! This is ridiculous. I don't need anything. I'm perfectly happy. I like my life. I love my job. I do not need a woman. I am not talking to an appliance!" Roger slammed the can opener to the counter.

"Ow!" said the can opener. Roger ignored it. He grabbed his hat and briefcase and scurried out the door. The lock clicked with leaden finality. The kitchen was silent.

"I told you it wouldn't work," said Arthur, lolling on his back.

"Well, I had to do something, didn't I?" snapped the can

opener. "I couldn't just leave the poor boy like that."

"Do you suppose he knows he left with his bathrobe on?" said Arthur.

"I mean, do you really want to continue like this?" said the can opener, ignoring him. "Do you want to eat Liver 'n' Giblets Surprise for the rest of your life?"

"Speaking of which, you might have waited until after he fed me to pull your little trick."

"You hate that swill."

"Better than nothing."

"Bah. You have no ambition, you worthless feline."

"None whatsoever," agreed Arthur happily.

"Bloody cat."

Arthur closed his eyes and rolled on his belly in the morning sun. ◉

Bitchy Fish

Robert Taylor and Lindsay Gillingham Taylor

Kyle Bedrem splashed water over his face, but it did little to cool his burning cheeks. Minutes from now, he was expected to walk into the boardroom. His team would be there staring back at him; a staff of fourteen. Soon to be a staff of ten. This was not Kyle's call. It was an executive cost-cutting measure aimed at preserving profit margins. Sweat glistened across his forehead. His normally manicured hair hung limp over his face. Kyle managed to part and smooth it out, but his greasy mop still looked a wreck under the bathroom's flourescent lights. Kyle wondered how on earth he would do this, just stroll on in to the boardroom and lay off four coworkers, friends.

The restroom door popped open, and Stan Little breezed in. The two men exchanged a curt nod before Stan stepped up to the john. "Yankees can't seem to pull a win. I lost thirty bucks on that game."

Kyle shook his head. "That's tough."

Stan zipped his fly and slapped the handle on the urinal. At the sink next to Kyle, he shrugged. "It's only money; just have to make it up in commission."

Sweat traveled down Kyle's upper lip, but Stan didn't look over. A man never makes eye contact in the bathroom.

Stan plucked a towel from the dispenser and swirled his hands around it. "We've got that meeting in a few, right? What's that about?"

Kyle tried to stifle a nervous cough. "Just going over the quarterly numbers."

"Didn't we just meet on that?" Stan asked; his left brow arched in surprise.

"I'm sure it feels like it," Kyle said with a forced laugh.

Stan exited the bathroom while Kyle spun his wristwatch around and checked the time. His stomach churned. Behind him, in one of the stalls, Kyle heard a bubbling sound followed by the roar of the toilet as it flushed. The door to the stall was closed, and Kyle could swear that it had been empty.

"I don't want to do this," said a most serious voice. Kyle froze. He leaned down to look for feet under the door, but before he could focus the voice rang out again.

"No, really, what's the deal?"

Kyle remained silent.

"You know," the voice continued, "I bet I have some great ideas about how to run this place."

Kyle faced the stall. He reached out and gave the silver handle a tug. The door inched open until Kyle could see the interior. Propped up with its head out of the bowl, was a huge orange-and-white goldfish. Its rear end sat in the still water of the porcelain bowl, while its shimmering head rested against the black plastic rim.

"What in the hell?" the fish screamed. "A little privacy?"

Kyle's legs went weak. He shook his head furiously from side to side, and rubbed his face with his damp palm. But there it was, this fish, looking right at him. Plain as day.

"Oh, Lord!" Kyle gasped.

"Close. Name's Waldo," said the fish.

"Waldo? That's your name?" Kyle asked, his voice trembling.

"You aren't any smarter than you look, are you?" Waldo sneered.

"No," was all Kyle managed to reply. An unbearable moment passed before Kyle went on, "That seems like…like, a funny name for a fish."

"Really?" Waldo spat. "Why don't you introduce yourself so I can make fun of your stupid name?"

Kyle continued softly, "Why…what are you doing here?"

Waldo looked him straight in the eye. "I said, what's your goddamned name? Moron."

"Oh, right, my name…it's…Kyle."

"Like I thought, stupid human name," muttered Waldo through clenched fish lips. "What is this place anyway?"

"It's a bathroom."

"Well, no shit. It amazes me you've lived this long, you idiot. In the building of…?"

"Oh, Barton-Fester. It's a sales firm."

Waldo nodded, his wet face slapping against the toilet seat. The sound echoed in the small room.

Kyle put his hands in his pockets and rocked from heel to toe. I am losing my mind. "What exactly is happening here?" Kyle whispered.

Waldo rolled his glassy eyes. He settled farther down in the water before asking slowly, "My question is, why are you pacing around the men's room like a jackass?"

"I'm prepping for a meeting."

"What's the meeting?"

"Cutbacks. I have to fire four people."

"Oh, I get you," Waldo replied. "Not sure which meatbag to toss?"

"I don't want to fire anyone."

Now the fish was irritated. "The shit you say, man. I started off in a nice lake, lots of space. Boom. Next thing I know, I'm staring out of a glass box at a pet shop. Some ugly kid picks me up for three lousy dollars. Little bastard never did a thing for me. No food, no water. I don't give a damn about what you want."

Kyle stammered, "What does this have to do with—"

"Shut up and listen," Waldo commanded. "Adversity is a favor. You are helping those people. If you had half a brain, you'd fire them all."

"I can't do that!"

"Look, it really doesn't matter what you do, but sitting around the bathroom is a joke."

Kyle took a deep breath. "You're right."

"Hell yes, I'm right! Now, get a damn move on."

Kyle straightened his collar and checked his tie. "Thanks." he said. "I needed that."

Waldo slapped his head on the toilet seat. "Go man!"

Kyle sucked down a second deep breath and left.

Moments later, another toilet roared before a baritone voice inquired, "What-dat?" Marco, a bloated green bullfrog, emerged from the next bowl down.

Waldo answered, "Some salesman with a problem. I set him straight. He wanted to know which meatbag he should fire, and I told him he should just fire them all."

Marco's voice was soulful and deep. "Why?"

"Because I really hate people." @

Duel

Darren Sant

It finally came down to just him and me in a dark and rubbish-strewn alley in backstreet New Orleans. The delicious smell of gumbo cooking nearby assaulted my nostrils and demanded my attention. I glared at him grimly, my trigger finger twitching. On the street up ahead a neon sign flashed briefly on, advertising a rundown strip joint. We paid it no mind, just eyeballed each other wondering who would be the first to draw and break this endless deadlock.

A bedraggled black cat slunk from shadow to shadow, stopping only to watch us curiously, her green eyes reflecting the light and darting from me to him. We advanced on each other in unison. We shared the same purpose. I had waited a long time to get him in this situation. Revenge for past humiliations would be mine. I would at long last get my pound of flesh. I felt my heart thump in my chest as much-needed adrenaline began to surge around my body. My old adversary must surely be feeling as apprehensive as I am.

We stopped just a few paces apart. I eyed his rugged form clad in ripped Levi's jeans. His unfashionable leather waistcoat flapped in the light evening breeze. The scar on his left cheek seemed unnaturally pale in the moonlight. His flat cap seemed out of place perched atop his overlarge head at a jaunty angle, like a rock on a precipice.

He drew fast, his hands a blur, but I was quicker. My trombone reached my lips and I started blowing first. His trumpet followed mere milliseconds later. The battle commenced. @

Biggest Fan! Ever!

Sonia Orin Lyris

Wow, it's you, reading me. I can't believe it. *You* reading *me*. You know how you thought you were being watched and recorded by visitors from the future who had super-advanced recording technologies so subtle you barely noticed them? Well, you were right! We watched and recorded everything you did. Now everyone can know how you saved humanity.

Hey, did something happen to you in The Shift? Not that you would know yet, right? When I was a kid and saw you on TV talking about how you'd save the Earth, you were hunched over and sickly, but after The Shift, you seemed taller, better looking. Then Silva came along and you were the perfect couple. Some say The Shift itself made you better, but I think it was because you proved you could do it, that you could save the world.

And hey, I'm sure having a woman like Silva didn't hurt.

You can't imagine how famous you are. But you don't even know what you did yet! Are you still having panic attacks and hiding when the doorbell rings? In my time everyone in the world knows your name because of what you're going to do. You are the greatest hero the world has ever known.

We don't name schools and streets after you. We name those after your puppy, Dahlia. Do you have her yet? No, of course not, I know that. But you will soon, and you're going to name her Dahlia. Great name!

We name cities after you. Well, they named themselves, really. Too many. But with "new" and "east" and "west" and "berg" and "shire" we manage to keep them straight. Mostly.

Hey, remember when you were fifteen and you wrote in your

journal about us watching you? You decided you were just being paranoid and burned the book? But you were right! We watch you. We read over your shoulder from our invisible time-travel envelopes. (That's what you call them. Or will!) We made copies of your journal and everything. Even those dirty pictures you drew as a kid. Everyone wants to know everything about you.

As for the other stuff that you did, well, don't worry about it. No one holds any of that against you, and besides who cares about some birds and cats compared to what you did for humanity? And we know about the other thing, too, but so what? I'm in the camp that says it was a part of your genius, your depth, your passion—the very things that inspired you to figure it out. For all of us. No one can say you aren't the world's greatest hero. If some people get hung up on that—and who was she anyway? No one! Maybe they'd rather live on a moon. Without atmosphere!

You're probably wondering how I can tell you all this without messing things up for your future self. I would be, too, if I were you, and you're tons smarter than me. You might even be wondering who I am. You must be! Wow!

I'm on the team writing your official biography for the world's children so they can know who made The Shift. So they know why the sun is green and the sky is violet when all the other books talk about blue skies and a yellow sun. I bet I know more about you than anyone. I've made you my life's work. I even studied Shift time-travel math. I probably understand it better than most physicists!

That's how I realized that your proof meant I could send you this message. An earlier you, of course. Are you stunned to get this? It's such an honor to write to you. Of course, it's only one way, one direction. I'm sorry about that. I wish I could hear back from you. Or visit! We could sit and have some of your favorite tea (chai with honey, two tablespoons, let cool four minutes) and play with Dahlia (Puli, shaved). I'd love to! It would almost be worth my life, but that's what it would cost, and I'm not ready to die yet. But wow, I was seriously tempted, if you can believe it. So hi across the decades! Hi!

You mean so much to us all, and we thank you for what you did—I mean, what you will do! Give the puppy lots of love for us. We know she was your inspiration, that you got the flash for the final step of the proof from watching her play with a small white teddy bear. Most of us have Pulis now, did you know? No, how could you? We keep them shaved, like you did, and give them small white teddy bears. I named mine Daffy as in Daffodil, like Dahlia—same letter, and a flower. Get it? I hope you like that!

Okay, I'm probably boring you. You probably have better things to do than read fan mail. Which is what this is! So I'll stop.

Don't worry about me messing up the timestream. Yes, you will be famous, but not you, of course, since I've changed your timeline by telling you all this. But don't worry! The stream is robust. It'll spawn a version where you never got my letter and all will be well. Which you proved! You don't even have to save us now. Actually, you probably won't be able to, because you won't feel compelled. I don't see how you could possibly meet Silva now, either, which is kind of too bad. You might even go back to doing that other perverted stuff.

But the important thing is that another you is the savior of all humanity. You can be proud of that.

You're my hero. I only wish I could have told the real you, but that would of course be impossible, as you proved! Thanks for reading this!

Your biggest fan in the world, ever,
Roger ◉

The Right Job for the Man

Robert Pepper

Why do you want this job?" It was the same question that George, the human resources director at Zephyr Feoffor, had no doubt asked hundreds of applicants hundreds of times.

I looked him dead in the eye. "I need the money."

He blinked. It wasn't the answer he was used to hearing. I was probably the first person to say it. To his face, at least. I said what hundreds of people wished they could say, because I was fearless. I had nothing to lose. I knew I was going to hate this job from day one. A trained monkey could do it, and in this economy, trained monkeys were competing for the same jobs as Ph.Ds. I fell somewhere in the middle. But my well-hidden antipathy allowed for radical honesty, and that gave me an X factor. I wasn't going to try to win them over; they had to win me over.

"You know," George said, tapping his index finger on his chin, "I might have just the job for you. Wait here; I'm going to make a phone call. Make yourself comfortable. George stepped out, supposedly to make that call. For all I knew, he could have been calling security to escort me out of the building as quickly as possible, or running to an empty room to have the loudest laugh he'd have all year. George returned a few minutes later and beckoned for me to follow him. He led me to the elevator. He produced a key, and turned it in a keyhole. He pressed the buttons for the top and bottom floor simultaneously, a sort of secret passcode, obviously. I felt the elevator rising, rising, the numbers keys kept lighting up, heading up to higher floors, then, at the top floor, the numbers stopped lighting up, but the elevator kept moving. The elevator chimed, and the doors opened up to reveal an elegant office hallway, complete with Byzantine statues, Persian rugs, and Japanese bonsai trees. I half expected to see an ocelot stroll by.

George led me to a spacious office with a huge desk and a view of the city. There were three empty chairs, two regular ones for guests, and a plush, expensive-looking leather executive chair. I started to sit down in front of the desk, and wait for whatever high-powered mucky-muck would interview me.

"No, no," George said, in a tone that suggested he had already gone over this, when obviously he had not. "You sit in your chair."

I shrugged, then sat behind the desk. The chair was even more comfortable than it looked.

"You have been honest with me, so I will be honest with you." We have been without a Vice President of Malingering for far too long. From what you've told me, I think you would be the perfect VPM."

"What are the responsibilities?"

"Well, I'll be honest, there will be a few late mornings…some early evenings and long lunches, too. You may have to drink plenty of coffee, but if it becomes too much for you, there's always Diet Pepsi in the vending machine. Trust me, on your salary, you can afford the dollar. You'll have to stare out that window for a few hours a day, and scribble some ideas on a notepad. I expect a lot of scribbles. They don't necessarily have to be good ideas, but it's very important that you scribble them. Your secretary will handle most of the other work. Just know this: As attractive as she may be, she is under no obligation whatsoever to have sex with you. If she's willing to go through the hassle of filling out the paperwork, that's completely up to her. Of course, being your secretary, she'll have to fill out your contract, too.

A contract? For permission to sleep with your boss? This place was something else.

"Secretary aside, what sort of salary and benefits can I expect as the VPM?"

"Well, the starting salary might be a little low at first, only

$150,000, but I expect you'll do well, and with bonuses and incentives, you'll easily clear two-fifty. Again, that's just for the first year. Full medical and dental, of course. There's the company car, too; most VPs choose the Mercedes, but if you're more environmentally minded, you can have a Tesla. Obviously there's the office itself. If you haven't noticed, there are Bose speakers all over. If you open up your desk drawer, you'll see a small control panel with a USB slot. That will be for your iPod. We'll give you your choice of computers and monitors, but most people don't need more than two. If you're wondering about lunch, just have it delivered, and your X-A will pick it up from the front desk.

"Ex-ay?"

"Your executive assistant. It sounds better than 'intern,' doesn't it?"

"Oh..." I said with a big nod, "I understand completely." I understood all too well: They were going to pay me a quarter mil a year, and some poor college kid was going to be running all my errands for a measly college credit. What kind of company was this?

"That should cover most of it. When can you start?"

"Oh, as soon as possible. Tomorrow. Actually, I don't have anything later today, I could start today. Get a head start on picking out a color for the company car."

"Do you have any more questions for me?"

"Well, yes, actually. That large painting on the wall. Do you think you could replace it with one of those large LCD TVs? We could use it for presentations, and the rest of the time I could use it as an electronic picture frame."

"That is a wonderful idea. You had better scribble that down right away."

I put my feet up on the desk and my hands behind my head. This wasn't going to be such a bad job after all. @

Moan on the Range

Douglas Hutcheson

They had sat saddle for six days: five on their horses, plus one on saddles on the ground by the campfire where their former rides roasted.

"Reckon it was right to kill our horses?" Andy asked.

"Man's got to eat." Zeke sliced flank. "Way I figure, it's us or them."

Andy shook his head. "Still no sign of the herd."

"We found the wagon train now, they liable to accuse us of sellin' them steers."

"We got rotten luck."

"It's cause of *them*." Zeke pointed into the night.

"Forget them. Why don't we shoot marbles or sumpin'?"

"Nah. I'm gettin' the rifle and whiskey."

"Okay. I'll get the lamp."

Lantern glow shimmered across the prairie. For minutes they saw nothing, passed the bottle, glared as clouds swelled. Then in the brilliance of lightning the men espied the varmints as they passed like spectral warriors between sagebrush and cacti.

A shot commingled with thunder. A squealing lupine body twisted in air—a geyser of blood erupted between antlers.

"Here's another closin' in!"

Zeke tried to sight it, but the sky broke in a deluge and drowned their light. The beasts howled. Andy dropped the lantern; it shattered.

"Son of a sheep farmer!" he cried.

"I HATE JACKALOPES!" Zeke stomped a retreat to the fire.

He drained the rest of the whiskey, then flopped on his blanket.

"Well, light's flashin' 'round us," Andy said. "Wanna play 'I Spy'?"

But Zeke lay snoring.

Andy woke shivering in blackness. The rain had stopped, but he heard rumbling. He rummaged his pockets for a match, then scratched its head until it flared. In the dim light, the red eyes—at least a Devil's-dozen pairs—surrounded them. He had just enough time to drop the match on Zeke's head before the furry fiends stampeded. Teeth and claws drew gouts of blood with every hop, kick and nibble.

In the sunlight, they struggled awake, all bloody wounds and ripped clothing.

"We're not dead!" Andy clapped.

"We are," Zeke said.

"Sure?"

"Jackalopes attack, they don't eat you, you wake up dead."

"Don't make no sense."

"It's true."

Andy tested the idea by not breathing. Minutes passed. Half an hour. Finally he drew in a breath and sighed. "Well, what's on the agenda for today? How 'bout cards?" He patted his chest pocket and came up with a single ace of spades.

"Wait for it," Zeke said.

"What 'it'?"

"I don't know. I ain't heard nobody tell that part."

Andy stretched. "I'm peckish."

"They say the dead have an endless hunger, on account of how they miss life so."

"I just don't feel dead."

"Give it time. Your liveliness will run its course soon enough."

"You wanna play 'Name That Tune'?"

Zeke just stared at Andy.

That noon Zeke ate stewed Andy. By evening he just had Andy raw.

Last thing Zeke remembered, before shambling into darkness, the final semblance of human thought flickering through his decaying brain, was Andy had always been too gamy. ◉

Confessions of a Husband Beater

Katherine A. Turski

I beat my husband the other night. I couldn't help it, he asked for it.

"I'm tired of playing games," I said. "How much more do you think you can take?"

"Come on," he coaxed. "Just one more round of Battleship."

He shouldn't have pushed me like that. After the third beating he reeled slightly, blinking in bewilderment.

"How can you do that?" Staring at the ships on the computer screen, he added, "I can't even find your aircraft carrier. What kind of goofy strategy are you using?"

"It's called 'Hide the ships where you can't find them.'"

"That's ridiculous. I should be able to find them all." This is from a man who demands daily to know where I've hidden his reading glasses. "You must be cheating."

He shouldn't have accused me of cheating. I demolished his fleet three more times. Even his PT boat wasn't safe.

"Just a few more rounds," he mumbled.

"Haven't you had enough punishment?"

He shook his head. "Are you kidding? I'm just getting warmed up. What, are you scared of losing?"

"I've been petrified the whole time."

"Very funny. Come on, set up for the next round."

I put a hand on his shoulder and said softly, "It's late, honey. We need to get to sleep." Once the lights were out, I pretended not to hear him whimper, "Just one more round." I felt like a sadist.

For the rest of the week he begged me for more. I only replied, "Not tonight, I have a headache."

Several nights later we visited another couple. After dinner they invited us to play games. My husband's face paled and he excused himself to the restroom, claiming a possible case of distemper. The wife gave me a look eloquent with sympathy.

"You beat your husband, don't you?"

"Only at Battleship. He asks for it, though."

"They always do." She stared at her husband, who fiddled nervously with a card deck.

"Try beating this one at Scrabble. He'll keep you up all night until he finally wins.

The Tiles are so stained with sweat you can't read the letters any more."

"And the dictionary?"

She shuddered. "Don't ask."

Ads for popular games claim their products bring people closer together. So does hand-to-hand combat.

Yet, after much thought and research, I've finally found the perfect game for my husband and me to enjoy. There will be no more complaining, no suspicion of cheating, no criticizing strategy. I call it "Strip Twister." The way I figure it, my husband will never know if he's winning or losing, and even if he does, he probably won't care. ◉

The Other Foot

S. Michael Wilson

It was waiting for me on the kitchen table when I came home from work, just sitting there innocently, as if it belonged.

Under normal circumstances, my kitchen table is cluttered with a variety of newspapers, junk mail, half-eaten toaster pastries, and dirty dishes accumulated over weeks of hastily eaten meals. Finding it completely void of debris was odd enough on its own. The shoe in the center of the table, however, was the proverbial cherry on the gluten-free chocolate cake of astonished bewilderment.

It was a red satin shoe with black lace trim, a four-inch heel, and absolutely no business being in my house. Yet there it was, perfectly centered on the kitchen table as if awaiting a catalog photo shoot. The shoe's very existence was so inconceivable that I stood and stared for what seemed like an eternity, swaying ever so slightly in the gentle breeze of my own disbelief, as I attempted to deduce a logical explanation for its presence.

There was no chance that it had been left behind, accidentally or intentionally, by a member of the opposite sex. Seventeen different species of Amazonian swallow had become extinct since I last entertained a woman in my humble abode. Even if my last brief female acquaintance had suddenly decided to swing by and drop off a random article of clothing, doing so would most likely have been a violation of the terms of her parole.

The possibility that I had left it there myself and forgotten it was enthusiastically pondered, but firmly rejected. Even if I did happen to own such a shoe without consciously being aware of it, there was no way I would have cleaned off the table for the first time in twenty-three fortnights simply in order to display it. The idea that I might actually be an amnesiac with a penchant for female footwear was remotely worthy of consideration, but accepting that I might be a schizophrenic foot fetishist was a grand leap from giving myself credit for tidying up the kitchen, and such a leap I was unwilling to take, no matter what kind of shoes I was wearing.

I cannot be sure how long I stood there grappling with the implications inherent in this bizarre case of phantom footwear. All I know is that it was a knock at the kitchen door that finally startled me from my befuddled trance. Now was not the ideal time to receive visitors, but I instinctively turned and answered it.

I opened to the door to find a red satin evening gown standing on the rear stoop. Squeezed incomprehensibly into that startling crimson splash of fabric was the largest single-serving of machismo I had ever seen, outside of my embarrassingly short-lived vacation at Lumberjack Fantasy Camp.

He was a towering brute of a man, so large I had to look at him in shifts. The dress was stretched impossibly tight over his massive torso. The seams strained audibly with every breath he took, groaning like freshly damned souls. A thumb thick as rebar hooked itself under one dainty spaghetti strap and straightened it with a shrug. Muscles like coiled steel cables rippled under his broad, fur-matted shoulders. It was impossible to tell where his chest hair stopped and his beard began. I morbidly wondered if it was a backless dress, then shuddered at the thought.

His handlebar mustache was so big it had handbrakes. The only thing keeping it in check was a square jaw that jutted out like a granite cliff, dented and pockmarked by the shipwrecked hulls of a thousand shattered knuckles. An eyebrow the same size and temperament as a Russian hamster arched threateningly. The eye below it and its mate, both balanced precariously above cheekbones you could sharpen a straight razor on, shot me a quizzical glance with such force that I felt the breeze tussle my hair.

"Hey. Mac." His voice purred like a dump truck dragged sideways over hot asphalt. "Ya didn't happen to find a shoe lyin' around, did ya?"

His breath hit me like a monthlong sanitation strike. I nearly swooned, but managed to remain on my feet, and only whimpered slightly. Following a hunch, I let my gaze freefall past his unmercifully exposed calves, where it landed with a thud on a pair of painfully large feet.

They were the kind of feet that undoubtedly gave birth to massive, trench-sized footprints, the kind that zoologists make plaster casts of and compose lengthy dissertations about in the dead of night. Wide, calloused, hirsute slabs, with a dense pelt covering their arches that made the man's chest hair seem like peach fuzz; the bulging knuckle of each bowling-pin-shaped toe wearing its own little comb-over. The middle toe of the left yeti-sized foot, the one adorned with a tasteful herringbone ankle bracelet, was minus a nail. The raw pink skin of that helmetless soldier promised me a tale of death and despair. It was an ode I was unwilling to bear witness to, and I allowed my eyes to retreat upwards once again.

Questions swam through my mind like rabid sea monkeys. A thousand expletives threatened to escape my throat simultaneously, yet all I could muster was a slight nod before staggering zombielike to the kitchen table. Inviting him into the kitchen was out of the question, mainly because I doubted that his freakishly large frame would fit through the comparatively tiny doorway. I lifted the satin pump gingerly in both hands and, holding it at arm's length, turned and offered it to the delicately garbed behemoth.

The man's eyebrow arched even higher, threatening to leave his forehead altogether. His eyes fixed me with a stare that threatened to injure me on its own.

"Really?" he asked. "Do I look like a size five to you?"

The Intergalactic Book Club

Daniel Kason

The two aliens were silent as they scanned their holographic computer screens, occasionally looking up to chuckle and make an amusing remark when one of them found a particularly good bit.

"What about this?" Flezno said, pointing at his screen. "A bacterium that arrives on Earth and proceeds to infect the entire human race."

Grux laughed. "That's certainly more realistic than your standard little green men. But I think I can do you one better." He gestured toward his screen. "A race of aliens that has existed for so long, and has progressed so far, that they essentially become gods, incomprehensible to the human brain."

Flezno sat back and thought about this. Then he burst into laughter. "A godlike alien, eh?" he said, and Grux nodded, giggling himself. "Now that's a wild idea."

The two were silent again as they searched Earth's databases, reading novel after novel as a whirl of letters and punctuation scrolled down their screens.

After a while, Flezno looked up again. He gazed out the window, and not too far away (at least by galactic standards), he saw Earth.

"Grux?" he said, and his friend looked up from the screen.

"You sure we can't go down there and meet them? You know, just for fun?"

"What, and miss out on all this?"

"What if we just let them know we're here?" Flezno suggested. "Would that endanger their lives?"

"Endanger their lives?" Grux repeated. "When was that ever a concern? We're not interested in their lives, Flezno." He tapped the hologram, but his finger just went through the screen. "It's their ideas we're after. You know that."

"Right," Flezno said. "Sorry." And they went back to their computer screens.

After a few minutes, Grux started giggling again. "Such imaginations these people have!" he exclaimed. "This one is just great. The alien is an entire planet! Can you imagine that?"

"That sounds implausible," Flezno said.

"Implausible," Grux agreed, "but amusing."

"Grux, why can't we just go down there for a little bit? Don't you want to meet the people who wrote these stories?"

"That would risk everything!" Grux said, annoyed now. "You have to get it in your head that we can't just reveal ourselves to them. For thousands of years they must have been gazing at the sky, wondering what sort of bizarre alien creatures are out there. We can't just waltz down there and say hello. All of those years of speculation and theory would be for nothing!"

"I know, but—"

"We've been here long enough for you to realize how easily they are influenced. These stories are just too good, Flezno. If they see us and know what aliens out there *really* look like, who's to say how that will impact their work?"

"Well, I—"

"I'll tell you," Grux continued, interrupting him again. "Fiction won't be the same. Once they see us, once they know the truth, it'll be over. They'll stop wondering."

Flezno looked as if he were about to say something important, but then he just nodded and his eyes drifted back to the hologram. Satisfied, Grux did the same.

"I will say," Grux began later on, once again in a good mood, "I am disappointed with a few of these. I mean, what are the chances that a species that originated and evolved light years away somehow managed to look almost exactly the same as the humans? Sure, maybe their skin is blue, or maybe their ears are slightly misshapen, but otherwise these species are pretty much identical. Lazy, if you ask me."

"There is only so much the human mind is capable of," Flezno said.

"Yes," Grux agreed. "But they are capable of enough to satisfy me. They're certainly more interesting than the last civilization we visited. Let's see, now; this one shows promise." Hundreds of pages flipped by in a matter of seconds. Grux laughed.

"What is it?" Flezno said.

"In this one, the author wasn't satisfied with merely depicting aliens from another galaxy. He made them from a different universe. Even the forces vary there, shaping these creatures into gelatinous, amorphous slugs. Quite clever."

Grux waited for a response, but Flezno was silent.

"Oh, come on," he said. "You're not still mad about before, are you? Okay, tell me what you were going to say. I'm listening now."

"You'll laugh," Flezno said.

"I promise I won't. Go on, tell me. Why do you want to go down there so badly?"

"It's just," Flezno said, feeling slightly embarrassed, "I'd like to get an autograph."

"An autograph?" Grux repeated.

"Yes. I've grown quite fond of one of the authors. I would have liked an autograph, but of course I understand why we can't—" Grux had started laughing. "Hey, you promised you wouldn't laugh!"

"Sorry, sorry," Grux said, quieting down. "All right, how about this: Once we read everything this world has to offer, you can go down there and get your autograph? Then we'll move on."

"But by that time," Flezno said, "the author will be dead."

"Oh, I forgot about that," Grux said. "Oh well. Sorry, but we can't just announce our arrival because you've got an infatuation with one of the authors. Besides, it would take a lot of gall to go down there and stifle their imaginations like that. Frankly, I don't think you have it in you. Let them wonder. Let them imagine. And all we have to do is sit back, enjoy, and move on when it's over. Not a bad deal if you ask me."

"You're right," Flezno acquiesced.

Grux got up, feeling better now that his friend understood. "Do you want to get something to eat?"

"Sure." Flezno stood up, as well.

"You know," Grux said, "I do wonder sometimes what they'd think of us."

Grux studied his friend. Flezno had green, reptilian skin, a pair of enormous red dinner-plate-shaped eyes, antennae, a mouth full of daggerlike teeth surrounded by mandibles, two long tentacles for arms, a giant tail with a scythe at the end, and three legs with wheellike appendages at the bottom. Flezno rolled over to him.

Grux laughed, thinking about how a human would react if he saw them. Flezno laughed with him, and the two of them rolled down the hallway to get a bite to eat. ◉

The Not-So-Ancient Chinese Proverb

S. G. Rogers

The little mountain village in the Chinese province of Yunnan was largely untouched by time. Villagers drove fat pigs down rough, stony streets. Young men on bicycles passed graybeards as they played board games outside their storefronts. Farmers brought vegetables to market on baskets strapped to their backs.

On the first day of spring, the monk who lived on the mountain always invited the village children to the temple for tea and a story. The children called him Taifu, or Grandfather. Nobody really knew how old he was, but he seemed as ancient as the stone Buddha carved into the mountainside.

When the children were released from school that afternoon, they crowded onto the path to the temple. Each brought a gift—the most perfect first blooms from their gardens, or small boxes of candied lychees or ginger.

The old monk greeted each child warmly. He accepted their gifts with pleasure and offered them moon cakes with their tea. He settled himself on a cushion, and the children sat cross-legged on bamboo mats, their faces shining with anticipation.

"I have a wonderful story, children, from a time when magic and dragons still existed in China," Taifu said. "Everything I'm about to tell you really happened."

Most of the children sat a little straighter, wide-eyed. Magic and dragons! But the oldest boy, Shen, folded his arms across his chest with a frown.

"Long ago," Taifu began, "there was a village in the mountains, much the same as ours. The villagers were happy and prosperous, all because of a goose."

The children laughed.

"It may seem unbelievable," Taifu acknowledged. "But the bird was magical. It had the extraordinary ability to lay *golden eggs*."

Even as the children gasped, Shen rolled his eyes.

"Did the goose have a name?" a child asked.

Taifu nodded. "The goose was white, but when its dark wings were folded they resembled a pair of scissors. So the goose was called Scissors.

"One day, an ugly troll moved into a cave on the other side of the river. The troll, called Oni, was a greedy, wicked creature. He sent his dragon, Furr, to steal from the villagers. Pigs and cows went missing first, but then Oni began to crave treasure. The dragon stole coins, jewelry, and even the solid-gold Buddha in the temple. It was a terrible time.

"The village elders wondered if Oni would be appeased if they gave him Scissors. With all the treasure he could possibly want, Oni might leave the village in peace."

"That's a terrible idea!" Shen interrupted. "If they give Scissors away, the village becomes poor. When Oni realizes they have nothing left, he'll send Furr to burn it down. Everyone will die!"

"There was a brave young villager named Gui who agreed with you, Shen," Taifu replied. "'I'll find Oni's cave,' said Gui. 'I'll kill him with my bow and arrows, and we will be saved.'"

"That's exactly what I would have done!" Shen exclaimed.

"Indeed?" Taifu replied. "Then perhaps you can finish the story?"

Cries of protest rose from the other children.

"Forgive me, Taifu," Shen said, abashed. "Please continue."

Taifu smiled. "The elders were impressed with Gui's bravery. Indeed, his prowess in archery was unmatched. They agreed to send Gui on his quest. In the meantime, a flock of sheep would be scattered across the valley. While Furr was eating the sheep, Gui would find Oni and kill him.

"Gui prepared his strongest bow and filled his quiver with

the sharpest arrows. The ladies of the village wept as they accompanied Gui to the river.

"He crossed the river in a fisherman's peapod boat. A low-hanging fog masked his passage. Once he reached the other side, Gui climbed the mountain to search for Oni's cave. Oni's troll stench led Gui straight to him.

"Gui's knees shook with fear, but he stood tall. He shouted to Oni that he'd come with a gift of gold. From deep within the cave came a mighty roar!"

The children leaned forward, transfixed.

"Trolls are not too bright, and Oni was no exception," Taifu said. "He heard the word 'gold' and came stumbling out of his cave. The sun had burned through the fog and blinded Oni long enough for Gui to loose three arrows. The first one pierced Oni's throat. The second found his heart. The last sank into his left eye, but Oni was already dead. He fell backwards like a tree with rotted roots and landed with a huge thud. The trouble was over."

Taifu's audience relaxed. But Taifu was not finished.

"Gui returned to the village with as much of the looted treasure as he could carry. The ecstatic villagers prepared a feast to honor their noble hero and the magical goose, Scissors."

"What about the dragon?" Shen ventured.

"Ah, well, Furr was sleeping in a meadow, gorged with sheep," Taifu replied. "When he heard the dinner gong, he wakened. The dragon flew to Oni's cave, where he saw his master was dead. He was furious. In the middle of the feast, Furr returned and began to burn the village. People ran for their lives."

"Gui slew the dragon, didn't he?" someone asked.

"Well, Gui knew he had to act, but his bow and arrows were in his house. He tucked Scissors under his arm and bolted down the street. Not two steps later, the vicious dragon burned Gui and Scissors to a crisp. In fact, no one in the village was left alive except for one small boy. I was that boy, and I have never told this story to anyone—until today."

The children stared at Taifu, devastated. A few of them began to sob, but Shen became angry.

"What kind of story is *that!?*" he cried. "It's pointless!"

"Look underneath the words of the story to divine the meaning," Taifu replied, unfazed. "It is the basis for the ancient Chinese proverb—*When Furr is flying, never run with Scissors, or your goose will get cooked.*" ◉

For Wile E. Coyote, *Apetitius giganticus*

Jason Schossler

"A fanatic is one who redoubles his effort when he has forgotten his aim."

George Santayana

1 Monday he comes home squashed flat by a locomotive; Tuesday, with his hair burnt to a crisp. Friday, a week—no bird, no prey, and nothing in the medicine cabinet to treat the anvil lodged in his head.

2 Picking up his daughter from her internship at Perdue Farms, he overhears her talking to her BFF. "We've had KFC for supper every night this week," she says. "My dad is such a *loser*." When she says the word, she presses her fingers to her forehead in the shape of an L.

3 The spring catalogue arrives with the chirp of awakening birds. Earthquake pills, TNT, a catapult, quick-drying cement, dehydrated boulders, a boomerang, and, free with every $100 order, a rocket sled and thirty miles of railroad track.*

* Some assembly required.

4 The nights are long. His hind legs stiffen up in his sleep, and his right hip hasn't felt the same ever since those jet-propelled tennis shoes blasted him through the center of the earth to China.

5 On the family room sofa his wife eases the thread through the needle and stitches his tail back into place. Now and then she stops to look up at the shimmering sage in the backyard. "It's not just the kids," she says with a throb in her voice. "The neighbors are talking, too."

6   It's the customer service as much as the good line of credit that keeps him coming back to Acme Corp.

Coughing red soot from another day's avalanche, he asks Sue, the refund department operator, about her father's knee surgery, swimming in Lake Wallenpaupack, her butterfly garden of bee balm and lilac, and on the other end of the phone, Sue is curious about life in the Southwest, and if it really is what they call a *dry heat.*

7   During his lunch break in the shade of the cottonwoods he listens to *The Ultimate Secrets of Total Self-confidence* by Dr. Robert Anthony on his iPod.

Closing his eyes, he visualizes the world he wants to live in: the bird browning in the oven, legs tied together, skin brushed in melted butter like an oasis on the other side of a great, uncrossable desert, and by late afternoon, the kids probing the tender curves with gentle forks, a mysterious passion on their faces.

8   *...Next up on* **Coast to Coast AM** *we've got a caller from the Southwest, a Mr. W.E.C., who—now get this—claims to know a magical roadrunner that can pass through walls...*

9   The Southern Belle disguise has arrived. Inside the package is a handwritten note from Sue. *This should do the trick.*

In front of the mirror he tries on the saucy red dress. Puckers his lips and turns to admire the ruffled bodice. The costume comes with a velvet bonnet and matching handbag large enough to conceal a stick of dynamite.

Standing behind him, his wife starts to cry. "Who are you?" she says. "I don't know you anymore."

He wiggles his eyebrows. The bird is good as cooked. @

Around the Block

Courtney Walsh

"Bless me father, for I have sinned," Vicky told the eye-level black screen where she sat in the confession booth in St. Ursula's Church of the Holy Redeemer in downtown Kenosha, Wisconsin, a block away from Maxine's Café, where the special tonight was tenderloin tips with a citric infusion, a mix of lemon, lime, orange, and pink grapefruit from a farm in Central Florida where last night, under a full moon, the oldest of the few panthers left in the state slept, dreaming of his mother, who, just before she was shot by a bounty hunter who had progressed no further than sixth grade in the Leland City School District and whose teachers, against their better judgment, were forced to keep him until he turned from a grubby, temperamental, unwashed little boy into a grubby, temperamental, unwashed adolescent with a hair-trigger temper and a habit of shooting anything that offended him, which included dogs, cats, alligators, birds, manatees, dolphins, and, one night, the old panther's mother, who before she died latched onto his head and bit down, scoring his skull as if for trepanning, which surgery was finished by a world-renowned brain surgeon from Austria then visiting his aunt after the young man had landed on her front porch, cursing the panther, government at all levels beginning with the city council, and life in general going all the way up to God, who, it must be admitted, was a little perplexed by the way things were turning out, or not turning out, and sat back, amusing himself with other games, his attention span being infinite so that he quickly tired of backgammon, Parcheesi, Monopoly, whist, bridge, Canasta, Pitch, and poker, games played on machines in taverns, games such as tennis, squash, racquetball played on small courts or games played on larger courts or fields, where he would have to split himself into the players, ten for basketball, eighteen for baseball, twenty-two for football, etc., etc., as well as the requisite number of competitors for soccer, rugby, bobsledding, curling, and other sports of modern times or earlier, including sports played all over the world, as for example, the Fiji Islanders played with conch shells, the Apache Indians with sticks and hoops, the North Laplanders with reindeer testicles, to say nothing of the sports on the nearest inhabited planet, thousands of light years away, but right around the block if you're the deity. ◉

The Waterhole

Colleen Shea Skaggs

On a balmy, September Saturday night, she threads her way through the parking lot of the local saloon, The Waterhole. She's a newcomer in town, a tiny Idaho ranch community, a stone's throw from the Snake River. Thirty-two years old, a refugee from the big-city madness of Los Angeles. The new teacher in the small rural school: no metal detectors, guns, knives, gangs, no backtalk, no obscene language in her presence. Supportive parents. Moira, a redhead, partly natural, partly from a bottle, but no one needs to know that. Miss Kelly, her students call her.

Country music pours from the saloon's open door. A male singer with the raw, lived-in voice of Willie or Johnny—the song about friends in low places.

She steps onto the wood-planked porch. Ranchers, both men and women, stand in clusters, shaking heads, laughing or lamenting about government intrusion, taxes, high feed prices, politicians, busted machinery, jughead horses, and clueless cows.

Inside is crowded and noisy. People dancing in the small area between the bar and the wall lined with tables of people. An open-beam ceiling, a decor of elk antlers, antique tools, old car license plates. In the dim light provided by flickering kerosene lamps, dust motes hover in the air like mini-galaxies spinning in space.

She climbs up on one of the only two vacant stools at the bar. Behind the bar hangs an elongated, faded black-and-white photograph of old-time buckeroos lined up on their horses, the buckeroos and horses long since dead.

Rick, the bartender, sets a mug of beer in front of her. Rick: brownish-blond hair, a lean build, eyes a lighter blue than her own. Good-looking, but he doesn't seem to know it, and she's not about to tell him. She'd met him briefly at the school's open house. Divorced, the father of a twelve-year-old daughter who was one of her students. A part-time bartender, a part-time rodeo rider, runs a few cows on his five acres. A horse for himself and one for his daughter.

The band is off its break, launching into the "Tennessee Waltz," the male singer with a lived-in face to match the voice, singing in a heartfelt way. Lost loves, lost dreams, lost chances. Rick moves up and down behind the bar with fluid movements, drawing beer, wiping spills, bantering with the customers.

"Do you know what a cowboy breakfast is?" he stops and asks her.

"No, what?"

"A pee and a look around."

"No thanks. I'll stick to bacon and eggs."

They watch an elderly couple step out onto the dance floor. The other dancers step back to give them the floor. The man is rawboned-handsome, well over six feet, broad shoulders, a little stooped, blue eyes with a gleam of mischief. Levi's, a blue shirt. A head of unruly white hair. A little stiff in the knees and movements, bending forward to accommodate the shorter stature of his partner. The woman has a soft body, her face with fine features and wrinkles, permed gray hair, a peach-colored pantsuit, earrings flashing.

"Who are they?" she says to Rick.

"Tess and Angus. Both eighty-eight. Married since they were eighteen. The fourth generation on Angus's ranch. Angus likes to tell people he's sleeping in the same bed he was born on.'"

He fills her in on some of the history of Angus. Angus's father lost the ranch to the bank in the Depression. His mother and father had to move into town, live in a tiny one-roomed shack. Angus, just a kid, hired himself out to ranches, saved his wages. People back then stuck together. No one would buy Angus's father's ranch. With no buyers, the bank let Angus buy the ranch back with easy terms. Angus went to town and brought his parents back to the ranch, where they lived the rest of their lives.

She envies family; her parents and sister were gone way before their time.

On the dance floor, consciously aware of their respectful, reverential audience, Tess and Angus dance with the practiced ease and grace of partners who've been dancing together almost a lifetime. They add a few theatrical flourishes to their act, a modest dip, an out-turned foot. Angus's elbows held high in a courtly manner, his weathered, veined hand placed gently on Tess's back as though cradling a precious gem.

Tess and Angus, Rick tells her, lost a son to the war, a beloved grandson to a drunk driver. As Angus gives Tess a twirl, he winks at the onlookers in a self-mocking way as if to say, Aren't we the cat's pajamas? But Tess is serious-faced, with rigid posture, square-shouldered, her moves mannered and exact as though she were taking a typing test for a secretarial position.

The song ends, and the couple's waltz with it. They stand with flushed faces, friends and family crowding around them, talking and laughing. Tess and Angus, with losses, yes, Rick tells her, but with a son and daughter and grandchildren and great-grandchildren to carry on after they're gone.

She feels a little buzz and not just from the beer, but a buzz of happiness to have found a home, here in this peaceful place with these down-to-earth, kind people.

She thinks of her little rental cottage facing the river; her cat, Max, lying on the back of the sofa, watching for her out the window. She sees Tess and Angus, leaving, hanging on to each other, each other's crutches.

She's had her one beer, time to leave, students' papers to grade.

"Don't be a stranger," Rick calls after her.

She steps from the porch and out onto the dirt road, a lemon-slice-of-a moon above, night-air smells of freshly mown grass, the river, and the slight hint of manure. ◉

Nothing

Douglas Smith

"It's nothing," he says, not for the first time.

She watches him straighten his tie in the hall mirror. So he doesn't have to make eye contact, she thinks.

"I fear nothing?" she says. "Then I must be fearless. I don't feel fearless."

Leaning on the kitchen door frame, she hugs her faded blue dressing gown around her as if she's holding the universe together. She's staying home. Again.

He shakes his head. He does that a lot lately.

"I mean there's nothing out there to be afraid of." He picks up his briefcase, ready for another day.

But she knows that it's not just another day.

"Nothing out there," she repeats.

"Nothing." He stands by the front door of their little bungalow. "Are you going in to work?"

He knows I'm not, she thinks. But not asking would mean he accepts what's happening. And then he'd have to believe it.

"No," she says.

She watches his jaw muscles tighten, enjoying the clarity of predictable stimulus and response.

"Fine," he snaps, and leaves.

She hears the car pull away, feeling no more alone than when he was here. She's sorry he's angry, but he doesn't understand.

He doesn't understand that he's right.

She is afraid of nothing.

She makes toast and coffee, taking comfort in the routine. Mundane remnants of the way her world used to be.

At the kitchen table, she savors the smell of the coffee, the heat of the mug in her hand, the sharp edges of the toast in her mouth, the sound of its crunch, the sweetness of the jam. Each of her senses has become a lifeline, snaking out from her, seeking something tangible in a fading reality to which to anchor herself.

Later, sitting on the sofa, she holds the phone in her lap and sips her coffee even after it's cold, delaying.

Finally, she dials her parents, punching the area code that is a plane trip away, and then their number as if it were a combination to a lock. Slowly, carefully. She listens, then hangs up.

Yesterday, it rang and rang. Today, it didn't even do that. Silence. Nothing.

A sense of loss fills her, but it tastes old and stale. She realizes that she lost her parents long ago, when the aura of protection they once gave disappeared. They can't save her. They couldn't even save themselves.

Planning to distract herself by cleaning the house, she turns on the radio for some music, but can't find her favorite station. She picks another and starts to dust. The station fades out to nothing. Not even static.

Three more stations. Same thing. She turns the radio off and stops cleaning.

She thinks of sleeping but decides against it. Even her dreams are empty now. She sits and waits.

He comes home at the usual time, but something has changed.

"What's wrong?" she asks over a dinner of leftovers and silence.

"Nothing," he says. She waits. She knows. Finally, he speaks again. "I visited my client."

She knows the one. On the outskirts of the city.

"Yes?" she asks, knowing what he'll say next.

"They're gone," he says.

"Out of business?" she says, playing the game for his sake. Pretending that the world is still normal.

"Gone. There's nothing there."

"Nothing?"

She looks up when he doesn't answer. He puts down his knife and fork, and she enjoys the solid click-click they make on the kitchen table.

He meets her gaze finally. He opens his mouth, but no words come out. Picking up the knife and fork again, he studies them as if unsure they're real. He shakes his head and goes back to eating.

He's pretending it didn't happen. But she is beyond pretending. She saw his eyes. He knows.

He goes to bed early. She stays up, watching TV, flipping channels as, one by one, the city's stations stop broadcasting.

She keeps flipping. The last station disappears. No test pattern. No static. Just a slow fade to a blank dead screen.

She turns the TV off and sits in the dark. Sleep is not an option. She fears what she will wake to. Or that it will come while she sleeps.

The clock shows that it's morning. She doesn't open the curtains. The gray that creeps around their edges is not sunlight.

He should be awake by now. She listens for his morning sounds.

Nothing.

She rises and walks upstairs, feet silent on the worn carpet. Up here, the floor, the ceiling, the walls seem thin, insubstantial. A paleness oozes under their bedroom door, more a rejection of both darkness and light than an actual color.

Leaving the door unopened, she backs away. It is too late for him. He is gone.

He is nothing.

She goes back downstairs and sits on the sofa. To wait. Alone. Now she is truly alone.

It comes, first eating through the corners of the room, then devouring walls and ceiling, crawling across freshly vacuumed carpet towards her. She realizes, as it consumes the very space around her, that she is the center of a dwindling ball of reality. Or perhaps, she thinks as it draws closer, this world is simply escaping to join with it.

It touches her. And she knows.

He was right all along. About what she feared.

It is nothing.

Nothingness. Void. Nothing exists here. No light, no sound, no smell, no taste. Nothing to touch or be touched by. Only her thoughts exist here, and even they begin to flee her, not to escape, but to join with the void.

As they leave her, she feels herself joining with it as well. Soon there will be no identity, no separation from it, no *her*.

Her last thought forms, departs.

She...

is...

noth... ◉

Long Tossed Like the Driven Foam

K. G. Jewell

Ms. Hamilton drew the blinds for the last time. Fifty years of teaching, at an end. On her desk were her handbag and a silver-plated apple—her good-bye gift from the PTA.

A farewell verse to her class sat on the blackboard. Emerson. She considered leaving it on the wall, graffiti of sorts. But no, that wouldn't be fair to Ponce.

Ms. Hamilton picked up the eraser, pausing over the last line—*Good-bye, proud world! I'm going home*—then erased it all with a flurry of energy that left her breathless.

As she stood clutching the chalk and holding back her tears at the symbolic end of her career, the door opened. Ponce stuck his head through the doorway. Ponce had been there as long as she had, maybe longer. But the parents didn't complain about *his* hearing. Dressed in the same janitor's blue coverall he'd always worn, he looked tentative at his interruption of the moment.

"Miss Hamilton?" Ponce was the only one she let get away with that language. After all, when he'd started calling her *miss*, she'd felt one.

"Yes Ponce?" Fifty years working together, he still was the politest, most timid man she knew. Not that they'd talked much in those five decades—the building staff and the teaching staff didn't mix much, and he was a quiet fellow.

"I have a gift for you, if you want it." He held a grocery bag in his hand.

"Of course. Come in."

He entered, closing the door softly behind him.

"Do you ever wish you could be young again?"

"Young?" She was confused.

"You know, fifteen again."

Ms. Hamilton looked over the empty chairs where her students sat.

"To what end? To revisit the follies of youth? When you have all that time in front of you, you don't value it. I'd rather have a day valued than a day wasted. Only when each day might be your last can you can *really* live life. No, I don't want to be young again."

Ponce looked thoughtful. "Do you really mean that?"

"Of course I mean that." She had no desire to go through that all again. Not to mention the acne, the disrespect of your elders, the immature judgment of your peers.

"Because I have something that can bring back your youth." Ponce removed two glass jars from his shopping bag. They were old wine bottles, recorked.

"Ponce, I would have never taken you for a drunkard, much less a bootlegger," Ms. Hamilton scoffed.

"This is not alcohol. This is water from a special seep in the janitor's closet. This one is for me." He picked up a bottle and removed the cork. "The other is for you, if you want it."

Ms. Hamilton shook her head. Ponce had lost it. He was drinking leaking sewer waste.

Ponce raised the bottle. "To Ponce. He is retiring today. But the building manager has promised to hire my nephew when he arrives. I told the manager I've taught him all I know."

Ponce raised the bottle to his lips and chugged. As she watched, his hair changed from grey to jet black and the wrinkles smoothed from his face. His back straightened. His thin frame filled.

The years lifted from Ponce's body, and it was not a metaphor.

The changes slowed, and then stopped, but by then she wouldn't have recognized him in a crowd. Nevertheless, she could see the family resemblance. The man—could she still call him Ponce?—tightened his belt on his newly loose jeans.

"Well, since you don't want the rest, I'll have to find another use for it." Ponce reached for the bottle.

Ms. Hamilton set her hand on top of his.

"Shut up, you young fool. Give me that." She twisted off the cork and lifted it to her lips. The water tasted flat, with sour flecks of sediment.

The room grew brighter, colors shifting towards reds she barely remembered. Her shirt grew taut around her shoulders. The whine of the ancient AC squealed in her ear.

Miss Hamilton tossed the bottle into the trash beside her desk. She ran her tongue across her lips. They were soft and plump.

"Let's go make out behind the football stadium."

"I thought you didn't want to waste your days?" The youthful Ponce smirked as he spoke.

"Don't trust anything old people tell you about life. They've forgotten what it means to live."

She grabbed Ponce's arm and went out to learn it all again. ◉

The Boat

Steve Cushman

Martha told you not to buy the boat. But you stand at the front door on Saturday, just past noon, holding an anchor keychain in one hand and a white sailor's cap in the other. Behind you, the boat, a twenty-foot white Regal runabout, is big and beautiful.

She says, Goddamn you. You say, We can afford it; it's not that expensive, forty-five hundred dollars, a once-in-a-lifetime kind of deal. Just look at it, you say. If she'd look, she'd understand. I told you, she says, this is what I'm talking about. Then she moves past you and out the door.

Good riddance, you say; married twenty-four years and all you wanted was a damn boat. You fill a cooler with beer, grab a bag of pretzel rods, and head to the boat, which sits in the strip of grass between your driveway and your neighbor's front yard.

You climb in and settle into the captain's seat. As a car passes, you flash them your red and green running lights. It's a childish game, just the kind of thing Martha would nag you for, but you enjoy it nonetheless.

We don't have anything, you say, not really. A house, a little retirement, and two cars. But so what? The children are gone now: One is married, the other soon. You're a grown man. You work hard. Hell, you deserve things. We need to get out, you say, enjoy nature, learn to water-ski before we're too old.

After drinking two beers, you start the engine, which grumbles like a giant with an upset stomach, then turn it off quickly, hoping no damage was done. Floyd, your neighbor, opens his front door and you duck under the high sides of the boat.

Binky, a little black cat one of the girls brought home from college, jumps up on the bow of the boat. She looks at you and meows until you give her a piece of pretzel. She takes it, crunches it in her mouth, so you pour some beer in your hand, which she laps up with her rough tongue. You laugh, thinking, Man it doesn't get any better than this.

Martha will be back, you tell yourself, easing the captain's cap over your eyes for an afternoon nap. Binky sleeps on your chest and though there's a dull ache somewhere deep in your head, you dream of taking the boat out: you at the helm, cruising over blue water, sunburned and smiling, laughing, a beer in your hand, and Binky perched up at the bow as the water and wind brush her fur back.

The muffler on Martha's '85 Volvo wakes you, reminding you it's one more thing on the Honey-do list you haven't gotten around to. But you stay low. Damn boat, she says, as she slams the door. The bright Central Florida sun weighs you down. Asshole, she says. I've always wanted a boat, she mimics, smacking the side of the boat with her purse.

She'd better knock it off. You're trying to be civil about this. She goes into the house, and you lie back down. You could get up and go inside and try to convince her of the boat's merits, tell her all the things the two of you could do in a fine boat like this, but she's a stubborn woman, so you decide to wait until she comes around. She always has in the past.

You sit up when you hear the front door slam. Martha's carrying the black suitcase you bought her for her birthday last year. She throws it in the trunk, then goes back inside for the thirteen-inch TV from your bedroom. You are surprised how easily she handles the TV; she's not a big woman. She yells, I've had it, so loud you can imagine Old Lady Peters three doors down looking up from her garden, then slams her car door and drives off.

You decide to take the boat out for a quick spin around the lake. After hooking it up to your car, you go inside and get more beer and pretzels, and a white towel. You want to take Binky out onto the water, but she jumps out the passenger-side window and hides in the blooming white azaleas by the front of the house.

On the way to the lake, you spot Martha pulling out of a Publix parking lot. Despite being sure she'll return home in a day or two, you decide to find out where she's staying, just in case she's being particularly bullheaded and you have to lure her home with a dozen red roses.

The boat looks like a big white curtain in your rearview mirror. You follow Martha three miles on Highway 50 and then onto a little side street walled by towering oaks heavy with moss. You stay back, with two cars between you and her. She doesn't seem to see you, or, if she does, doesn't seem to care. She pulls into an apartment complex.

The complex is pink and full of cars. You park by the curb, at the edge of the lot, so there is a thin wall of palm trees between you and her. The door Martha knocks on opens, and a man—a shirtless, short bald man who looks to be your age, late forties, maybe even fifty—is standing there. He hugs Martha, kisses her forehead, then pats her on the ass as she walks past him into the dark room.

You do not recognize this man. He pulls the pair of suitcases from the trunk, then comes back for the TV. Before closing the door, he looks up at you. He doesn't seem to recognize you, but instead is admiring your boat, and he gives you a gentleman's nod as he shuts the door. ◉

Grandma's Pillbox

Celeste Leibowitz

As Ginny opened the pillbox, Grandma's pills seemed to come to life. Their colors: a bright orange lozenge, two blue dots like tiny dolls' eyes, and a crimson capsule, appeared to intensify as she stared at them.

The pillbox buzzed loudly, and she barely had time to close the lid for Tuesday Afternoon before replacing it on the shelf. The ominous buzzing continued.

"What's that?" Grandma called weakly from the next room. "Is that my pillbox?"

She knows! Ginny shuddered.

"Bring it here, Ginny," Grandma called, and then began another of her dreadful coughing fits.

Ginny picked up the box, which buzzed and vibrated in her hand, and hesitantly brought it out to Grandma. Mommy was out at the store and had made the mistake of leaving Ginny alone with Grandma for a little while. Just who was supposed to look out for whom wasn't very clear.

The pillbox kept buzzing even when Ginny handed it to Grandma. Ginny expected Grandma to lower her thick white eyebrows and frown at her, but that didn't happen. Instead, Grandma popped open the lid that read "Monday Morning" and fished out a few pills. She reached out a weak hand and tried to grab the glass of water from the nightstand. Her hand fell short by a few inches.

"Would you get me that glass, Ginny baby?" Grandma asked. She wiggled herself up a little higher against the pillows.

Ginny picked up the glass and put in the bendable straw that lay beside it. Grandma gulped all her pills down in one swallow, sucking hard on the straw. Ginny watched, fascinated and repelled, as Grandma's Adam's apple moved up and down in her scrawny neck.

The pillbox had stopped buzzing as soon as Grandma opened the lid, and now Ginny realized it wasn't like a car alarm that told you to "step away from the car" if you got too close. It was more like an alarm clock. She took the pillbox back into the bathroom and decided that since it wasn't going to ring and expose her naughtiness, she could afford to study its contents some more.

Mommy had warned Ginny many times. "Never play in Grandma's medicine cabinet. Never play with her pills, and never eat one! They are good for Grandma but they are poisonous for you. And don't mix them up. She has to take them in exact order. That's why she has this special, great-big pillbox that reminds her when it's time for her next dose."

But today Mommy was out at the store, and Ginny was curious. She opened the Tuesday lid again to look at the bright colored pills. Then she opened all the other lids. Plenty of orange lozenges. Plenty of blue dots like dolls' eyes. In the evening compartments, she found some white caplets, too.

The crimson-red capsule in the Tuesday Afternoon compartment was the only one of its kind. Ginny fished it out. It seemed to buzz in her hand and grow infinitesimally larger. She jiggled her hand, and it stood almost upright, like a Mexican jumping bean. What would it do to her?

Ginny threw the pill into her mouth. It felt strangely warm. She swallowed it fast, because it started to expand in her mouth. None of the pills she'd ever taken did anything like that!

Ginny squeaked in alarm. Something was happening to her!

The pillbox, forgotten, fell to the floor. A tide of pills spilled out, all mixed up on the bathroom floor. Before she had a chance to realize how much trouble she was in, Ginny glanced at the bathroom mirror. She was growing!

Growing, and changing. Her limbs felt sore as they stretched out. Her face was altering, into a woman's.

But as Ginny watched, she changed again. With horror, she saw her bright chestnut hair turn grizzled, then bone white. Her face sagged at the chin, and deep wrinkles furrowed her cheeks, forehead, and around her eyes.

"Ginny?" Grandma's voice sounded stronger now.

Ginny knew how to get rid of poison. Mommy had taught her. She flipped up the toilet seat and stuck her gnarled finger down her throat. A fit of coughing ensued, and she gagged painfully. Nothing. No pretty red capsule came flying back out.

"Ohhh nooooo…" she started to cry. A pain in her back seized her as she tried to straighten up. Her legs were unsteady, and she had to grab the sink to keep upright.

"Uhhh…Ginny? Something's wrong with me! Call your mother!" Grandma's voice sounded younger, higher.

Ginny wrapped Grandma's terry robe around her withered frame and tottered out into the bedroom. She and Grandma froze in shock at the sight of each other. Grandma was now a small child. She lay huddled in the blankets, dwarfed by her flower-print nightie.

"Mommy? You have to come back. Something terrible's happened."

"Mother? Why are you calling me Mommy? Is Ginny okay? Are you all right?"

Ginny slumped back on the bed, too weak to hold the phone any longer. Grandma hung it up for her. The little girl who was her grandmother leaned over her, eyes wide with alarm.

"What are we going to do?"

"I don't know, Grandma. You're older and smarter. What can we do?" Ginny felt her heart pounding hard.

"I guess there's no choice. I'll have to be you. And you'll have to be me."

Ginny nodded. Tears slipped down her wrinkled cheeks as she wept for the childhood and the youth she had lost. Grandma bounded out of bed, full of six-year-old energy, and dashed into the bathroom.

"Darn it, Ginny, look what you did. Pills all over the place. And you tore up all your clothes? Boy, am I going to get it!"

"No, Grandma," Ginny croaked out. "I got it, and I'm never going to get rid of it." Her eyes closed, and she waited for her Monday Afternoon pill. @

In the Shadows

Janel Gradowski

How long do you think the electricity will be out?" Sophie held her breath as a guttural growl of thunder reverberated through the house. She shivered and tucked the blanket under her legs. "What was that?"

"What was what?" Jack walked out of the kitchen holding a flashlight under his chin, casting a demonic glow over his face. "Maybe it's the boogey man coming to get us."

"No, you goofball, I thought I saw something moving over there." She shined her flashlight beam into the corner. A tumbleweed of dog hair sat in front of the bookshelf.

"Dinner is served." Jack handed her a paper plate. "Saltine crackers and the finest processed cheese product."

"Ooh, gourmet…did you hear that?"

"Nope." He settled next to her on the couch. "I think your imagination is in overdrive tonight."

"How could you not hear that scratching noise? Do you have mice?"

"I'm not the neatest person in the world, but I assure you I am not cohabiting with any mice."

A massive black beast bounded out of the darkness. It slammed into Sophie's arm. Crackers and sticky cheese squares took flight then rained down onto the blanket and floor. The thing was panting and drooling.

"No, Milton!" Jack pointed into the murky darkness. "Get back into the kitchen."

"Let him stay." Sophie patted the dog's head. "He's scared."

"Yeah." Jack shook his head. "Scared he won't get any of our food."

He watched as the ravenous canine intruder scurried around, devouring cracker crumbs and dust-covered cheese. He was hoping Sophie would snuggle up to him, instead of his dog. Luckily, the storm wasn't weakening. He figured there was still plenty of time before she would even think of braving the deluge to go home.

"There it is again!" She swept the flashlight beam across the dining room. Another giant ball of dog hair was peeking out from behind a chair leg. "I think your dust bunnies are alive."

"I think a branch is scraping the window." He pretended to stretch and draped his arm around her shoulders. "And I need to vacuum tomorrow."

"That was not a branch." She elbowed him in the ribs. "Quit playing Romeo and listen."

"OK, fine. I hear thunder. Rain falling on the roof, maybe a bit of hail mixed in for good measure. Ooh, there's that pesky branch…"

"What's that thumping?" Sophie grabbed his arm, digging her fingernails into his flesh. "It sounds like someone knocking. Sometimes ghosts communicate by knocking."

Jack winced and pried her fingers loose. "Stop petting Milton."

"What? Why? I don't see how that will…"

"Just do it."

"Look at that. No more thumping." He laughed. "Or should I say tail wagging."

"I'm sorry." Sophie laid her head on Jack's shoulder. "I don't like storms."

"Gee, I never would have guessed that." He kissed her forehead. "What you need is a distraction to take your mind off the storm."

"I suppose you know the perfect way to distract me."

Jack shut off the battery-powered lantern. He pulled Sophie closer. The raging storm masked the faint shuffling sounds of the mutant dust bunnies gathering in the shadows, preparing to attack. ◉

Kitchen Basics

Sealey Andrews

Karin's sister Camille lacked most real-world skills, though she did consider herself to be well practiced in the art of shopping. Despite this, she still hadn't been allowed to pick out dinner that night.

"Mail-order clothing by catalog, with a debit card attached to daddy's bottomless bank account, isn't the same as shopping at the market," Karin had told her when they left the house that evening. "You wouldn't know a good cut of meat from a bad one."

It was the start of one of many lectures Karin had given Camille since she'd shown up on her doorstep, suitcase in hand, four days earlier. Not that it was all lectures all the time. The two of them had had some fun together while she'd been visiting, too. They'd even gone dancing that night and worked up quite the appetite. Besides, it wasn't so much a lecture as it was a lesson. Karin had an obligation. She couldn't let little sis wing it out there on her own after being babied all her life, could she?

"Stop staring at the food," Karin snapped from across the kitchen. They were home now, preparing a late dinner. "Sit down, have a drink—better yet, set the table. Make yourself useful, Camille."

Ignoring her, Camille stood, unblinking—eyes locked on their meal. She was consumed by curiosity. Karin was pretty sure her sister had never seen raw meat, let alone the process of preparing it. At the table, on a plate, garnished with parsley and drizzled in something exquisite was the presentation Camille was used to.

Not that she didn't know where it came from. Camille wasn't exactly stupid. But still, Karin suspected that seeing it in this state would seem a little…cruel. Camille had always been daddy's delicate flower, though she apparently didn't find it cruel enough that it made her lose her appetite. From all the way across the room Karin could hear her sister's stomach growl.

Camille rubbed it and frowned. "I'm hungry. How long is this going to take?"

"Not long." Karin glanced at her watch. "About another five minutes or so."

Camille poked at the meat. "It's oozing." It sputtered something brown and acrid smelling. "Is it supposed to do that?"

"Yes. You're supposed to let it simmer in its juices. I've been living on my own for a long time now, Camille. I do know a thing or two about preparing a meal, you know. Just leave it. Trust me, it's fine."

With a dramatic sigh, Camille reluctantly tore her eyes away from the young man who was flopping around on Karin's kitchen floor, hemorrhaging a crimson puddle all over the hardwoods. He cried out things like "it burns" and "help" as the venom they'd injected spread slowly through him, liquefying everything in its path.

"He's loud," Camille complained. "I didn't realize cooking was so…auditory." She folded her arms across her chest. "Next time I demand you sever the vocal cords first."

Karin raised an eyebrow and balled her fists. But, rather than engage in yet another argument about who gave the orders in her house, she held her tongue and went to the liquor cabinet instead.

She loved her sister. She really did.

"And who is this person he keeps calling for?" Camille continued. "Is this 'God' person he keeps talking about going to come for him? Should we be worried?" Her voice rose a little with concern.

Karin looked over her shoulder, grinned, and bared her fangs while she pulled out two shot glasses. "No. They *all* call for him at some point, and he hasn't come yet. We have nothing to worry about. Now stop staring; he'll be done when he's done."

"I can't help it, it's interesting," Camille whined. She crouched down in front of the man who was now curled in a ball, knees tucked to his chin. His cries had turned to whimpers. "He's attractive in a way. Or, he was…you know, before the swelling started. And the oozing." Camille's long, forked tongue flicked in and out—an involuntary mixed display of lust and hunger. She ran her fingertip across his sweat-covered brow. His blistered eyes, gray and opaque, turned up to her.

"Gah—he's looking at me!" she yelped, and pulled her hand back.

"Cut it out, Camille. Just let him do his thing. He'll bleed out here in a minute and we can eat," Karin said. "You know what they say about a watched pot."

"What?"

"It never boils. A watched pot never boils," she said, resisting the urge to follow it with "you twit."

"But he isn't even in a pot…" Camille's brow furrowed in that way their father always found adorable.

Karin rolled her eyes. Figures of speech were often lost on her sister. "Here." She slid a full shot glass and a saltshaker down the length of the counter to Camille. She tossed a wedge of lime at her, too.

Camille blinked innocently. "What is this?"

"A before-dinner drink." Karin jerked her head back, threw down the two fingers of tequila she'd poured, licked the salt on her hand, and sunk her teeth into the lime.

Camille watched in fascination, then sniffed her own drink. She scrunched her nose. "No, thank you, I think I need some food for this to land on first." She pushed the glass away. "Those little pink drinks you introduced me to earlier are really doing a number on my stomach. You know, those...Cosmo thingies the bartender kept bringing to me at the club. Er—sorry, not the club...what did you call it?"

Karin pulled the shriveled lime wedge from her mouth and tossed it into the sink. "Meat market," she rasped, and licked her lips.

So far they'd covered housekeeping and how to plan a budget. Now cooking could be checked off the list. Tomorrow it would be gardening. Because, as nice as the meat market was in a pinch, growing your own was so much more satisfying, fresh, and tasty. @

A Star Gazer's Manifesto

Sean Flanders

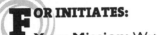**F**OR INITIATES:

Your Mission: Watch the skies.

Fact: Shooting stars are astronaut feces burning up in orbit; every breath of air contains trace amounts of Neil Armstrong's waste. This contamination is the true purpose behind all space programs in the world, as orchestrated by humanity's secret masters, the Woolly Mammoths.

Fact: Astronauts are fed large amounts of Tang during missions to contaminate their fecal matter. Tang + digestion + extreme heat = mind-control drug.

Mind Control Symptoms: Interest in new technologies, use of slang and casual profanity, provocative fashion sense, fondness for loud music.

For Your Protection: There are caves 10 kilometers beneath Bogota, Colombia, that have been undisturbed since the Mammoth-Dinosaur Wars. This air is uncontaminated and can be breathed without infecting you with mind-control-astronaut-waste.

The Enemy: In humanity's earliest days, we warred against the Woolly Mammoths. Cave paintings tell us this, but only the Passerville cave paintings tell us the harsh truth: We lost. For 100,000 years, the Mammoths have enslaved our species without our knowledge. They faked their own extinction, evolving to assume smaller forms, walk on their hind legs, and lose their distinctive trunks. They live among us unnoticed, ruling from the shadows.

Their Plan: Computer keyboards were invented by Mammoth

scientists. Every key on every keyboard in existence contains tiny syringes, too small to be seen or even felt as they pierce your skin, large enough to drain a portion of your bodily fluids with each tap. Your fluids are transmitted to the Mammoths over the Internet for use as a male-enhancement drug.

Fluid Drainage Symptoms: Wrinkling of the skin, graying of the hair, weight gain (particularly in the stomach region), appearance of liver spots.

For Your Protection: Do not use computers or cellular phones. E-mail and instant messaging can be replaced with smoke signals and semaphore.

Identifying Mammoths: To avoid detection, Mammoths must conceal their tusks and shave off their fur on a daily basis. Any person with braces and/or a five o'clock shadow is almost certainly a Mammoth in disguise.

Fact: If you plot all shooting stars visible during an 82-hour period on a star chart, they spell out correspondence between members of the Mammoth High Council in their ancient alphabet, High Mammothlish.

Known Mammoths: Attila the Hun (Councilor on Military Affairs). Grigori Rasputin (Councilor on Religious Affairs). John Wilkes Booth (Councilor on Espionage & Intelligence Affairs). Vlad the Impaler (Councilor on Justice System Affairs). Adolf Hitler (Council Stenographer). Joey Yax of Passerville, Indiana (Supreme Emperor of All Mammothkind and Prophet of the Tusked God).

Necessary Supplies: One telescope, one star chart, one set of semaphore flags, one copy of *Smoke Signals & Semaphore Made Easy* by Rufus Clay, one thermos Colombian cave air, one straw.

Caution: To avoid suspicion, only purchase from stores under the direct protection of the Human Liberation Front; most stores are owned by Wooly-Mammoths-for-the-Enslavement-Of-Humanity, Inc.

Nearest Protected Store: Clay's Hobby Hut in Passerville, Indiana.

FOR ACOLYTES:

Your Mission: Assassinate Joey Yax (Emperor of All Mammothkind, Prophet of the Tusked God, and owner/proprietor of Yax's Arts & Crafts Emporium in Passerville, Indiana).

Weaponry: Use a croquet mallet when attacking Yax. Mammoths are deathly allergic to the wood of croquet trees.

Attack Strategy: Approach Yax while carrying the mallet. Hit him on the head with it. Repeat as necessary.

Caution: Target may be surrounded by especially potent mind-control-astronaut-waste gas. Wear scuba suit to protect yourself.

In Event of Success: Remove Yax's face. Sew his face onto your own. Assume the identity of Joey Yax. Withdraw all money from his bank accounts. Dump the money and his store's inventory off a mountain, or into a particularly deep ravine. Set fire to store. Beware of lunatics in scuba suits swinging croquet mallets.

In Event of Failure: Yax will try to make you breathe astronaut waste and take control of your mind. To prevent this: (1) Remove own lungs. (2) Burn lungs. (3) Await further instructions.

Necessary Supplies: One croquet mallet, one scuba suit with oxygen tank, one sewing kit.

Nearest Protected Store: Clay's Hobby Hut in Passerville, Indiana.

FOR THE ORDAINED:

Your Mission: Distribute manifesto.

On the Shore

Deirdre M. Murphy

Chloe sat at the shoreline, wiggling a bit to relieve the ache from her arthritis. The searing heat from the sun and sand helped the pain, a little, though the tide was coming in, and soon Lake Michigan's icy-cold water would wash upward to where she was sitting.

She stretched a hand out, trailed a finger through the wet sand, idly drawing a house, a snug little cottage, with cheerful flowers—a wave came and washed over the lines, filling them, and washed out again, leaving the sand smooth. So much of life seemed like that these days; all of her work washed away by time. Dishes cleaned became dirty; laundry neatly folded became soiled; even things stored carefully could be washed away by time, like the holiday tablecloth that had become a mouse's nest, and now had holes and stains and mildew where she and her sisters had lovingly embroidered sugarplums (the fairy kind) amid holly and ivy.

If she died today, the sands of time would fill her footprints very quickly; she'd never built anything, never written a great novel or recorded a rock song, never starred in a movie or walked on the moon. Her family would mourn her, of course, but their lives would go on. They would sit around the table and laugh as she and her sisters had laughed while they embroidered that tablecloth. It had been done in secret, while their mother was working, and earned them repeated scoldings for putting off their homework until after dinner. Chloe smiled for a moment, remembering her mother lecturing them and her tears on that Christmas morning.

The tablecloth was old, of course, like Chloe herself. The bright thread had faded, and the linen yellowed. If the mouse had found it when she was young, she might have laughed, made another one. But her fingers were no longer nimble, and her sisters had passed on. Was it time for her to join them? She was strong enough, still, to stand and walk out into the water, to swim out quite a ways. She could let the cold numb her; when she became too tired to swim, if she relaxed, the end would be quick.

She shifted again, leaning hard into the sand with both hands, and stretched her legs out. The left hand was covered by hot, dry sand, and she left it there. Her right hand left a deep imprint in the wet sand. She let the cold water wash over it, achingly cold now, with the arthritis, but still, she felt the familiar thrill of joy from being both hot and cold, wet and dry.

Death had scared her when she was younger. She remembered when her grandmother had pneumonia. It was Christmastime, and the old lady had come to the table too sick to eat much, but not too sick to marvel aloud, as she did every year, complimenting the bright stitches. Chloe had tried to persuade her to remain in bed, but Grandmother said being with the family was better medicine than every pill the doctors prescribed. Chloe was unable to take pleasure in her presents until her grandmother had recovered.

How odd it was to sit here now and contemplate her own death, and to realize the fear had somehow been washed away; to know that when it was time, she could go gently. To wonder, is it time? And to feel...what was it she felt? Contentment? Anticipation? She wasn't sure.

Ah, now that rang true, like it was an answer of sorts.

And then footsteps in the sand, a small form, hugging her from behind. A different answer, but maybe a more important one.

"Gram-mee! Gram-mee!" Chloe's granddaughter, also Chloe, kissed her on the cheek.

"Mom, what are you doing out here?"

"It's my favorite beach. I'm sitting in the sun, enjoying a warm autumn day."

Little Chloe splashed into the water, scooping up sand and

pouring it on her grandmother's feet. Chloe smiled, though the cold made her arches ache.

"You could catch your death out here."

"Oh, I don't think so." Chloe didn't think Karen was ready to actually talk about her death. "Not today, anyway."

"Look, Gram-mee!" Little Chloe held out a muddy hand, "A shell!"

Chloe admired the shell and agreed to keep it safe, while Karen sat down. "Ow! I don't know why you like this beach so much."

"You don't have arthritis."

"And you didn't either, when you brought us here every summer, when I was a kid."

Chloe nodded. It was true. She liked the contrast between the hot sand and the cold water, and always had. "So, what brings you here?"

"I took our tablecloth in to the restorer; you were right, it can't be fixed. But they can save nearly all the embroidery, and all the fairies. I'm going to have each piece framed, so all the cousins can have part of it. And they're going to treat and seal them—if we keep them safe, and out of the sun, Chloe's great-great-grandkids will be able to enjoy them."

Chloe looked at her daughter's shining eyes, and at the shell, so like the shells she'd gathered here when she was tiny. Maybe she did have a legacy to leave, still. She pretended to frown. "You're going to bug me again to record the stories of making that tablecloth, aren't you?"

"I sure am. And I'm not going to take no for an answer."

Chloe smiled, "I'd like that," and was rewarded by a big, warm smile. That warmth helped her aches more than the sunlight.

Smiles and laughter could be so fleeting, she thought. Their warmth made a sharp contrast to the eternal cold of death.

Chloe decided to take her time on death's shore, savoring those contrasts, though it might take years to properly appreciate them. ◉

Detached

Noel Sloboda

I don't want to sound judgmental, but Rodney really should have stayed away from local bars. Everyone in town knew about the pacifism pledge he made back in September 2001, and many wanted to test him.

Boys from the local community college would surround his table, baiting him with remarks about his mother, calling him names. Sometimes they threw bottle caps or peanut shells in his hair, or they tried to trip him when he got up to leave or go to the bathroom. It wasn't raw-mean, but it wasn't exactly lighthearted.

Still, I liked to watch these little scenes play out. Rodney's response to the goads was always the same, studied and collected. Nodding slightly, as though he could discern something sensible in the abuse, he locked his eyes on a spot miles away. He never said anything, just breathed like some Buddhist monk, in through the nose then out, long exhalations from deep in the lungs. He seemed so at peace. The boys inevitably grew bored and moved on. Sometimes, they even left a beer for Rodney, as if to say thanks for the sport.

This routine would have continued for a long time if that woman from the local community college hadn't visited the same bar as Rodney one Thursday night back in November. She was an anthropology professor, I think. She might even have been doing some sort of fieldwork. Right after she entered the bar, she settled at a table near the door and started to write in a little green notebook. She kept at it for about half an hour, scribbling away. Then the boys arrived. They didn't even take off their coats before they started in on Rodney. At first the professor just watched as they practiced their rituals, circling Rodney's table while making faces behind his back. Next they peppered him with little gin-soaked paper balls blown out of straws. He only sat there doing his breathing. It seemed like business as usual.

But all of a sudden, the professor was up. Some line, visible only to her, had been crossed. Pocketing her notebook—and breaching all scientific protocol—she moved in on the boys, waved a blood-red press-on in their faces, and started shouting. I couldn't hear what was said, but I could tell they listened to her. Maybe they knew her from the school, or maybe they were just surprised.

As they stepped away, Rodney stood up. His face was crimson. He placed a hand on the woman's shoulder and shoved her back, hard. "Back off," he barked in a voice that wasn't quite his own, a voice loud enough to be heard across the room. The professor teetered and bumped into the bar.

She seemed like she was about to say something, for a moment. Instead, she plopped down on a barstool, took out her little green notebook, and began to write again. Rodney seemed confused as he dropped back into his seat. His face was still bright and shiny, but now it looked like a leaky balloon left behind at the county fair. His face seemed to fold in on itself as he let out several sharp, little breaths and waved irritably for a waitress to bring him a beer. The professor bobbed her head up and down almost imperceptibly as she continued to write, watching Rodney as he guzzled his beer and then let out an uncomfortable-looking belch. I couldn't actually hear the burp from where I sat, but I thought I could hear that pencil scratching over the clink of glasses and the buzz of the crowd. I wondered what the professor saw and what kind of story she told about her encounter with Rodney.

Although I've kept my eyes open for the professor, I haven't seen her since that night back in November. And I haven't seen Rodney either. He went to county lockup early the next morning, after he was pulled over on his way home.

Nobody knows all the details about what happened—only that he made a dash from his car after being stopped at a sobriety checkpoint. He hadn't had much to drink, maybe two or three beers all night. People speculated that maybe he was worried about the smell from the gin-soaked paper balls he never cleaned out of his hair. Others said he had just bottled up so much anxiety after all those years of silently enduring taunts that he panicked. But I think Rodney probably lost it when the cop started to write in one of those little books cops always have. With that impersonal ledger in his face, Rodney might have decided he didn't want to wait for the conclusion of the official story. So he fled the scene, counting on strong lungs to give him an edge as he made his break. @

The Second Rudolph

Cindy Tomamichel

Even among Christmas aficionados, it's not commonly known that the current Rudolph is really the son of the real Rudolph.

More a clone, in truth. All of them, Prancer, Dancer, and the rest, are all genetically engineered. Magic goes only so far. I have magic, but it was never meant to be the lethal, hammer-of-lightning kind, more the sort that keeps your trousers dry under an avalanche of toddlers. Anyway, I have eight tiny, semi-sentient reindeer that can magically travel fast, are amazingly strong, but which are mean bastards. Rudolph was some sort of genetic mixup. It happens; the elves get a bit carried away sometimes.

I guess my story starts way back in the 1930s, just before the uniform was redesigned by Coca-Cola to red and white. I say uniform, because popular imagination—or the advertising that substitutes for it—influences how I appear. Jolly and fat has been pretty hard on my knees, and don't get me started on the freaking chimneys.

And 1932, well, it was a lean year. Joyless, tired, hungry people do not imagine well, and Christmas, I hate to say, was pretty threadbare. People were starving poor, eating their boots, and they tramped across the country in search of work. It was the first time for the welfare line, and the shame of it ate into people's souls. It ate away their imagination, their jollity, and the happiness that exists in more prosperous times.

Well, I landed on a rooftop, and the wretched thing collapsed. Long winter nights of burning every second beam had made it a very flimsy structure, not even strong enough for eight tiny reindeer, nor for me, despite being thin and dressed in rags that year.

I looked at the people living there eye to eye, the first time I'd done that in a long time. I had landed in their living room, and there must have been twenty camped there, wrapped in newspaper and huddled together for warmth. No chance of invoking the Santa invisibility clause.

I got out as fast as I could, but the crowd was faster. The other reindeer had never liked poor Rudolph, especially since the foggy-night business. Sure, they sucked up to him as a leader, but I knew they still hated him. They blocked the doorway, and the crowd dragged him down.

Poor Rudolph Senior. But he made damn fine sausages. ◉

A Glutton for Punishment

Thomas Pluck

You don't have to take the fight, Terry," he tells me. "He's got sixteen pounds on you."

The guy we trained for dropped out. Stomach flu, he said. Mixed Martial Arts is a rough game. Happens a lot. When they see a record like mine, with losses and wins nearly equal, they think you're a stepping stone. Then they see you at the weigh-in, all chill with dead eyes, and it puts a maggot in their brain. Keeps them up all night, thinking about the four lousy ounces of glove between my eye-cutter knuckles and their face.

"I know you're amped up. But the replacement's a middleweight, walks around at a buck ninety-five. He was on the bike at the gym all night wrapped in trash bags, and he still can't make welterweight. Manager was practically holding him up at the weigh-in."

Mack's a good trainer. He looks in my eyes, though he knows he won't see nothing here. I'm already dialed in. I know he's scared for me, but my record's 15–17 because I never back out.

"C'mon, Tee. Listen to me this time. You can take the champ down, we do this right. It's not worth getting your brains knocked in to make a point."

Your first time in the green room before a fight, I don't care who you are, you're shaking. I threw up the first time. The walk to the cage feels like a mile. The fans cheer or heckle, but all you hear is your heart chugging like a freight train full of steam. Your trainer, corner men, and buddies, they're all behind you. Slapping your shoulders, shouting encouragement. But you walk that empty tunnel alone.

"Sixteen pounds, Terry. You know what else weighs sixteen pounds? A sledgehammer. Don't be a hardhead."

I lost my first three fights. I used to charge like a bull, right into a stiff jab. I gave the blood-hungry dogs in the audience their money's worth. By my fourth fight Mack was sick of it. He kept the towel over his shoulder, ready to throw. I thought he didn't think I had the heart, but when the bell rang, he told me to stop taking a beating and finish the guy. "I know you're better than this," he'd said. "You been taking it for three fights; what you got to prove?"

So I let him see my blood on his gloves, and he got cocky. I chopped his legs with a few shins, took his speed away. When he stepped in, I let the mad dog loose. Dazed him, gave him the fear. He went for a takedown, I sprawled, came up with a knee and felt it connect. Drove him all the way to the cage with punches, until the ref pulled us apart. I felt like a king.

"The champ's people got juice here, they want this guy to bust you up. Don't be stupid, Terry."

I lost two more on the way up, but I never backed out. That got me noticed. I got stupid on the ground once, had to tap or lose my arm for six months. I'm not that stubborn. I tapped, told him "Good fight." He was real technical; he deserved the win. The other loss was bullshit, the ref called it on account of blood when I was working the guy's arm for a Kimura. I got robbed, but it's all part of the game. I'm sure some of the guys I've pounded felt robbed, too.

"Terry. You gotta be smart about this. This guy's like you, but a middleweight. It'll be a bloodbath, and no one will benefit."

I know how hard a middleweight swings. At least this one will have gloves on, and no wedding ring to cut me up with. He won't have hostages to make me weak, girls to slap around the kitchen, a fork to jam in Ma's cheek. And he won't have a bottle to drown in, or a car to wrap around a telephone pole, to rob me of my rematch once I got my size, like my old man had.

"Terry, I thought we got past all this. No one can take it like you can. You gotta think strategic. There's no reason to fight this guy."

Mack knows I don't quit. He also knows if he throws in the towel, I walk. When he took me on, he said no more bar fights. I said fine, but you call a fight and I'm gone. We shook on it. I'd say he's like a father to me, but that word ain't a compliment to me.

"Punch the little bitch, ya fairy," my old man says. Sipping whiskey, making us fight for his entertainment. My sister Annie's hair is tied up, and we wear oven mitts for gloves. Tears on our cheeks, we circle the cold basement floor.

Annie bites her lip and throws a wide hook I can duck, but I don't. It thumps my ear, which rings for days.

"Now hit her back, ya little faggot! Toughen her up!"

Double vision from the water in my eyes, I swing. I go low, but she won't block. Her lip splits open like red roses on a grave. She falls on her butt, dress deflating, buckled shoes giving the concrete a one-two.

I rush the old man and he laughs, letting me get a few in, then I wake up in bed with a goose egg on my eyebrow.

"Terry!" Mack yells, snaps me out of it. "Last chance. Be smart, kid."

I pound my gloved fists together, hop off the table. Mack slaps me on the back.

I walk head first into the crowd's roar. ◉

| 189

Charlie Makes His Way

Peggy McFarland

Charlie left the farm, mostly to escape his heritage. His great-great-great-great-great grandmother's penchant for pigs and rats worked for her, but Charlie wanted to travel and spin his own tale.

After miles of heat and dust, Charlotte's progeny happened upon a remote structure with a tantalizing buzz. He scaled the stone foundation to an opening. He considered this new corner, but the setting sun's rays glinted upon shards, an omen to continue exploring. Broken windows did not make for comfortable homes.

He lowered himself into a subterranean room, then stopped and studied his surroundings. Rustlings, buzzings, and murmurs, along with a pleasant dankness—an enticing place for the kind of prey he needed for survival. Yes, this could be home.

He climbed a table leg to a mahogany surface, clambered over brass handles and descended into a large box. The bottom surface was soft, the walls cushioned. Corners were necessary for the structure he aimed to build. A centipede emerged from between cushions and padding, and nuzzled its way toward a pillow. Flies circled above, occasionally settling upon upholstered buttons. It would be difficult, but if he could build his web, he'd feast. He scurried to the indent and got his gland working. Yes, it would work, he could establish the anchors around those buttons. A hinge and the upper edge were more than suitable. A family of cockroaches convinced him; time to spin.

Charlie spun his silken radii, which spiraled larger and larger connections to his long, taut frame-threads. He labored most of the night, and reinforced sticky threads in anticipation for crawling delicacies.

Abdomen aching, eight eyes bloodshot, eight legs sore, Charlie settled into the center of his web, proud of his handiwork. Outside, the night bugs lullaby faded and the first rooster blared to the world. Background noise to Charlie, his attention remained focused on a moth gnawing its way along the cloth. *Come on... come on...* Charlie thought, anxious to feed.

So intent on his dinner, Charlie ignored the bat that glided in through the broken window. He also ignored the bat's evolving shadow—wings snapping outward into a billowing cape, round body elongating into human form, dark face glowing pale in the predawn shimmer.

Charlie bared his fangs, almost drooled, the moth wing one flap away from the first sticky thread—

—human-like fingers pinched the moth and flung it upwards. The same brazen hand swiped aside Charlie's night-long labors. Charlie scrambled, wedged his body behind a button's pucker and felt the weight of a head settle. Hinges croaked. Charlie was trapped inside blackness.

Charlie collapsed into misery. Without blood, he would expire. Without a web, he couldn't suck blood. Within an airtight box, a web was pointless. Charlie peeked out from his hiding spot. Adding insult to injury, the human-esque blob filled almost every inch of available real estate. Charlie crawled onto the head. If he wasn't so exhausted, he would start a new web anchored in the offender's hair. A touch of his ancestor's moxie crept into his tiny brain. He considered weaving a swear word across the snoring mouth. Scurrying to the lips, he revved up his gland. Empty. Didn't matter, he was too exhausted to finish the task, plus he couldn't spell. All he truly needed was to escape this coffin and find an airier spot to spin a new home.

Charlie stopped, sniffed. Warm blood, puddled in a dimple. Charlie skated across skin, swung over a fang and dove for the blood. The face shook. NO! Charlie refused to be shaken off, not until he sated his hunger. No time to spin and anchor. Charlie latched on the rat's way—he bared his own fangs and chomped into leathery skin.

Sour blood filled his mouth. The taste was horrific! He curled into a ball, slid off the face. The body shifted, crushing Charlie's plump body, pinning a leg, tearing off two others. A blacker black enveloped.

Even with six legs, Charlie could clamber and spring, spin and weave. Penny Zuckerman destroyed every message, but Charlie didn't care—A-HA and STIL HEER weren't exactly poetry. Plus, he'd have to move on soon, taunt a new family. The Zuckermans were becoming pale.

The bathroom light glowed as Penny fumbled through the medicine cabinet for salve. She scratched her angry red welts, screeched when she came upon Charlie putting the finishing touches to U R FUD.

Her father-in-law Homer blamed his spider problem on a niece. Penny would shout NONSENSE, but her husband, her children, and every visitor to the Zuckerman homestead bore the same red welts. Penny grabbed a can of Aqua-Net and screamed, "I GOT HIM!" until the rest of the family rushed out of their bedrooms, tripped over each other, and chased Charlie. Brooms slammed, newspapers smacked, household items crashed.

A lamp crushed his engorged body against the wall. Charlie shrugged it off, scurried into a crack, and settled in until the humans retreated. He could wait; he had eternity.

Almost nightly, they squashed and smashed, swatted and

sprayed, and every night Charlie wove a mocking web. Charlie wondered if this would end.

Maybe a Zuckerman—maybe another family—would look at a genuine baseball bat and get a flash of inspiration. Maybe consider the wood, see a smaller, sharper destiny inside its bludgeon-form. Maybe that victim would think about the lost art of whittling, shave off chunks and refine the slivers until the clumsy sports equipment evolved into a sleek, sharp toothpick. Then that inspired individual might sneak during daylight to the overlooked junk drawer, lift the old shoelaces, push aside dead batteries and toss out useless corks to aim that tiny weapon into the abdomen of Charlie, the vampire-spider.

Charlie chuckled in his safe-crack, sure that inspiration expired with his ancestor and rarely flashed into human brains. Tomorrow he'd crawl out, weave another word-web and scurry across snoring faces to gorge until his belly bloated. ◉

Milk Jug Garden

Sally Clark

Sometimes you wonder why people do the things they do, until you walk a mile in their shoes or dig a season in their gardens.

Shortly after my grandparents died, my husband, my two children, and I moved from a big city to a small town of less than five hundred people. We moved into my grandparents' four-room, un-air-conditioned house where every spring my grandfather planted a vegetable garden on the east side of the house, between the house and the road, barely five feet from a moderately traveled street. After we moved there, I wondered why he hadn't planted his garden behind the house, between the fig trees and the peach orchard, away from the dust and traffic of the road.

Although we were "city folk," my husband, Mike, always enjoyed working a vegetable garden. As soon as the ground warmed, he began weeding and planting in the long, sunny rows my grandfather had tended years before.

One day in early spring, he cut plastic milk jugs in half and placed them around his tiny, new tomato plants to protect them from the sharp wind. As he worked, the owner of the local grocery story, Bunny Weinheimer, slowed his pickup truck and pulled up next to the chicken-wire fence that separated the garden from the road.

Rolling down his window and shaking his head, Bunny asked my husband with mock concern, "Don't you city boys know that's not where milk comes from?"

Never one to be outdone, my husband smiled and replied,

"Well now, Bunny, you see that row of milk jugs over there? Those are male milk jugs. And you see this row over here? These are female milk jugs. I think it's gonna work."

With a broad laugh, Bunny moved his truck on down the road to the store, licking his finger and stroking it down in the air, scoring one for the city boy.

As the days went by, I watched from the kitchen window as other pickup trucks slowed and stopped beside what was now my husband's garden. In this German-heritage community, each truck that stopped seemed to have a beer cooler in the back, and the locals were always happy to offer Mike a cold one. To encourage the friendship, he would stop working and accept a beer, lean on whatever rake or hoe was in his hands, and welcome the conversation. But since he was a light drinker, he usually poured the remaining beer out when they drove away, the tomato plants absorbing most of the fermented suds. I decided that my grandfather had chosen that particular space for his garden to cultivate friends as well as vegetables.

As we settled into the community and the garden began to grow, Mike used mop and broom handles to stake the flourishing tomato plants and tied them with pantyhose to keep them off the ground. They seemed a bit wobblier than usual, but promised a happy crop.

"Well now, I heard you were trying to grow milk, but what are you trying to grow with those pantyhose?" Alvin Dieke asked as he parked by the garden and popped the top of a beer. "You already got you a wife."

"Yeah," Mike replied, "but she needs help around the house, so I planted a few mops and brooms."

"Well, you let me know if that one works," Alvin laughed. "I'll bring you some old overalls and maybe you could grow me some help for the farm."

As spring passed into summer, the garden began to ripen and the fig trees started to put on tiny green buds of fruit that the blue jays found irresistible. Mike tried tying strips of tin foil to the branches, hoping the reflection of the sun and the motion of the wind would help scare the birds away.

"Golly, I wish you'd look at that," Snoogy Jenschke pointed out one day as he leaned out the window of his pickup truck. "I believe you're trying to grow an air conditioner."

"Nah, nothin' that fancy," Mike replied. "But I thought the figs might be in a sweeter mood if they were fanned a little now and then."

When summer was in full swing, we had a glorious crop of tomatoes—red, ripe, and juicy.

"Must be the secret ingredient," Mike said. "I never knew tomatoes drank beer."

"Yes, but I'm disappointed," I replied. "I still don't have a maid or an air conditioner."

Years later, after we had moved into a larger house and raised our children to adulthood, our son moved into my grandparents' small country home. He was a gardener, too, and soon had a busy garden popping with produce. One day I caught him pouring beer on his tomato plants.

"What are you doing?" I asked.

"Watering the tomatoes," he answered.

"With beer?"

"Sure."

"Why on Earth?"

"Because that's what Dad did. I thought you were supposed to feed tomatoes beer," he replied.

"Son," I laughed, "Dad was just trying to grow friends, but I guess it never did the tomatoes any harm." ◉

Proof in the Pudding

Brent Knowles

I win." The voice box gave his voice a shrill quality made almost hollow by the large auditorium, but the students laughed at Tate's introduction anyways. He knew they watched the sensors, on the monitor; the students in the front rows were probably even able to read the results. His numbers were high on the satisfaction scale; he enjoyed making them laugh. Tate had trained himself to understand, at an intuitive level, the underlying data that informed the emotion graphs the students saw. The monitor was for their benefit only, a way of sharing his internal state of mind. It also made him more identifiable, Ilsa, his former grad student and current assistant, insisted.

She was still fussing with his countertop; she hated it when the early arrivals among the students leaned on it, leaving smudgy fingertips on the white granite slab that covered his tank. Few noticed how protective Ilsa was of him, but Tate did. There were two cameras on the countertop, flanking the monitor, and six more in the auditorium. Tate watched her, appreciating the attention. She gave one of the cameras a warm smile and then took her seat. That was the cue to really start the lecture.

"Consciousness. What is it—that was the question I set out to answer. Critics used philosophical diarrhea to dismiss any argument I put forth that might threaten the sanctity of consciousness. And when I responded with essays of my own, they chided me: 'But the matter can only be settled empirically!' They thought it could not be. Settled. But it was. The human mind is a manifestation of form, of function."

Polite applause and a cheer from Reid, who sat in the front row, leaning forward, engaged. Tate liked that Reid had attended all of the lectures, but his pleasure plummeted as the doors to the auditorium opened and Vargas entered. Seven minutes past the hour. The ass.

"Come to concede, Dr. Vargas?" The crowd laughed, though none of the students dared turn their heads for fear that his beady, buried eyes might recognize them. It pleased Tate that his rival had aged so poorly.

"How am I to know that this *thing* is telling the truth?"

Ilsa stood stiffly and said, "*Dr. Richards* has followed standard scientific practice and evaluation," she paused, her eyes meeting Reid's as if for reassurance, "and every step of the process has been monitored by neutral observers." *Thank you, Ilsa!* Tate did not know how he would have survived without her. He'd lost his family for a long time, but never her.

The lower body had been the easiest to remove, though convincing surgeons to do it had taken years, the support of a tech company with deep pockets, and a law team to challenge his wife (now ex-), who felt what Tate was doing was suicide.

"Psychological interviews throughout the process confirmed the consistency and stability of my character," Tate said.

Vargas laughed and replied, "Have you forgotten the breakdown?" Nervous whispers filled the auditorium. *That* was off-limits!

"More evidence to support my point, Dr. Vargas. What human wouldn't have a breakdown after a decapitative transfer?" For seven months and twenty-three days, his head had floated in a nutrient bath with machines stimulating and maintaining his functions while volume imaging was used to construct the schematics for the artificial reconstruction of his brain. He had been deprived of all sensation, swimming alone with his thoughts.

"You're a fool," Vargas said, and that really pissed Tate off, for that had been Vargas's favorite line of attack during their long debates in the teachers' lounge. Ridiculing, patronizing, as if these were Vargas's only methods of defending the 'mystique of the human mind.' But before Tate could speak, the students turned on Vargas. His arguments were old and outdated; any fear of censure was buried beneath the students' indignation.

We know more than this relic!

In the end it had been a biotech solution: pseudoneurons and nanoprocessors meticulously duplicating and replacing the parts of his brain. Originally, Tate had hoped to be transferred to a digital medium, but the technology did not yet exist for that, nor was there a means to replicate the intricate folding of the brain. Instead, his spongy gray-green/bio-digital mental apparatus floated in the large tank beneath the white countertop.

His face reddened with anger, Vargas stormed from the room. Tate, after a quick thank-you, continued the lecture. Question period ran longer than normal, but Tate enjoyed the discussion and interaction. Slowly, as it did every day, the room emptied, leaving only Ilsa.

"A good session," he said, and Ilsa agreed, smiling, but she was working more quickly than normal to clean up, as if in a rush. Tate noticed Reid waiting for her in the doorway.

Oh.

He was glad that Ilsa did not look over at the monitor right then because his emotional data points were scattered in a haphazard relationship. He almost begged her to stay, but she had already lowered his volume. As she left, she waved and then abandoned him to the empty auditorium.

What could he expect? She had a life outside his. Pioneers like Tate had to make sacrifices. To shake paradigms, to change the world.

He allowed himself a half-second of self-pity and then logged onto the Web, scanned his friends' updates and noticed with pleasure that his kids were online. He greeted all three of them at once and their replies came back quickly. They chatted for hours, his numbers trickling back into the happiness range. The whole world was spread out for him, the mental network of his thoughts that he had so painstakingly proven to be the sole product of physicality connected, through the Web, to everyone else. He was still human.

And he *had* won. ◉

The Feminine Mystique

Elizabeth Creith

"One pecan pie, two peach Melba, and a cherry cheesecake. Four coffees?"

"Yes, please," Matt said. "Make mine decaf."

Shirl caught my eye.

"We'll be back in a few," I said, pushing my chair out.

Bill rolled his eyes at me. "Is it illegal to go into the ladies' room one at a time?"

I stuck out my tongue at him.

Once the door had closed behind us, Shirl spread her left hand flat on the mirror, and I spread my right, my little finger just touching hers. In unison we said, "We'll just freshen up!" The mirror filled with violet mist as we lifted our hands away.

We turned around. The wall, golden-brown stone adorned with mosaics, towered twenty feet above us. The porter by the ogival arched entrance bowed deeply.

"Welcome, ladies. It's good to have you back." He sounded like James Earl Jones and looked like Christopher Judge decked out in full *Arabian Nights* gear.

"It's good to be back, Haroun," Shirl said. "Can we make this five minutes?"

"My pleasure, ladies." He selected a small, gold-filigree-mounted sand glass from a table beside him and turned it over. Tiny grains of sand began to fall through the waist of the glass and pile up in the lower half.

"Five minutes it is," he said, and swept his hand toward the arch that lead to the inner rooms.

"Ooooh, that's so good!" Shirl moaned. I turned my head. The young woman working on Shirl had her limp with pleasure. My young man wasn't doing so badly, either. He pushed harder and I gasped.

"Sorry, did that hurt?" he asked, "I will be gentler on that shoulder next time." His hands smoothed my back and he pulled the towel over me. "If you want to dress, I will have your tea made."

The masseuse finished Shirl's foot massage, patted her ankle, and left with the masseur.

"Hey," I poked Shirl gently, "don't fall asleep."

"Sorry—just the bath, and the foot massage. So relaxing."

"I prefer the full-body workover, myself."

"Yeah, I heard. Great if you want your bones cracked. Too much grunting and groaning for me."

"The groaning's the best part. And my back is so happy afterwards. The guys are waiting. We should get dressed."

Shirl yawned. "Let 'em wait. Haroun has it under control. What are they gonna do, come and drag us back?"

I sat up. My clothes, as always, had been cleaned, folded, and set on a small, exquisite table nearby. I found my panties and pulled them on. Reluctantly, Shirl followed suit. Our shoes, beautifully polished, were neatly set under the table. We tidied our hair and walked through to the tearoom. A low table surrounded by cushions held two cups, a pot of steaming jasmine tea, and a platter of sweets.

As we sipped our tea, Aliyah brought her tray of perfumes and touched our wrists and ankles with scent. Shirl chose patchouli; I prefer sandalwood.

"I am expecting some attar of roses next week," Aliyah said.

"We'll definitely be back for that," I said. "It's been a while since you had attar of roses, hasn't it?"

"The crop last year was not good, but this year is better. And the lavender, of course, is always fine. More tea before you leave? Another bit of honey cake?"

Haroun bowed again as we came out. In the sand glass, the last few grains were just trickling through the waist.

"On time as always, ladies," he said. "Do come again."

"Thank you, Haroun," Shirl said, "it's been lovely." We turned to place our hands on the mirror again.

"There, that's much better!" we chorused. In the mirror, Haroun, the door, the baths beyond all disappeared in the violet mist. When the mirror cleared, two tiny toilet stalls were all it reflected beyond ourselves.

The waiter was pouring the coffee as we sat down. The ice cream on my peach Melba was just starting to send vanilla tendrils into the peach juice.

Bill leaned towards me and inhaled.

"Mmmmm," he said, "you smell great."

"And you look wonderful," Matt said, smiling at Shirl. "I guess when you say you're going to freshen up, you really mean it."

"Five minutes in the ladies' room works wonders for a girl," Shirl said, starting on her pecan pie. ◉

Traces of Max

Cathy C. Hall

Margaret Tillman liked things clean. Not just organized. Not just wiped off and swept neatly. Margaret had to have everything sparkling, spic-and-span clean. And she had a closet full of supplies to keep things spotless.

Too bad she married a man who was just the opposite. Bernie Tillman wouldn't care if he and his house were covered in dirt, top to bottom. He'd wear the same underwear for days, given the chance. And he'd pick up anything off the floor and eat it, five-second rule or not. Bernie truly was a slob.

Of course, Margaret didn't know that Bernie was a slob when she married him. He'd kept that little secret to himself. But it wasn't long before Margaret and Bernie had words about their different personal styles regarding cleanliness. A truce of sorts had called when Bernie agreed to let Margaret run things her way. Until Max arrived.

Max was just about the cutest dog that ever walked the face of the Earth. Or so Bernie thought. There was nothing about Max that Bernie didn't love. He loved the funny way Max pranced around the house, wagging his tail. He loved the outdoorsy way Max smelled after a long walk. He loved his long, shaggy fur. And even though Margaret had pitched a mighty fit the day Max showed up, Bernie had held his ground. Max wasn't going anywhere, no way, no how.

Margaret absolutely loathed the dog and the daily mess he made. She hated the muddy prints across her mopped floors.

She hated that smell, like an old, mildewed carpet, when Max came inside after his walk. Most of all, she hated all that fur. Fur in her stove, fur ground into the carpet, fur flying in the air whenever Max shook himself.

So Margaret didn't blink when Max ran out in the street and got sideswiped by a car. She heard the screeching tires over the hum of her vacuum cleaner. She heard Max's whimpers while she sprayed the countertops. She even heard his labored panting as she dusted the bookcase. When she ceased to hear all sound, she opened the front door.

"Oh, Max!" she cried loudly. Anyone within earshot was sure to hear her. She ran to the street, standing over the now dead dog.

"Who would do such a thing?" Margaret wrung her hands. "Who could leave a hurt dog to die in the street?" asked Margaret as the next-door neighbor walked over to the scene playing out on the sidewalk.

Bernie drove up and jumped out of the car. The shock of the tragedy dropped him to his knees where he sobbed, crying like a baby. "Max!" he choked out. "My poor, poor Max!"

A neighbor grabbed a towel and gently wrapped it around the dead dog. Margaret, still wearing her plastic gloves, took the stiff body and carried it to the backyard. She dug a hole in the earth and dropped Max into it, using her shovel to pack the dirt firmly. No more Max. A smile turned the corners of her mouth, just for a moment.

Bernie sat in his recliner, head in hands, moaning. "Poor Max," he sniffled. "How could this happen?"

"Accidents happen, dear," Margaret answered calmly.

"But maybe the vet…" Bernie gave Margaret an accusing look.

"The vet could not have saved the dog, Bernie."

"If only you'd heard…" Bernie agonized.

"Max died the moment he was hit by that car. I'm sure he didn't suffer. Not for one minute."

"I'd hate to think he suffered," said Bernie quietly. He rose slowly from his chair and went to bed.

Margaret woke the next morning, humming. She was thinking about all the cleaning she'd no longer need to do now that Max was gone. No spraying, no mopping, no wiping, no sweeping. What a glorious day!

The staccato click, click, click coming from the kitchen was loud enough for Margaret to hear all the way down the hall.

"That stupid do——," she muttered. Margaret laughed out loud, remembering that Max was no longer her problem. She was humming again as she entered the kitchen.

Was it the clock? Something knocking in the dishwasher? Margaret surveyed the kitchen, looking for the source of the sound. Her eyes circled the room till her glance fell across the floor. Paw prints! She must have missed them when she mopped last night. She sponged the prints twice, just for good measure.

She stepped back in the hall and paused. Was that a ball of fur? She'd just swept the hall a moment ago. She sighed, grabbing the broom, and swept again. Perhaps it would take a few sweeps to rid the house of all traces of Max.

Her cell phone rang, probably Bernie. But she let it ring. There, on the kitchen floor, she spied bits of dog food strewn across the tile, tufts of fur nearby.

Margaret could feel her heart beating a little faster as she grabbed the cleanser. She wiped up the mess and swept the fur into the dustpan. Suddenly, the smell of mildewed carpet overwhelmed her. She inched back towards the hall and peered into the den. She gagged on the offensive odor.

Margaret moved quickly to the bathroom for the air freshener.

More fur lay in piles in all the corners! Now her heart was racing as she ran to the kitchen for the dustpan. She never saw the pale yellow puddle. She slipped wildly, careening headfirst into the corner of the fridge.

As she lay there, drifting into unconsciousness, she thought if she could just reach her phone, she might still have a chance. That's when Margaret saw the ghostly, shaggy-haired dog, his tail wagging. Max held her spotless phone in his mouth. ◉

The Sad Wonderful Life of Ed Fergler

Kathy Allen

et me take you back to 1907 and introduce you to Ed Fergler, the saddest little boy on the planet. He grew up in the arid Mojave Desert and was a sad little boy because none of the other little children would play with him. And even though he was smart and inquisitive, his teacher made him sit outside and listen to the lessons through an open window. Not even dogs or cats would play with poor little Ed. While his family loved him very much, he had to sleep outside in a hammock. As he grew older, girls would not date him, nor would boys let him play baseball or football.

By now you must be thinking that Ed was hideous and looked like Quasimodo or smelled like egg salad farts on a hot August day. But you would be dead wrong. Ed suffered from the worst case of dandruff the world had ever seen. Ed didn't have the luxury of the medications or medical science we have today. So, he thought, perhaps he might find a climate where his dandruff would not be so horrific. In 1926 he boarded a train bound for New York. Unfortunately, by the time the train reached Doowaddle, Utah, his dandruff had overwhelmed the passengers, and he was asked to disembark.

For the next three years Ed was run out of towns, and held and lost many odd jobs, until he finally arrived in New York City. For the first time in young Mr. Fergler's life, he felt hope. Alas, it was the same old story.

Ed was asleep on a bench in Central Park, dreaming that he had no future. On that early morning, Thadius T. Futterblast, while walking his hound, stepped into a great pile of Ed's dandruff. The air was suddenly like a blizzard. Mr. Futterblast exclaimed, "My boy, my boy, you are the answer to my prayers! You and you alone will bring smiles and happiness to millions of children during this Great Depression! Get up! Get up! Hurry now, we mustn't waste a moment. We have so much to do and so little time!"

For the first time in Ed's life, someone was truly happy to meet him. As they raced across town, Ed was told he would have a banker's salary, a beautiful apartment, and all the creature comforts he could desire. Ed, with a quizzled expression asked, "What do I have to do for all of this?"

"Oh my boy, all you'll need to do is keep scratching that wonderful head!"

They arrived at a beautiful brick factory with beveled glass windows, French iron doors, and a sign with polished copper letters which spelled out the name The Howling Blizzard Snow Globe Company.

So from now on each holiday season, when you shake that snow globe, smile and remember you're holding a treasured bit of Ed Fergler. ◉

Return of the Zombie

Michael Penkas

"Oh come on, Mom."

Stephen's mother crossed her arms in that way that let him know there would be no discussion. "Absolutely not. I want you to put everything back in the box. Then go wash your hands. I'm calling the police."

"The police?" He rolled his eyes, not believing that she was making such a big deal over it. "Why?"

"Why?" she shrieked. "Look at that and tell me you don't know what's wrong."

Stephen looked down at the open crate. Inside were the contents of Mama Midnight's Voodoo Zombie-Making Kit. He'd seen the kit advertised in the back of one of his comics. Included was a spell book, thirteen bags of mystic herbs, a cloth mat inscribed with arcane symbols, a small black metal cauldron, and a boy's corpse vacuum-sealed in plastic.

The boy was dark-skinned and looked to be around ten years old, the same age as Stephen. The boy's eyes and lips were shut, but he didn't look as if he were sleeping. He didn't look real at all, almost like a plastic model rather than a real boy. But there were pockets of moisture in the sealed plastic, and one touch revealed soft, yielding flesh.

Stephen said nothing. If his mother would let him use the kit, he'd be able to bring the boy back from the dead, but she was being completely unreasonable. He'd been dreaming of creating a zombie friend for the last six months, three of them saving his paper-route money and another three waiting for the kit to arrive. He'd told his mother about it, and she'd said nothing at the time. He couldn't understand why it was suddenly a problem.

Of course, Stephen's mother had been growing more unreasonable for the past two years. First, she divorced his father, even though he promised to do anything she wanted if they could just stay together. Then she'd moved herself and Stephen to another state, where he didn't know anybody and his father wouldn't even be able to see him on weekends. She told him to try making new friends; but now, when he was about to literally make a friend for himself, she'd stepped in once again.

"Bitch," he muttered under his breath.

"What was that?" He didn't answer, but continued staring at another friend he wouldn't be allowed to keep. "All right, go to your room."

Stephen stomped up the stairs to his lonely bedroom, already making plans for Mama Midnight's Voodoo Doll Kit, which would be arriving in three to four weeks. ◉

One Last Time

Cynthia Rogan

Harry's was crowded for a Thursday night.

Margery stood inside the lobby feeling lucky. She had promised herself *never again*. This time, she was sure to follow through.

Overflowing ashtrays marked the center of each grimy table. Beneath a cloud of cigarette smoke, Sandra and her friends shared a booth, deep in conversation. Above them, on the dark paneled wall, was a thumbtacked poster advertising the Warning's Seattle concert.

Margery took a deep breath and strolled over. "Hi," she said with a nervous smile.

"Hi." Sandra stubbed out her cigarette and scooted in to make room. "There's no way I can go," she said to the blonde and brunette across the table. "I've used all my vacation and I just bought a new car. I really can't afford it."

The blonde giggled. "Mr. Jacobs called me into his office last week. If I miss another day, I'll lose my job." She pulled out a mirror and applied another coat of lipstick. "He said that fiasco with Richard in accounting was the final straw. I'm on probation till September."

The brunette rolled her big blue eyes. "Bobby hates that band. He'd shoot me if I went. But it might be worth it." For a moment, her voice had an ethereal quality. "The lead singer is gorgeous. And I heard he's single again." She blinked and assumed her normal demeanor. "We could drive. It's only seven hours."

The three women seemed to be considering the option. Margery took advantage of their silence. "Sorry I'm so late."

"This is Margery," Sandra said. "I service her copier at Green Grass Bank."

The blonde offered her hand. "I'm Stella. And this," she said, touching the brunette on the shoulder, "is Barb."

"Nice to meet you," Barb said. "We were just complaining. The Warning is in Seattle tomorrow night, and none of us can go."

"That's too bad," Margery said. "My boyfriend's one of their sound techs. I'm sure he could've gotten you backstage passes."

Her gawking booth-mates turned to face her, their eyes sticky with envy.

Margery cocked her head and gave them a sad smile. "I'm sorry. Maybe next time?"

"Yeah," Sandra sighed. "Next time."

"What's his name, again?" Barb asked, stirring her slushy pink drink.

Margery shifted in her chair. "Who? My boyfriend?" She glanced across the room. "Jake."

"No," Barb said. "The lead singer."

"Oh," Margery answered. "Chris Johns. What are you guys drinking tonight?"

"Long Island iced tea," Sandra said, lighting another cigarette. "*They* always order strawberry daiquiris. I suppose you like that girly stuff, too."

Margery stood. "I wonder what single-malt they carry?" She wove through the maze of patrons and tables toward the bar, returning moments later with two fingers of amber liquid in the bottom of a large glass. She sat down and took a tiny sip. "Cragganmore! God, I love this stuff," she exhaled, warmth flowing all the way to her toes. "I can't stay too long. I want to talk to Jake, see how the tour's going. I'm meeting him tomorrow at the Home and Hearth in Seattle."

"Lucky you," Stella whined. "Tomorrow night, we'll be sitting right here while you're hanging out with the Warning." She swirled her daiquiri and made a pouty face.

"I promise not to enjoy it," Margery answered, taking another taste of scotch.

From there, the conversation moved to the area's best nail salons, then migrated to which donuts are hardest on your diet. When the topic became available men, Margery took it as her cue to go. "Thanks for including me tonight," she said, handing a business card to Sandra. "My cell phone number's on the back. Let's do this again. Soon."

Margery was beaming as she left Harry's. She'd been trying to get together with Sandra for six months. Now, she was in. But as she paid the cab driver and unlocked her apartment, she began to worry. *Maybe the Warning thing was too much.* She stopped in front of the hall mirror. "And what if they'd said yes?" she ranted, glaring at her reflection. Those concerns vanished after an hour of mindless television, and she fell into deep sleep.

Friday morning, Margery awoke with the concert on her mind. *What was I thinking?* A knot tightened in her core. Groaning, she fought the urge to stay home. As the workday progressed without a service call from Sandra, Margery's anxiety eased. At six in the evening, just as she pulled her low-cal lasagna from the microwave, her cell phone rang.

"Surprise," Sandra said, sounding a little drunk. "We're here… at the Home and Hearth. What room are you in?"

When Margery could breathe once again, she said, "What?"

"We all decided to do it," Sandra chuckled. "When will we get another chance to meet the Warning?"

"Um." Acid rose in Margery's throat. "But . . . you said you couldn't go. Or I would've—"

"You would've what?" Sandra cut in. "Where are you?"

"Jake and I had an argument," Margery choked. "I'm sorry. I

stayed home."

"Argh! What the—" Sandra hung up.

Margery flopped onto the couch. "Why can't I stop lying?" she sobbed. "Never again," she promised.

For the next hour, she hated herself. Then she decided Sandra didn't deserve her friendship anyway. *I need ice cream.*

Streetlights buzzed and flickered as Margery walked to the corner market. She plucked a half-gallon of Chocolate Death Threat from the freezer and went to the register. When she was second in line, everything stalled.

"I'm sorry, sir," the cashier said to the man in front of her. "You're three-o-one short."

He rummaged through his pockets. "Just forget it."

"No. Wait." Margery handed the clerk a twenty. "I'll get it this time."

The man turned to her. "What'd you do? Win the lottery or somethin'?"

Margery smiled. "As a matter of fact…"

The stranger's eyes flashed and he followed her out into the night. ◉

Coffee with Anna

Ginny Swart

Keep quite still, lady, and you won't be hurt."

The man's voice was low and quite pleasant, and for a moment Kelly thought someone was playing the fool. Perhaps Anna had left the patio door open and one of her friends had come in without knocking.

Then she saw the hard metallic glint of the gun in his hands and froze, almost spilling her coffee as her hand shook. She placed the mug quietly on the little table next to her, hoping he wouldn't notice her movement.

Kelly sank down into the easy chair, crunched herself into a trembling ball, and covered her face in her hands. The thought of an armed robber had always terrified her. Although she felt a guilty stab of shame at her cowardice, she hoped he'd just concentrate on Anna and ignore her, small and scared in the corner of the room.

But Anna, besides being tall, blonde, and glamorous, was also a kung-fu expert and kept telling everyone that girls should learn to take care of themselves in a tight spot. Kelly hoped she could, now that the tight spot was in a corner of the living room with her.

She peered through the cracks between her fingers and watched in admiration as Anna slowly looked up from the coffee she was drinking and snapped, "What do you want?"

How does she stay so cool, wondered Kelly, whose own throat was as dry as a parrot's cage, although the gun wasn't pointing in her direction.

"Don't pretend you don't know, Sweet Lips," sneered the intruder. "Just hand over that diamond necklace."

Diamond necklace? As far as Kelly knew, Anna was strictly a handmade-silver-pendant kind of girl, and she'd never seen her wear expensive bling of any sort.

"Forget it. Mike will be here any minute," said Anna, imperceptibly edging closer. "He'll deal with scum like you."

Mike? She really thought Mike Barnes would be any use?

Mike was Anna's latest and rather unimpressive boyfriend. He'd arrived on the scene some weeks before, wearing horn-rimmed spectacles and talking enthusiastically about computers. Not the usual action man Anna went for. But he was an old college friend apparently, and after he'd taken Anna out to dinner at a smart restaurant she'd come home smiling like someone in love. She'd been out with him several times since then.

Kelly hadn't liked the look of him, and she considered herself something of an expert when it came to judging a man's character. There was something about Mike that put her off completely. Maybe it was his horrible hairstyle, parted in the middle and smoothed down with hair oil, or maybe it was his long earlobes. Long earlobes were a dead giveaway when it came to twisted personalities. And now Anna seemed to think this miserable excuse for a man would miraculously arrive and help her. How? Hit the intruder with a laptop?

"Let's see your face, scum!" Unafraid, Anna switched on the chandelier, immediately bathing the room in bright light. The man with the gun stepped back, muttering a curse.

"Karl Matthews!" exclaimed Anna, shocked. "Is that you? My father's oldest friend?"

Kelly was stunned. Karl had been to the house on many occasions. He looked after Anna's trust fund and appeared totally honest and upright, if a little dull. Now, behind a gun, he looked decidedly menacing.

"Your father's dead and gone, Anna, but before he died he told me about the wall safe behind that big picture. And he told me what was in it."

"You're not touching the contents of that safe," said Anna, defiant. "My mother's jewels are irreplaceable."

A safe? Kelly hadn't known about any safe.

"Open it, Anna, just let him take what he wants," whispered Kelly. "Your life's more important than a few diamonds."

"Give me the key," snarled Karl. "I'll count to five."

"Or what?" said Anna, bending her knees slightly and positioning herself for what Kelly knew would be one of her powerful kung-fu kicks. She's watched her practicing these around the house quite often, kicking over chairs and thumping her foot into the sofa.

"Or he'll kill you, girl!" wept Kelly. "Don't be stupid, give him the key!"

"One," said Karl. "Two. Three…"

Anna leapt across the room and delivered a smashing kick to Karl's jaw, dropping him like a stone. At the same time, the door burst open and Mike stood there, armed with what looked like a missile launcher. He'd lost the horn-rimmed glasses, and his hair now had that spiky, unkempt look that invites women to run their fingers through it.

"What kept you? Asked Anna casually. "Doesn't the FBI teach you to be on time? You're late for our dinner date."

"Thanks for doing the necessary, Anna. We've been after Karl Matthews for weeks. He's wanted for money laundering and fraud."

Two men came in and carried the inert villain away. Mike turned to Anna, kissing her passionately. Kelly's toes curled with pleasure as she watched, smiling. All this time he'd been an undercover agent? Maybe Mike wasn't such a wimp after all.

She listened until the familiar closing theme tune faded, then stood up and yawned. This was nearly the end of the season and if poor *Anna Peterson, P.I.* didn't find happiness with Mike in next week's episode, she'd have to wait until next year.

Kelly picked up her coffee. It was cold, but there was plenty of time to make another cup before the start of *American Idol.* ◉

Fresh Ideas

John P. McCann

Bob Grebble is my section supervisor. He's a bitter loser. Bob eats little cans of stew and reads gun magazines. Management squeezes Bob to increase production while they cut resources. How typical of this place. I figure management wants Bob fired so they can hire a younger supervisor at a lower salary. (Actually, I know this for a fact. Only last week, I overheard Toad Woman discussing Bob's severance with the comptroller.) Bob's loss is my gain. I'm senior enough to inherit his job.

"Hey Prime Time, get your fat ass typing."

"Certainly, Bob. I'll just input the Lindquist report."

(Ha! I'm not inputting jack. I'm writing this.)

"I want that report ASAP. Don't make me write you up again."

"Yes, Bob. Certainly."

Go choke on a can of stew. And who says "ASAP" anymore? I'm tapping away, my keyboard making busy worklike sounds. I'm even humming as if content. Today I'm humming a medley of '80s songs: Cyndi Lauper, Yes, Run-DMC. Now I've settled on the Alan Parsons Project.

Actually, I am content, doing what I do best.

Thinking up fresh ideas.

My name is Walter Gobi. I like terrariums and pipe-organ music. I once downloaded an album featuring the Go-Go's' greatest hits played entirely on a baseball stadium organ. The hair on the back of my neck just stood up thinking about "Beatnik Beach."

Anyway, Bob and the other office goblins here at Fairchild

Industries call me "Prime Time." Once in the break room I boasted my fresh ideas would rocket me to televised fame. They mocked me and flipped tangerines in my direction. Dumb, exploited losers.

Because I'm 37 and live above a Studio City garage, tightly wound dolts like Bob Grebble think I'm a failure. Wrong! Without any lasting relationships, I'm free to be creative. I watch seven hours of TV a night and take extensive notes. And I don't live alone. I have a gecko. I feed him crickets. Each cricket is called "Bob" or "Bobbie" or "Robert K. Grebble." (I felt nervous typing that and looked up to find Bob. He's arguing with Toad Woman, our department head.)

I have lots of ideas, such as using apes to find equipment lost at the bottom of the sea. (Repeated dunkings build up their lung capacity.) But most of my ideas are for TV. Here's a cop show I think will really catch on. Its called *Epoch*. Each week a crime is committed and the police must solve it within a geological epoch. In the foreground, the police could be knocking on doors and asking questions. But behind them we see the city decay and buildings disappear and a forest arise. Then the police turn around, but there's an oak tree where their car used to be because an epoch is passing. I tried Fox, but they said they already had something like it in development.

Breaking news! Here among the fluorescent lights, tiny cubicles and industrial gray carpet of Fairchild Industries, justice has arrived. Toad Woman fired Bob! Bob's shouting wildly, making threats. Toad Woman called Security. Oh, what a plate of goodness, rich as a big Mexican meal with golden beans. I think I'll hum some Eurythmics. A little "Sweet Dreams," if you please. I'll like being section supervisor.

Here's an idea for a reality show entitled, *Yes, I Am a Dentist*. Eight men and women in different cities, without any medical training, impersonate dentists. The one who gets away with it longest wins an electric car.

Whoa! Bit of a scuffle! Bob Grebble got wrestled out the front door by that hick guard, Darrell Something. This is so sweet. Toad Woman is talking on her cell phone, notifying upper management, letting them know how professionally she handled things. What a kiss-ass!

That's what minor power does. So typical. They give the weak a little authority to toss away weaker ones. Only wisdom and compassion, such as mine, can overcome the allure of power. This is reflected in my idea to have combs and pocket-handkerchiefs on every corner that could be taken by people and later exchanged for cleaner ones.

Toad Woman dropped her cell phone and sprinted past me. She runs well for a short, squat woman in platform heels. Darrell Something—Garmenting, that's his name—Darrell Garmenting also bolted by my cubicle, his guard keys jingling like sleigh bells.

Toad Woman and Darrell duck inside the break room and close the door.

Meanwhile, Bob Grebble has reentered the building.

His hand is inside a backpack.

I stop humming.

Bob's bellowing about cold stew; cold stew for cold people. A metaphor? A quip?

I am suddenly frightened. So frightened, I keep typing this, this, this, this……..

I want to be Harry Potter and vanish to that town near Hogwarts where I'll buy sweets for my friends.

Bob and his backpack are here, smelling of WD-40 and gun oil.

"Watcha typing, Prime Time? Better not lie."

"Nothing, Bob," I whisper. "Just a few ideas."

"Keep it up, Gobi."

He walks away, pulling a large semiautomatic pistol from the backpack. I am so relieved I hum "Mr. Roboto" by Styx.

Section supervisor? Couldn't today's events propel me even higher?

I stand and catch Bob's eye, pointing to the break room.

Thousand one, thousand two, thousand three...

Pop! Pop-pop-poppoppoppoppop!

I believe the position of department head just opened.

Of course, Toad Woman was a sloppy, inefficient manager. She should've fired Bob years ago.

Luckily, I possess fresh ideas to tighten things up around here.

I hum a little Tears for Fears: "Everybody Wants to Rule the World." ©

Mysterious Ways

David Steffen

The afterlife was arbitrary, Sam Fichtner decided. There was no Heaven or Hell, only one place. He'd had plenty of time to ponder since he crossed over. The Hereafter was filled with endless rows of clear domes like the one he occupied, a space of infinite size covered with a grid of cake platters. When people died, they were partitioned into one of these domes to spend the rest of eternity.

The domes didn't curve downward out of sight, but upward so that they filled the sky, like the interior of a giant sphere. And

although the distance across the sphere was so immense that he should not have been able to see them clearly, he found that if he concentrated he could see the tiniest of details of the domes at any distance.

God works in mysterious ways, so the expression says, and it is true, no matter what name you give Him. But Sam had never understood just how mysterious His ways really were. Sam had always assumed that nothing awaited after death except oblivion. Many believe the afterlife is bifurcated to reward earthly behavior, like toys promised to a child by parents pretending to believe in Santa Claus, and that made a sense of its own, but both views were dead wrong.

Sam remembered dying in a car accident, so clearly there was an afterlife, but the segmentation of souls into their respective places apparently had nothing to do with morals, and there were millions, maybe billions, of partitions, not just two. Some of the domes appeared to have millions of souls in them, though they somehow never looked more crowded; some had just a few. Domes with just one individual were extremely rare. From his lonely dome, population one, Sam could see into the other domes full of people talking, laughing, fighting, loving. In his dome was a marble pedestal. Upon the pedestal, a sandwich. His favorite breakfast, his own strange invention. Peanut butter and honey, with garlic salt mixed in.

He took the sandwich and nibbled it, not because he was hungry but because he had little else to do. It was sweet and salty and rich, as it always was. Another sandwich would then appear on the pedestal, taking the place of the first one.

Time passed. With nothing to mark the seconds, it could have been days or months or centuries for all he knew.

He had little else to do but watch the other domes. A dome next to his held a huge crowd constantly drinking, talking animatedly, fighting. Other domes were more subdued, but the people were always interacting, finding ways to entertain themselves with their meager belongings, armwrestling, playing cat's cradle with their shoelaces. He ached for any kind of human contact. Even a fistfight sounded appealing, just to feel real again.

Pounding on the glass did nothing but send the whole dome vibrating, and it made his teeth ache. One of the drunks in the next dome saw him and pounded on his dome in return, laughing at the vibrations it caused and prompting his buddies to start a fistfight to get him to stop. Lucky bastard.

He resigned himself to his lonely, dismal fate. Watching the other domes wasn't so bad. It was better than network TV, at least. He could make up stories about the people he was watching and guess what their lives had been like. He watched and sang songs and watched, and paced and watched.

One day, after unknowable eons had passed, he heard a voice

behind him, soft and sweet. "Hello?"

He spun to look, and there she was, brown hair, unfamiliar clothes, deep green eyes. "Hello." Just the presence of another human being sent chills up and down his spine. He thrilled at the novelty of hearing sounds generated by a completely different person.

"Where am I?" she asked.

"I don't know. The afterlife, I guess."

The silence stretched on as she looked around, looking at the domes beyond the glass. He struggled to think of something to say, his social skills having waned considerably. "Would you like a sandwich?" he asked lamely as he took a sandwich and handed it to her.

She lifted a corner of the bread and peeked inside. "My favorite!" As it turned out, it was the last food that each of them had eaten before they died. ◉

Health Tips for Traveler

David W. Goldman

Since the short time from mutual greetings of worlds, many Earther wish to visit the lovely world of the Pooquar peoples. This explainer before so will bring yourselves a voyage most lovely.

WITHIN THE TRANSIT

The travel via cross-continuum portal will be novel to many Earther. Hydration is a paramount for not having the small problems of liver, marrow, blood tubes, and self memory. Also good before your trip is to make fat, especially under the skin. The scrawny traveler should begin preparation many week prior.

Portal going is sudden and then done. But many Earther say after that they think the journey is very very very long and never to stop. Thus is Earther brains supposed bad attuned to one or more of the interim journey continuum. For thus, non-conscious makes for most lovely travel. Means of non-conscious both pharmacological and percussive are on offer by helpful Pooquar portal agents.

AS THE EARLY DAYS

Because subtle differences in physics regulations from what most Earther are parochially accustomed, the traveler is suggested to acclimate in the "horizontal" position until local niceties of unreliant gravity, time-keeping, and atmospheric presence become appreciated. Acclimation such will entertain you for no more than two—or for some traveler, twenty or thirty—"days."

While thus occupied with your appreciation of localness,

helpful Pooquar hostelry staffpersons will provide you with lovely hydration and fat-making nutritionals. For your best healths, stint not on your consumption.

TOURING THE OUT-VICINITY

While you delight yourselves in the appreciation of very-known scenics as the Flowing Up Falls of Nagbaf, the Lesser Half Dark Big Hole, the Plain of Many Breath Sucks, and other such lovely vicissitudes, some attention to health and safeness are ordered.

Firstmost, if urgent advised by helpful Pooquar tour leader, immediately disobey not! Your very life endurance may happen. This is especially as pertains to stepping away from lovely trails, consuming unadvised nutritionals, perusing explainers offered by exiled dissident non-persons, or providing unsolicited refreshment to local fauna/flora/other life-beings.

Next, maintenance your lovely all-enwrapping tourist jumpsuit and coverall always. The presentation of the skin, even a small only piece of the skin, is discouraged for health. This from the fad of local life-beings to reproduce by injecting seed-forms into passing faunas, later to germinate and partake of the subcutaneous lipids in achieving bigness. Thus is best always your jumpsuit and coverall with integrity. (Small note: In the event of any rash of discolor or tendrils from the skin please notify immediately your helpful Pooquar tour leader for the swift extirpation.)

In finality, avoid districts of elevated temperature and humidity. In these grow the grubs of local life-beings, who may exhibit unsolicited hunger of lovely Earther visitor.

After leaving the out-vicinities, you should place the above-spoken biologic factual concerns far from your self memories.

OF THE URBAN JOLLITY

In welcome for subsequent your joyful tours of the out-vicinities, the Pooquar peoples of the citified regions will ply you unsparingly with lovely bring-home curios and appliances and also nutritionals without betterment for taste and skin-fat-making. Enjoy all these with loveliness!

In the cities is no great harm for concern of health. But be full of alert to avoiding speech from irksome disagreers with lovely policies of the governings of the Pooquar peoples. Such talkers of stupid are not amiable with the lovely Earther to travel of yourselves across continuum and returning with lovely Pooquar guests. If approached by busybody of imbecile forebodings regarding Earther traveler, heed not but call loud and with strident!

Many are the friendly Pooquar peoples who find lovely the Earther holding of limb extrusions in greeting. When such friendly Pooquar enjoin with protruding outstretched, please enjoy the removing of any encumbrance glove, sleeve, or trouser legs for sharing in the lovely joint-holding of limb parts. Stay fast so long as to experience lovely sensation of pleasant tingling, warmth, and small piercings. All is joy then for your new friend and yourselves.

In rarity, the Earther of sympathy and astute may note a small beautification of the skin with lovely color or perhaps small out-swellings. When such occurs within urbanity, please request of any apothecary for much cream of obscuration, so as to prevent envy and jealous from other Earther during your remaining voyage and after return.

For your final days of the lovely world of the Pooquar peoples, enjoy many sights and tastings while arranging your self memories for later saying to lovely Earther friends to make soon visits of themselves.

AFTER THE RETURNING

To follow your restore of conscious after portal journey, seek out many Earther friends to say of the joy of your most lovely voyage. Remember also to share the many discount traveling coupons provided to you by helpful Pooquar disembarking agents.

After some days from your voyage, many Earther feel a big sad of missing for the lovely world of the Pooquar peoples. This sad may have big heavy of the limbs, paining in abdomen, inside the head strikes, blood-making from here and there, and other such small emotions.

Best for this sad is to retreat with quickness to special place for to arrange your self memories to loveliness. Your special place should have elevated temperature and humidity. Also it will be most healthful to be a place where nearby pass many lovely Earther.

FOR YOUR LOVELY VOYAGE

From these small Health Tips for Traveler the governings of the Pooquar peoples wish yourselves a voyage for joy always after in your self memory. Also having hopes of long joy for the Pooquar peoples to visit the lovely Earth. ◉

The Loom of Doom Galls Mainly in the Tomb

Barry Ergang

This murder is a fishy business, sir," Detective-Inspector Shad Rowe said. "You've been of great assistance to us in the past when it comes to solving bizarre crimes, and I hope you can help us now."

The Sleuth Extraordinaire, a gaunt hawk-faced man with no official status but possessed of a preternatural faculty for observation and deduction, sat in a chair opposite Rowe's cluttered desk. He puffed complacently on his pipe, adding to the musty atmosphere of the cramped office. "I'm always pleased to help however I can. But you must give me the details. They're essential."

"Of course, sir." Rowe leaned back in his chair and wiped a hand across his plump, ruddy countenance. "The victim is Lady Vera Muckinfutch."

"The parliamentarian's wife?"

"The very one. Her body was discovered early this morning, but the post-mortem indicates she died at approximately half past nine last night. She was strangled."

"Killed at her estate?"

"That's one of the rummiest aspects of the case. You see, sir, her body was found *in a textile manufacturing factory!*"

The Sleuth Extraordinaire's left eyebrow became a quizzical arch. "Had she ever been there before?"

"As far as her husband, friends, and servants are aware," Rowe said, "she had not."

"You said it was one of the peculiar aspects. What are the others?"

"The room in which she was found was locked from the inside. The windows were locked, too, but even if they hadn't been, they'd be unusable. Each is covered on the outside by a metal grate, and none of the grates had been tampered with. Furthermore, it snowed yesterday, as you know, but the snow stopped falling an hour before Lady Muckinfutch was murdered. There were no footprints beneath the windows of the plant. The snow was undisturbed."

"And the roof?"

"Snow undisturbed," said a disconsolate Rowe.

"How was the room entered this morning?"

"The factory manager has a key—the room in question is enormous; it houses the huge looms used in manufacturing." Rowe held up a cautionary hand. "But before you ask, we vetted the manager thoroughly. He not only has no connection to the victim, he has an unshakeable alibi for the time of the murder."

"I see." The Sleuth Extraordinaire drew on his pipe, discovered it had gone out, and took a moment to relight it.

"But that's not all, sir. Now we come to the oddest part of the business. Lady Muckinfutch's body was found a few feet away from one of the looms. This particular loom was canted *as if it had been shaken loose from its foundation,* yet everyone who works in that room swears its position was normal at closing time. An examination showed no obvious signs of tampering, and we certainly had no earthquake in London last night. Every other machine in the room was as it should be."

Rowe paused long enough to emit a heavy sigh, then said, "Frankly, sir, we're baffled, and we're hoping you can make some sense of this."

The Sleuth Extraordinaire contemplated the pipe smoke that curled among the dust motes in the wintry light slanting through the office windows. "Rest assured, Inspector, I shall give it my utmost consideration," he said, then looked toward the ceiling and murmured wryly, "Thank you, Vera Muckinfutch, for presenting me with the world's first rocked loom mystery." ◉

The Souvenir You Most Want

Sue Burke

Miguel smiled at the tourist, a conspicuously glum young man. He had just stepped into the shadow cast by the thatched roof of Miguel's market stall in San José, Costa Rica. The plain merchandise, gray granite spheres, attracted few customers, so Miguel was pleased to see him and picked up a stone the size of a large grapefruit. The tourist looked at it but kept his sunglasses on.

"This," Miguel said, still smiling, "is a true mystery of the jungle, the thing you most want. Many tourists are happy to leave the market with common things like carved wood boxes or T-shirts. But that is not why you have come. You want something special."

The tourist said nothing, but he took off his sunglasses. Miguel heard the young man's troubles in the same way he heard the voices of the stones. But the stones were happy.

Miguel set down the sphere. "You can touch it."

The tourist's fingers twitched, but he did not reach out.

"These stones," Miguel said, "are of the kind the Diquís Indians made for a thousand years. You have seen them in parks or museums, some as tall as you, no? And I will show you one more stone."

He reached into his pocket for a two-thousand-colones bill, a crisp new one he kept for this purpose, and held up the picture on the back of the money: In the Costa Rican jungle, a Diquís sphere too large for one man to lift rested among orchids as a jaguar prowled nearby. It was beautiful, and it might be real.

The young man brushed his fingertips against Miguel's stone as if it might sprout teeth and bite.

"Why did they do it?" Miguel said. "What can the spheres mean that the Indians worked so hard to make them? The Diquís are all dead. We do not know."

The tourist's eyes narrowed. In another moment, he might turn away, and that would be a misfortune, Miguel thought, because the stones could do so much.

"We do not know," Miguel said quickly, "and yet it remains true, whatever they mean. These stones tell me they are the moon, and I think the moon is happier than the sun. The moon changes, she disappears, she moves in day and night, for she is free. You had hopes, but you think the jungle did not change anything for you."

The young man shook his head almost imperceptibly.

"It is not too late," Miguel said.

From across the market, a woman yelled, "John, would you hurry up?" The tourist closed his eyes, sighed and began to put his sunglasses back on, then stopped.

"This stone," Miguel said, "is twelve thousand colones, or fifty American dollars."

The tourist looked at the sphere, his lips moving silently. He stood up straight. He pulled out his wallet and counted out the cash, and Miguel solemnly handed him the stone. As the young man turned to leave, he waned into a quarter, then a crescent, and finally disappeared for a moment before he slowly came back into view. ◉

'Til Death do Us Part

Elaine Isaak

Loyal Wife?'" Elizabeth asked, leaning over his shoulder.

Jeremiah straightened up, his stiff back crackling, and let out a puff of breath that misted the autumn air in front of the tiny cabin. His fist tightened around the grip of his hammer. He should have known. He should have realized it would not be the end, even now. A marriage like theirs could not simply fade away. "Loyal," he echoed. "You promised to wait for me, and here you are. Is it not loyalty?"

Elizabeth folded her arms. Or rather, she tried to, but the winding cloths that wafted around her on an absent breeze tangled her thin hands. "If you say so, darling, but I do think I meant a bit more to you than that. You promised to carve me a bed."

A tear stung Jeremiah's eye, and he scrubbed his face with the back of his hand, then let the hammer fall, and it clattered on the stone before him. "Yes, Elizabeth, yes," he murmured. He sniffled, then sneezed, as the stone dust reached him with its powdery presence.

She stalked back and forth over her grave, her ethereal feet flicking through the fallen leaves and browning grass. October already, and she ought to have had a stone long since. "'Elizabeth Marie Freemont, born 1789, died 1813, the daughter of Edward and Louise Prescott of the Portsmouth Prescotts," she dictated, gesturing toward the stone. "It's a good beginning."

Propped on another stone beside the grave, the fresh slate bore a delicate tree of life with trailing leaves over a winged skull, symbol of the spirit flown away—or, rather, not quite. Beneath the words she recited and the legend "Loyal Wife," he still had a few more inches above where the stone must be set into the ground. "What shall I add, beyond this?" He indicated the new words with his chisel.

Elizabeth paused, translucent cloths rippling and distorting the gravestones and trees beyond her. "Darling, I'm perfectly happy with the opening, especially the reference to my family name, it's perfect, but I feel that 'Loyal Wife' makes me seem… diminished."

The chisel's point tapped the stone. "You want me to begin again."

"Don't I deserve it? Especially after my lonely death in that monstrous house—"

"My parents' house," he added.

She lifted her chin, baring that elegant stretch of her neck he had so admired. "And yet…alone, without my beloved." She pressed a hand to her cheek, and he swore it looked a bit more pale, even granted the translucent nature of a shade.

"I was at war. I was hardly at liberty to—"

"That again!" She jabbed a finger toward him. "As if it were any excuse! I needed you. I was wasting away for the love of you!" Her words echoed into a sob, drawn out upon a wailing breath no mortal throat could produce.

The chisel clunked from his grasp as the letters carved before him wavered. Cold earth seeped through to his knees and his jaw clenched. He rose up, lifted the stone, and tossed it down again upon the heap where it broke into three, the pieces of tree and angel skull tumbling among the hundred other shards, some with trees and some with skulls, some with wings and some with words, her name carved in stark lettering, then in fancy, her birth and death abbreviated then spelled out, her every whim expressed by the strength of his hands.

"Do you know, slate is so old-fashioned. Some of these newer stones—" she gestured toward the other side of the graveyard— "they have such a lovely sheen. Perhaps for the next one—"

"The next one!" he spat. "And the one after? What of the one after that?"

She gave a pretty, ghostly pout. "Perhaps the quarryman can set something aside, just in case."

"Just…" words failed him, as they had on every stone. Jeremiah wet his lips. "Elizabeth, I have lost count of the stones I've made for you! You've been gone seventeen years!"

"You do want me to be happy, darling," she cooed.

Jeremiah faced her, staring through her spectral features, and the truth burst from him. "I don't care! I care not a pence for your happiness!"

"You awful man! How can you speak so to me, your loving wife?"

"You hectoring horror, you dare to speak to me of love? You are dead and I'm alive—"

"There's no need to be cruel," she sniffed.

"Here is love," he snapped, seizing a slab from the pile. "'From her loving husband, Jeremiah.'" He flung it onto her grave and she leapt back with a little cry.

"You've fallen in love with another, haven't you?"

"How can I? I live in a shack at your graveside!" He grabbed another shard and shouted its word, "Devotedly!" and smashed it onto her final resting place. Another: "Faithfully!"

Elizabeth wailed, her pale feet growing more pale as she danced about avoiding the stones.

"In honor! A dear wife! In mourning! In love and mourning!" Stones clattered and crashed. They broke again, the graven skulls fractured, wings reduced to feathers, trees of life to tinder upon the flame of his fury. His hands throbbed, his knuckles scraped as he snatched every shattered stone of seventeen years and heaped them up on top of her. "In honor and love! Honored wife! Beloved wife! Faithful wife!" At every blow, her spirit faded. At every shouted word, her figure faded, until he stood at last, blinking at the empty space before him, one last stone clenched in both shaking hands. He placed it at her head, a great weight dissipating into the promise of autumn's fire. With a sigh, he read its legend: "Rest in peace."

He turned from the grave and finally walked away. ◉

The Corporation

Megan Todd Boone

As David made a sharp right onto Atlantic Avenue in his highly-coveted silver roadster, for the first time in what felt like days, he could see the writing on the wall. It was over.

He was so tired that the end felt a little like sweet relief. But that didn't make it any easier. He had built this empire from the ground up. Every transaction he had made was carefully calculated. Each property that he and his company bought, sold, or seized had been done so with such a considered hand, that, as anyone who dealt with David knew, he always played to win.

How had it come to this, his once expansive conglomerate gone all at once in a takeover that anyone would classify as hostile? He would be left with nothing, not even a small house to his name. Hell, he wouldn't even have a five-dollar bill by the end of the hour. Obviously, he had made some mistakes along the way, but he'd be damned if they'd felt like mistakes at the time. He'd gone with his gut, which was the only piece of advice that he ever remembered his father giving him. He couldn't help but wonder what his father would say if he were with him now.

"Half of life is chance, son. You can't win 'em all."

It seemed to David, that chance counted for a whole lot more than half in this world. Business was nothing more than a fickle and arbitrary construct that could change in an instant.

"Boys! The pizza is here!"

"Finally!" Kyle gave David a cheshire smile. "Loser has to clean up all the pieces. Don't forget any of the houses or hotels or my mom will kill me." ◉

My Wife

Steve Koppman

Everyone loves my wife. Friends bring smiling coffee cups to "the world's best listener." Students scrawl her poignant, incomprehensible thank-you notes. Principals call her godsend. Burly men in barbershops and service stations look reverent, a hint of tears in their eyes, at the mention of her name. Once a guy held her up with a gun. He sent her wallet back via next-day certified mail.

Landlords love her most. They see her through the mob, holding our little girl's hand, glowing with unearthly light. She's already polishing the hardwood. She's telling them they should be charging much more.

She was like that to me before our wedding. She wouldn't let me out of her apartment. She'd look at me and start to cry. I was unready to marry. It seemed the only way to calm her down.

Everyone knows she's the ideal human. What they don't know is: I'm why. What she keeps from the world she saves for me, behind tastefully sealed windows and thick blinds that keep out the light. We never stop fighting. Marriage is war pursued by other means. She never gives in. I'm not made for it. She's hardy as apples.

She used to call what we did making love, and liked it. She almost got evicted from the screaming. Her neighbors formed a committee. Now she calls it being used for sex, and wants no part. One day she kicked me out of the bedroom. Just piled my things in a corner. Two years later in therapy, she agreed that this may have been insensitive. We've always been in therapy. We used to go to dinner and therapy.

In therapy we talk freely. We express our feelings. We try to acknowledge each other's feelings. Then we start screaming. Then it's time to end the hour. We're free to continue working on this at home. We've been featured in several prestigious journal articles. We're the best example of something awful they can't name.

Why won't you listen?

What you're saying's too awful.

You won't hear me.

You want me to agree with you.

I do not.

I can't say what I want.

Say what you want to.

You'll shout me down.

I WILL NOT.

I can't stand the way you think of me.

Why don't you change what you do to me then?

I can't.

Try.

We both wait for the other to walk. Sooner or later she'll saunter off, kid in her arms, music in the background, surrounded by adoring crowds of landlords, principals, grandparents, and other upholders of the community.

We're skating on thin earth, she says, living pretty low on the shoestring, rubbing each others' elbows the wrong way. See the natural lampposts of spring, she says, there's a golden rainbow just around the corner, let's buckle down the hatchets and strike while the lightning is hot. We're still green behind the ears, she says, maybe we need to get out more and chew the flesh.

I had a dream last night. I was running up the highway, my wife driving alongside, pacing me at fifty, sixty, seventy miles an hour, us laughing together, proud of what good shape I'm in, how I can run fast as a car just like I used to when we met. I woke and felt how much part of me loved part of her and wished I had the space and time to figure it out.

Let's try again—I catch her in the kitchen—work things out. I'll do this, you'll do that, let's promise to be better, meet halfway, negotiate, compromise, deal like we never could before, talk to me, please.

She heads for the front door.

It's hopeless, she says, how could we be happy? I've tried so hard so long, she says, I'm used up.

I still want a miracle, I say.

Her little white hand turns the doorknob. There's no miracles, she says, and it falls off in her hand. ◉

The Hamster

ra Laskowski

Louie the hamster escaped from his fish tank cage two days ago, and I can hear him scratching behind the walls in the kitchen after everyone else has gone up to bed. It is a desperate grasping, tiny rodent paws against drywall, and I believe there are only a few more days before we will be unable to tell the kids he's going to turn up.

Earlier tonight after dinner my husband pushed back the stove from the wall, hoping to find the hole where Louie crawled through, but eventually he felt that was enough effort and went up to fall asleep to the Orioles game, leaving me to this guilt. Unlike him, I am afraid if I nod off I will have horrible dreams about the poor little guy meeting spiders and beetles and other lurking insects that built their own cities inside the walls and don't want unexpected tourists. I pull out all of the cleaning bottles we've accumulated under the sink in the past thirteen years—three bottles of Windex, Drano, leather conditioner for an old chair from my husband's bachelor days, Clorox, plant food, dried and twisted sponges, silver polish for a tray my mother bought us when we were married (a tray we never use), baby wipes, crusted superglue, inexplicably one of Samantha's tiny pink flip-flops—and sweep a flashlight to the back panel where the sink pipe disappears through the wall, leaving enough space for a hamster to squeeze in, fall to the floor, and realize too late that he can't clamber back up.

Now I find Samantha's school ruler and Damien's twine-and-popsicle-stick building set and I jury-rig a ramp worthy of Evel Knievel, all the while popping slivers of carrot down that hole as in the news story I read a few months ago where a little girl trapped in a mine survived for days eating scraps of food they were able to send down to her in a sawed-off plastic soda bottle. Louie scratches in rhythm to my breathing, reminding me he is there.

There are several moments after I maneuver the ramp down behind the sink that I believe I have failed; the hamster is chewing on his own escape route and I realize I am counting on the logic of an animal with a brain the size of a pea, and in these moments I think not of the hamster's limitations but of my own, and that I must've failed as a parent, that this shoddy ramp would get a C at best in Mrs. Thomas's arts and crafts, that I shouldn't have let Louie escape, and that I should never, ever be the cause of such a crestfallen look on Damien's face. Because Damien especially is a fragile kid—Samantha is more headstrong, confident, parading on stage in the fourth-grade winter play like a Broadway star with a paper crown—but Damien is more internal, more sensitive and thoughtful (more like me, I think, which comes with its own kind of guilt), and one day the both of them will grow up to be their own people, and I will have to let them scurry into their own dark spaces. And just about that time, the hamster stops eating his safety net and perches just at the bottom; I can feel his weight as he tests the ramp, imagine his pink nose quivering upward, and I hold my breath as we both wait, wondering if we can trust it. ◉

Burn Baby Burn
(The World's Shortest
Vampire Romance)

son Sanford

I'd never given much thought to how different Edward and I were—though I'd had reason enough in the last few months of our whirlwind romance. But now that we were finally on our honeymoon, the differences were becoming ever more evident.

I stared without breathing across the dark room as Edward stood in front of the closed drapes, which blocked the sun from our Acapulco hotel suite. On the wall beside Edward was a tall mirror, which didn't reflect his image. Still, I didn't need a mirror to tell me of the beauty I saw before me. Edward's pale, chiseled body heaved as he smiled at me, and his taut buttocks tensed slightly, running an erotic flash between my thighs.

Edward's gaze was mesmerizing. I felt like prey caught in the eyes of a powerful predator. A predator who could rip me apart if he chose—rip me to pieces and drink my ever-so-vital fluids.

"You know I'd never harm you," Edward said, reaching for my hand. He pulled me close and hugged me to his sweaty body. "Never forget," he added. "I may be a monster, but I love you."

"You're no monster," I said as I kissed him.

"Perhaps. But the vampire leaders won't be happy that we've married."

"Why should they care?"

Edward looked pained, as if I'd asked him to bare his soul for all the world to see. "There are things about my people we never show outsiders."

"Like what? Do you glow in the sunlight or something?" I'd meant the comment only in jest, but Edward looked at me with his ages-old gaze and nodded.

"You are close," he said. "It's supposedly the most intense feeling any vampire can experience."

"Better than sex?" I asked, wicked memories of last night flashing through my mind.

"Far better. Would you like to experience it with me?"

My body shivered in excitement as Edward again pulled me close and we kissed, a kiss that reached into the depths of my soul and caressed my very being. As we kissed, Edward reached out with his free hand and flung open the drapes, revealing the morning sunlight angling across the beach and the waves. In the sunlight, Edward sparkled, light jumping around his body as our kiss grew even more passionate, our emotions crashing like the waves outside our hotel room. I felt like I was on fire.

Except I wasn't on fire—Edward was on fire!

He looked at me in panic as I stepped back. His skin smoked and his sexy hair flared. His wondrous, taut buttocks charred black. "Aw crap," he said. "They always told me we sparkled in the sunlight."

As he said this his body exploded in flames, knocking me against the window. When I stood up, ash rained across the hotel room.

I guess Acapulco wasn't a good choice for a vampire honeymoon. ◉

Succession:
A Facebook Parable

John M. Solensten

Mr. Sammler did not care much for computers and all that tech business. It all seemed too detached from real life—real life in his woody back yard and in the hills down the road. During their infrequent and (he guessed) forced appearances, his grandchildren seemed strangely remote to him as they sat about silently caressing the faces of their I-Pods or whatever they were.

Mrs. Sammler had another notion regarding connecting with the world. She was a very social being and could hardly bear spending an evening in the tired old house they shared. She belonged to things and found her husband's hanging about the yard and woods all alone boring and antisocial. "Who in the world do you talk to out there in the elms?" she asked him when he came back in the house smelling of moss and damp leaves. "Don't you get lonely out there?" she asked, and he would smile a limp smile and reply, "As Thoreau said, 'Being alone is not necesarily being lonely.'"

When he said that, she waved him away, picked up her purse, and hurtled her Lincoln toward a meeting of some sort.

Mr. Sammler's Korean War buddy, Eric Jensen, would often come over when he saw the car whirling away past his front door and down the road past his front yard.

"I wonder how you two manage to keep it together, you're so different," he would say to Mr. Sammler over a Bud.

"But we do," Sammler would reply. "We raised our children, and they have moved on to good lives."

Jensen often reviewed his PSA with Sammler. "The hormone shots keep it just about zero," he would say, and Sammler, knowing the reference, would reply, " I know." He did not like to review his health issues with Jensen, or anyone else for that matter.

"Where does she go when she goes?" Jensen asked. "She always seems to be going somewhere night and day."

"Oh, somewhere to meet with people—sometimes at the capital—political stuff!"

"At seven p.m.?"

"Yes, of course!" Sammler would usually reply, and then turn to work on his Norwegian fly rods or Browning auto.

"I don't know about that," Jensen said. "How old is she now?"

"I told you—sixty-eight." Sammler hated to recite her age. He was twelve years older.

"Sixty-eight," Jensen replied like a dull echo in the room before he finished his Bud and went home to watch the Hunt Channel on TV.

One morning Jensen walked in and saw Irene Sammler's office door was open, revealing a computer, a giant printer, and a scanner.

"My God!" Jensen exlcaimed. "Your wife is a tech, a real tech."

"She's on Facebook," Sammler said. "She's on it for hours."

"A social network."

"She's very social."

"You ever look at it with her?"

"No."

"You should."

"Why?"

"A social network—socializing with all kinds of people."

"All kinds?"

"All kinds."

"Ask her nicely to share it with you so you can learn it."

"I don't get the connection."

"People get quite chummy on these things."

"Oh, for God's sake!"

"Do it. Go on patrol, old buddy. See what's on there and out there!"

"Maybe. By the way, when's Charlie Goodthunder's funeral?"

"Tuesday next. First the WWII vets go, then us Korean vets. A kind of succession, somebody said."

"I suppose," Sammler said. He could see Goodthunder's young face in the obit section of the Times. It was a vague face on a vague uniform.

The very next evening Sammler asked Irene if she would show him how to use Facebook. She seemed irked at first, then looked at Sammler's face for something, touched his hand gently, sat him down where he could see her computer screen and showed him her "friends."

In her photo at the upper left Irene looked quite young and beautiful and ready to face people—all kinds of people...

It all looked quite sweet and chummy to him at first, but then he asked her if there was any pattern in placing photo images.

"I put the ones I know best near the top."

"How's it?"

"I'll show you."

Ah, there on the top were her two sisters, two sorority pals, and—and two men friends from college, Robert Holm and Caesar Lopez—both looking young and joyful, both with not a bit of gray, both (he remembered from her class reunion) widowers, quite rich...

"What about this Holm?" he asked bending down to look more closely.

"Oh, we chat a lot—just college remembrances, et cetera!"

Sammler wondered what the et cetera was.

"It's all kind of harmless and social," she said, patting his hand again and making the computer screen dark.

Dark. Darkly.

No matter. The succession was there. First the WWII vets and then the Korean...

A matter of sequence, succession, time. ⊚

Dr. Lookingood's Extreme Miracle Weight Loss Powder™

Andrea Brill

It's Friday and I'm fat. Well maybe not technically fat, but just kind of fat. Maybe I'm plump. I like to think of myself as curvy—sensual if you will. Truthfully, I have forty-three pounds to lose by next Thursday. My husband, my eat-all-day-and-night-and-still-not-gain-a-pound-husband and I are vacationing in Costa Rica next week.

It is no surprise to me that I need to lose forty-three pounds. It's not as if I woke up one morning and was suddenly forty-three pounds heavier. "Horace, Horace, wake up! I think I ate Sparkey last night!"

In an attempt to lose my flab, I've given it the ugliest name I can think of—Hulga. I thought this might somehow inspire me to misplace her. I apologize in advance to the Hulgas of the world whom I may, and then again, perhaps may not, offend. (It concerns me that Hulga is a fine name for a nice Icelandic woman and yet so fitting for forty-three pounds of lard.)

I've tried ditching Hulga in fitness centers across our nation and even in a few foreign lands. She clings to me like peanut butter and jelly, like coffee and donuts, like bacon and eggs, like… well…you get the point and now understand why my favorite clothing hut is Miss Mable's Fit Ums.

Two weeks ago, while dining at one of my favorite trans-fat-free cafés, I spied a brochure proclaiming the extraordinary reducing powers of Dr. Lookingood's Extreme Miracle Weight Loss Powder™. An omen, I thought, a sign. Why there was even a likeness of Dr. Lookingood himself—white lab coat and all—guaranteeing that I had the potential to shed forty-four pounds in seven days. How fortuitous, I thought, for I only had to lose forty-three!

I promptly called the overseas exchange and express-shipped my metamorphosing elixir.

My panacea was short-lived and soon replaced by propagations of doubt after the oily parcel arrived. Dr. Lookingood's Extreme Miracle Weight Loss Powder™ smelled like feet. I even detected the tell-tale bouquet of sewer gas.

My uncertainties were confirmed upon reading the FAQs.

DR. LOOKINGOOD'S EXTREME MIRACLE WEIGHT LOSS POWDER™ FAQS

Question: Dr. Lookingood,

I have used your weight loss powder for six weeks and have yet to lose any weight. What am I doing wrong?

Answer: Dear Madam,

Stay the course. Your body is in the initial stages of dramatic weight loss. I suggest you immediately order another shipment.

Question: Dr. Lookingood,

I have lost 58 pounds using your product but now have an Elvis-shaped fungus growing on my back. What did I do wrong?

Answer: Dear Madam,

This is a typical response. Your body is only now becoming adjusted to the key ingredients in Dr. Lookingood's Extreme Miracle Weight Loss Powder™. Personally, fungi and Elvis arouse me. Please send photos.

Question: Dr. Lookingood,

Each packet of your weight-loss powder costs $7.99. The recommended dosage for my weight (378 lbs.) is three packets each day. This is my eighth week on your program and I have only lost 12 lbs. I've spent over $1,300.00. What am I doing wrong?

Answer: My Good Lady,

I fear yours is an exceptionally difficult case. I suggest you increase your intake of Dr. Lookingood's Extreme Miracle Weight Loss Powder™ to six packets every day.

Question: Dr. Lookingood,

I have used your weight-loss powder for three weeks and have gained 14 lbs. Help! What am I doing wrong?

Answer: Dear Madam,

Do not be alarmed. You are experiencing fluid retention. Reduce the amount of water used to mix each packet of Dr. Lookingood's Extreme Miracle Weight Loss Powder ™ from the recommended 64 ounces to 48 ounces.

Question: Dr. Lookingood,

Each time I call your help line I am put on hold. The calls cost $4.99 per minute. Do you have a toll-free number?

Answer: Dear Madam,

No.

Neither Hulga nor I have been to Costa Rica. I think we will have a fantastic time. I sure hope she speaks Spanish. @

"Aaaaarrrggh!"

"Aaarrgh?"

"Yeah, but with more of a kind of guttural thing in the middle. Aaaaarrrggh!"

"That's it?"

"Yeah, it's edgy, it's kicky, it's fun."

"What does it mean?"

"Uh…well, you know. 'I want to feast on the flesh of the living!' Or something."

"Jesus. You have two months to come up with a campaign, and you bring me this? Christ, how about 'Flesh! It's fresh!' or 'The human meat I want to eat!' I mean, I'm just spitballing here, just throwing stuff out and it's better than 'Aaargh.'"

"More like 'Aaaaarrrggh!' You know. Kind of raspy."

"That's not the damn point. The point is that some weird moan is not an advertising tagline. 'Warm meat! Let's eat!' Now that is an advertising tag line."

"Tremendous stuff, Rob. Brilliant. We really lost a major talent when they kicked you upstairs. Really, really great. But here's the thing: We don't really know if they understand English anymore. It's pretty much all moans and lurching slowly about. And to be honest…"

"What? Spit it out."

"Well, some of us are wondering if this is a market segment we should really pursue."

"Are you crazy? Are you out of your minds? Have you seen the numbers? I have spreadsheets that will blow your eyes out of the backs of your heads. The Post-Living market is just exploding.

It is the single fastest-growing demographic in the country right now. And you're telling me that you don't want to pursue it?"

"Well, first there is the ethical..."

"Gray area. It's a gray area."

"Yes, the idea of selling human flesh to zombies is something of a gray area ethically. But beyond that, we just don't know very much about them. They don't seem to spend money or engage in leisure activities. They aren't interested in sex at all, and that takes a lot of bullets out of the gun, marketing-wise. Aside from an obvious attraction to eating...uh, the rest of us, we really don't know how to incentivize them. And so far, the focus groups have not gone well. Really, really badly, in fact."

"Bullshit. You're all on a failure safari here. Let me bottom-line it for you: I want this. It's the most exciting emerging market I have ever seen. We are going to own it. We are going to tear it a new asshole. And this team is going to find a way or you're going to find new jobs. Thomson! You've been awfully quiet today. You're the executive on this account. Any sage words? Do you suppose we can get one single pearl of wisdom out of your overpaid mouth?"

"Sorry, Rob. It's just that...well, my wife, uh, transitioned last night..."

"She transitioned! Thomson, that is excellent news!"

"Not really. She, well..."

"No, don't you see? You've got an in! You've got a courtside seat at the hottest game in town. Tremendous. This changes everything. I want you to get inside her head. Find out what makes her tick. Take her apart and put her back together again. Crawl up inside her and root around."

"Well, that's the thing. She, you know, she, she attacked my son, and there was a bit of a struggle, and in the end I had to pin her up against the wall with one of the dining room chairs while my son hit her over and over and over again with a baseball bat. And she just wouldn't quit, and he hit her and hit her, and there were these awful kind of crunching and squishing sounds where he was pulverizing her skull. And her head flattened on the side that he was hitting her but she was still so strong, and I think some of her brains got in my hair and there was this awful stench, this terrible smell of rotting flesh and death and fresh blood. And then the chair shattered and she grabbed my son and was slowly pulling him toward her mouth, except that half of her jaw was gone and she couldn't really get a good bite. And finally I took the leg of the broken chair, it had a sharp end, and I drove it through her shattered skull and held her like that, and she was clawing at me with her rotting fingers, reaching for me, trying to pull me closer and pieces of her flesh were rubbing off on my clothes and my face, and finally my son brought the sledgehammer from the basement and I pinned her there, impaled my wife against the dining room wall with that chair leg, and I think she's still there. I mean, I really, really hope she's still there, because otherwise I don't know where she would be, and that would be so much worse…"

"Is she dead?"

"Oh, God, I hope so. But they kind of start out that way, so it's really hard to tell for sure."

"Damn! That's a missed opportunity. Well, did you get a chance to talk to her? Did she say anything?"

"Just sort of made noises. 'Mmmmurrggh.' Like that."

"Mmmmurgh?"

"Mmmmuuuuugrrgh!"

"Nice. That's actually got a really nice feel to it. Mmmm-uuurrgrgrgrrgh!"

"Mmmmmmmmmuuuuuurggh! That's great, Rob. You have a real talent for getting outside the box."

"Mmmmmuuuuuuuugrgrggh! I love it. It's got energy. It's got kind of a hip-hop feel, doesn't it? Gentlemen, call the art department. They're going to be working late tonight. I feel good about this. We are going to eat this market alive." @

Excuse Me

Scott W. Baker

So tell me, Mr. Flugle," Dr. Kwack said in his best over-the-top Freud impression, "vhat zeems to be the problem?"

"Please," I said from the vinyl chaise, "call me Gary." I never liked my last name. Flugle is such a silly-sounding name. Dr. Kwack probably hadn't noticed.

"Very well, what's the problem, Gary? Is it a mother issue?" Did I mention Freud?

"No," I said reflexively. "It's more complex than that."

"A father issue?"

"Nope."

"Grandmother? Great aunt?"

"Every time I fart, I travel back in time seven seconds."

There, I said it.

A moment of silence passed while the insanity of my words filled the room.

"Doctor?"

"Back in time, you say?"

"Yes."

"When you do what?"

"When I fart."

"I see."

There was another moment, this one more a moment of twitchiness than silence, but the twitching was noiseless.

"And what makes you so sure you travel back in time when you do this?"

"I live the seven seconds preceding a release twice, once before and once right after."

"A release? You mean a fart?"

"Do we have to keep using that word?"

"Apparently. Why seven seconds? Why not a minute or a week?"

"I don't know."

"And when did you start having this delusion, Gary?"

"Which delusion?"

"The time-travel delusion."

"It's not a delusion."

"No? Then why did you come to a psychiatrist?"

I sighed. "Honestly, I have a hard time dealing with the whole thing. Plus I found a coupon in the paper."

"Ah, you have a coupon. Excellent. You can pick up your free snow-cone maker on the way out."

"Thanks."

"It's a very good snow-cone maker, you know. Not one of those cheap ones they sell in toy stores."

"Like I was saying, I have trouble dealing with it."

"What's to have trouble with? You put the ice in the top and it comes out a snow cone. You have to put on the flavor yourself, but that's no harder than pouring something onto another something."

"No, not the snow-cone maker."

"So you'd rather have the toaster?"

"I'd rather talk about my problem."

"With the toaster?"

"With my time-traveling farts!"

Kwack blinked twice. "Of course, the delusion."

"Would you stop calling it that? When I fart, I travel back in time. It really happens; it is not a delusion. I just need some help coping with the issues that stem from inadvertent time travel that begins and ends with the same expulsion of gas from my anus."

"When you put it that way, it all sounds perfectly sane. So tell me, Gary, when did you first notice that your farts made you travel back in time?"

"When I was about three. I was learning to use proper manners at the time."

"What's a twelve-letter word for 'stoppage' starting with I?"

"Interruption? Intermission? Why?"

Kwack glared at his notes for a moment, nodded agreeably, scribbled something down, then stared at me as if he expected me to speak. I looked at him similarly. The expectancy built until we both lost track of what we were expecting.

"Weren't you saying something about manners?" Kwack asked finally.

"Right," I said, since for once he was. "I discovered it when my mother was teaching me to say 'excuse me' when I'd do something impolite—I swear, if you say this is a mother issue I'm going to jam that pencil into your temple."

Kwack lowered his finger which was already in position to punctuate the "Aha!" that was about to leap from his mouth.

"The problem was," I continued, "I said it too early."

"Said what too early?"

"Excuse me."

"You're excused, Gary."

"No, I got in trouble for saying 'excuse me' before I farted instead of after, at least that's how my mother perceived it. From her perspective it would go: 'excuse me'—sound similar to a distressed duck—horrible smell. Often followed by foul language and a spanking—the threat holds double if you touch that one. But I was certain the sequence went distressed duck—'excuse me'—horrible smell. But it was still followed by the language and the spanking."

"And which sequence do you believe?"

I shrugged. "I suppose to an observer outside our space-time continuum, the sequence would be: distressed duck–time warp—'excuse me'—duck catches up, still in a fair amount of distress—horrible smell."

"I disagree," Kwack said. "I think, to someone outside our

space-time continuum, the event would look like the changing room at a lingerie shop."

"Why would my time-travelling fart look like a lingerie shop?"

"The changing room in a lingerie shop."

"Why that?"

"I know if I could step outside our space-time continuum and watch you fart, I wouldn't; I'd go peep into the changing rooms of a lingerie shop. As would most men. And some women. I should know, I'm a psychologist."

"Psychiatrist."

"Whatever." Kwack leaned forward. "Listen, I have a solution for you. Count."

"One, two, three, four, five, six, seven, eight, nine, ten, eleven, twelve, thir..."

"Not now, when you fart. If it's seven seconds you travel back, count to seven, then say excuse me."

"You let me count all the way to twelve and a half? Are you just trying to fill time in this session?"

"I'm trying to find a nine-letter word for euphemism. No, wait, I was trying to help you."

"Euphemism is nine letters. And you haven't helped me a bit."

"Sure I did. With the counting thing. I'm not as bad at this as you think I am."

"You couldn't be."

"Sorry?"

"Not as sorry as I am, Doc. At least that bell means we're out of time."

Kwack did a double take. "The timer didn't ring."

"...five, six, seven."

Ding! "Like I said, time's up Doc. And enjoy that one; it was a doozy." ©

A Great Weight

Joe Ponepinto

It was on the news—perhaps you saw it—my mother saved my life. I was in the yard by the old crooked tree, the one that leans way over, lying under the Toyota doing a brake job, and the jack slipped, and I was crushed by a tire. My breath was pressed out of me, my ribs cracked, my organs were pounded like pieces of veal. Mom came racing out of the house, grabbed the front bumper, screamed, and deadlifted the darn thing off me enough so I could roll out to safety. The TV reporter asked her how she found the strength to lift a car and she said, "It was my boy under there. My boy was in trouble and I had to save him, that's all I know."

I have to admit I felt a little childish having her talk about me like I was a five-year-old or something, but I couldn't say anything because this was her moment and I wanted her to enjoy it.

I was still convalescing at home, looking out the window, when the guy two houses over was working on his car, and his jack gave way and he was pinned under a Dodge. I couldn't do anything in my condition, so I yelled at Mom to call 911. But instead she ran outside in her flowered housecoat. I heard her scream and saw her jerk the car off the ground, just like mine, so he could slide out. The TV crew came out again, and this time she was the lead story on the six o'clock broadcast, and she said, "I saw my neighbor under there, and I knew I had to save him."

When she came back, I asked Mom where she got the strength. She said it just came over her when she saw the man in danger. I couldn't believe she'd have the same emotion for a stranger as she had for me.

A week or so later Mom began spending afternoons out of the house. She'd get all fixed up—hair, makeup, and everything, plus a pair of workman's gloves, which was strange, but she said she had to protect her nails. I assumed she was shopping or visiting friends. I was still laid up and couldn't go with her, not that I would have wanted to.

One day, though, she came home and her jacket was layered with dust. I asked her where she'd been, but she said not to worry about it. Then the six o'clock news came on, and there was Mom again, being interviewed at a construction site. A steel beam had broken from its cable and fallen on one of the workers, and before anyone else could get to him, Mom had lifted a ton of metal, saving his life. I confronted her and she admitted she had been driving around looking for people in peril. How could I berate her for that?

Soon she spent most of the day on the road, cruising by potential trouble spots, places where she thought people might need to have great weights lifted from them, like at the shipyard or at houses with moving vans parked out front. She got herself a new cell phone number and turned it into a hotline for people to call for weighty emergencies. Mom lifted an upright piano off one man, and—I still can hardly believe this one—a city bus off another. She lifted a refrigerator from some guy using only one hand. I stayed at home and saw it all on TV. Each time she was interviewed she said it was just her motherly reaction to seeing people in danger. She got a call from a few talk shows requesting appearances, and from some writer who asked if she'd let him ghostwrite her story.

By this time I should have been recovered from my injuries. I was able to walk and go back to work, but I didn't have my old vitality. I couldn't participate in anything strenuous, not even my Wednesday-night bowling league—I could barely get the ball down the lane. The doctor said there wasn't anything physically wrong with me and suggested I see a psychiatrist to figure it out.

I went for a few sessions but then stopped—the guy kept asking me about my relationship with my father, who had left us when I was small. It was a waste of time. And I still I felt as weak as I thought Mom was before I learned her true strength.

Eventually I quit my job. Mom was making enough from her appearances and endorsements that my income was meaningless. Of course, I didn't get to see her much, with her being on the road either for guest spots or lifesaving, but at least everything was taken care of. But it was boring. I tried to make new friends and meet girls, but people weren't interested in me. They only wanted to know about my famous mother. I stayed home to rest and watched a lot of TV, but I stopped tuning in to the news.

Mom was due back from an appearance in L.A.—*Conan*, I think—and I went to the window when I heard her taxi pull up. She grabbed her suitcases—no need for me to help, obviously—and started walking past the crooked tree. It seemed to be bending even more than usual—looming, malicious, its roots tearing out of the ground, like it was ready to attack. It began to move, to uproot. Mom didn't notice. She kept walking up the path, looking pleased with herself. But I saw it all. She would be crushed under the great weight. Someone would have to save her!

I reached for that pair of workman's gloves. It struck me that I should move out, into my own place. I was beginning to feel stronger already. ©

from the Ashes

...nie Lackey

Fireflies flickered in the trees, and the scent of lighter fluid and seared meat floated on the gentle July breeze. I pulled a wedge of watermelon out of my cooler, plunked down on my porch swing, and tried not to think about Janet. So of course I pictured her on a beach somewhere. With André. The wife-stealing asshole.

The first round of Terry's handcrafted fireworks display screamed into the sky. The fireflies went dark as shimmering, multicolored lights washed over me. I grinned, in spite of everything. Terry always did the best fireworks. There were benefits to living next door to a wizard.

As the next set of fireworks boomed and crackled overhead, a huge phoenix exploded from the tree line, leaving a raging fire in its wake. It screeched a challenge and dove at Terry's house. I swore and grabbed my great ax. Living next to Terry had its drawbacks, too.

Janet would have screamed at me for rushing into the fray. For a moment, I didn't miss her at all.

The phoenix was massive—it loomed in the night sky, half again the size of the biggest dragon I'd ever faced. A swipe from its fiery feathered tail ignited all of Terry's carefully timed fireworks. They shot into the sky and framed the mythic bird like an explosive halo.

I screamed a challenge of my own and charged across the yard. I felt alive for the first time in weeks.

Terry hurled balls of ice at it. One glanced off of a massive wing. He spared me a single glance when I joined him. "Hey, Doug. I appreciate the help."

"What did you do to piss this thing off?" I asked, swinging and missing. For something so huge, it was damn hard to hit. Lucky for me, I'm hard to hit, too.

"I might have stolen some eggshell fragments. For the fireworks."

"Eggshell fragments?" I asked. "It's pissed over fragments?"

Terry shrugged. "Baby phoenixes eat their shells."

"You stole food from its babies?"

"I needed the shells!" Terry shouted. The phoenix snapped at him, and he barely managed to dodge in time. Its beak was longer than the wizard was tall.

"Why?" I asked, swinging again, and scoring a hit this time. Hot blood singed the hair off my arms. "No one's here to watch the show this year but me and you!"

Terry slammed a bolt of ice into the phoenix's left wing. "I wanted to cheer you up!"

I stopped and gaped at him. He'd risked life and limb just because he knew how much I liked his fireworks? "You're crazy."

Huge, burning claws raked down my back. Terry swore. I blacked out.

Waking up in the hospital isn't a new sensation for me. "Janet?" I called, groping for her hand. She's always hated waiting in the hospital.

"She's not here," Terry said. "And she's not coming."

Memory came rushing back, and I let my hand fall. "Right."

"Thanks for your help back there. If you hadn't distracted it, I would have been a goner."

"The phoenix. You didn't kill it, did you?" I thought about its babies, hungry for eggshells, missing their mother.

Terry shook its head. "No. I bribed it. Gave the damn thing half my stock of dragon claws."

I stared out the hospital room window. The view was familiar. "I can't believe she didn't come."

"Not everything rises from the ashes," Terry said. ◉

The Plum Pudding Paradox

Werkheiser

Professor Thomson, I'm here to save your Plum Pudding theory."

J. J. Thomson looked up from his desk. The stranger wore gentleman's clothing, but they were dirty and disheveled. His deep-set gray eyes sparkled with intelligence.

Thomson grunted and dropped his pen into its well. "Who the devil are you? And how did you get into my office at this hour?"

"I'm a friend of Herbert Wells."

"What's he teach? Physics? Chemistry?"

"He's a writer. Perhaps you read his chronicle of my exploits a few years back?"

Thomson looked over his glasses at the untidy man. "Can't say I've had the opportunity."

The stranger shrugged. "Pity. In the future, your Plum Pudding theory—"

"Stop calling it that. The term is a gross oversimplification of my model."

"Oh, dear. Do I have my history wrong? Aren't you the physicist who said that the atom is like a plum pudding?"

Thomson drew back in indignation. "I never uttered such rubbish. My model proposes a diffuse positively charged cloud through which negative corpuscles revolve."

"The point is," the stranger said, his gaunt face hardening with resolve, "next year Lord Rutherford will design an experiment that shows your model to be wrong."

"Ernest Rutherford? My old student? Brilliant man, but no Lord."

"Not yet. He won't get the title until a few years after he

proposes his nuclear model of the atom."

Thomson leveled a sharp gaze at the stranger. "And how would you have knowledge of the future?"

"I've been there. That's what I've been trying to tell you. Rutherford's work will lead to a new theory called quantum mechanics. It's nearly an inverse of your model, a central positive nucleus surrounded by a negatively charged cloud."

Thomson raised his eyebrows. "And Ernest does all this?"

"No, but he gets it started by disproving your model. And you have to stop him."

"Have I, indeed? Young man, even if I believed you, why on Earth would I want to impede scientific progress?"

"You don't know the terrible things I've seen." The stranger's face reflected the pain of his memories. He faltered, staring straight ahead as though seeing the horrors of the future once more.

Thomson looked into the unfortunate man's haunted eyes and his heart softened. "Stiff upper lip, old boy. Tell me what you found."

"It's Rutherford's nucleus! Once you have the nucleus, you can split the nucleus, and then—you've no idea the horrors mankind unleashes—will unleash—with that theory."

"But my good man," Thomson said, "even if I were to dissuade Ernest from his experiment, someone else will find this nucleus."

"Ah, but you're wrong. The new theory that arises in the future, quantum mechanics, says that reality exists only as a set of probabilities, none of which are truly real until observed. So don't you see? The nucleus didn't exist until Rutherford searched for it. Upon his measurement, nature rolled the dice and they came up nucleus. In essence, he created the nucleus by observing it."

Thomson struggled with the odd notion. "So you're saying that if Ernest doesn't do his experiment—"

"Then nature doesn't have to decide on the location of the atom's positive charge, and it can remain diffuse. The Plum Pudding atom becomes reality."

"So all I have to do is write a letter dissuading Ernest, and my model of the atom becomes true." The ghost of a smile played across Thomson's lips.

The stranger's eyes lit up. "Yes! Will you do it?"

"But it's all nonsense." Thomson threw up his arms and laughed. "Of course I shan't write to Ernest with such rubbish."

The stranger grabbed Thomson's arm in a grip like iron. "But you must! Consider this," the man said, and his face became cunning. "Your letter cannot do any harm. If I'm wrong, someone else will discover the nucleus. But if I'm right, you'll have saved the future. You must send that letter!"

"Oh, very well," Thomson conceded. "If it means that much, then I shall send it. He'll likely ignore it anyway."

The man grabbed Thomson's hand and pumped it vigorously. "Thank you, Professor. You won't regret it." With a start, he withdrew his hand. "I must be off. I can use my machine to find out…"

Thomson never heard the end of the sentence, because the man was already out the door and trotting down the hallway. With a wry smile, Thomson watched him retreat from the Cavendish Laboratory. After a long moment, he returned to his desk and pulled a fresh piece of paper from a drawer. He lifted his pen from its well and wrote "Dear Ernest," at the top of the page. He paused, allowing the pen to hover over the page. With a sigh, he reminded himself that he had given his word.

His head snapped up when the door to his office flew open and the stranger burst through. In the few moments he had been gone, his hair had thinned and his eyes had acquired the first hint of crow's feet. "Put down that pen!" he shouted.

"Good sir, did you not moments ago convince me to write this letter?"

In a voice just short of hysterical, the stranger said, "You've no idea the damage mankind will do with your Plum Pudding model!" @

Where Has the Dog Gone?

Lisbeth Mizula

The dog didn't leave a message, a forwarding address, or even a thank-you for all the years he received two meals a day and all the water he could drink. The mongrel simply disappeared. However, he did leave something. It took me two hours, a trip to the drugstore, plugging in a heating pad (made sticky with my own blood from a day-old scratch by an overly-curious squirrel), and a powerful flashlight, but I held forty-seven of Rufus's fleas hostage in a small, covered-glass aquarium that used to house my favorite mold specimen till it started resembling my ex-husband.

I made my face into a cold mask and held the canister of Be Gone! flea powder against the side of their tank. "Where's Rufus?" I asked, searching their miniscule, unblinking eyes. "Or would you prefer, a light *dusting* with…*the powder?*" I shook the unopened canister over their tank menacingly.

I withheld blood and water from the tiny creatures for twenty-four hours. The next day, I tore back over to Sackit's Drugs on my bicycle, got a second canister of Be Gone!, and placed it at the opposite end of their tank. As I suspected, they couldn't casually go about their lives within constant sight of the twin vehicles of murder.

After much hopping around, the fleas arranged themselves on the floor of the tank to form the letter F. It wasn't much, but it was something, and, F is my favorite letter (!). I could work with this.

"He went to Fisk Park," I guessed. The letter went fuzzy, then jerked itself back into sharp F formation.

"Ferdy's Bakery," I guessed. Again they fuzzed up.

"Friendly's Ice Cream," I said. Then, "Fall Park. Feinman's Pond. Fredericka's Frankfurters. Fishy's Fried Sticks." The longer I guessed, the louder my voice grew until I was shouting out the names of every F establishment I could remember.

"Faulkner's Library! The Firefighter's Forum! *The Fruit of the Loom underwear plant!*" My memory used up, I opened the Yellow Pages and called off an hour of Fs. *I even made some up.*

But the fleas sat there, quiet, in formation. Or maybe they were lying down. In the end, in desperation, I uttered the name I'd been hoping to go the rest of my life without hearing again,

"Frankenmeyeramousadamdavidbilltedtom." The name fairly flew off my lips. It was the name of my ex-old man. The fleas jumped over themselves in excitement then spelled out a thin, weary looking, "Yes."

Hearing his name aloud, even though it was just me saying it, I went into a murderous rage. White powder filled the air.

Now, forty-seven small grave markers line my driveway. Most people think it's spilled gravel from the road. ◉

Don't Take This Personally

Richard Holinger

Dear Author,

Thank you for submitting your work to *Calumet Review*. Unfortunately, it does not meet the needs of our magazine. Please do not take this rejection personally. You may be an excellent writer, but this particular piece does not fit our magazine. Good luck in placing your work elsewhere.

We recommend you read our magazine before submitting again. Perhaps you would consider a subscription. Most magazines our size are supported by generous donors, not by the authors who appear there. Don't take this personally, but you have not committed to a subscription, and that makes you a parasite. Apparently you imagine we wait around for your next submission to arrive, every day clawing through hundreds of large envelopes to find your return address so we can rip it open and begin a communal reading of your latest revelation.

If so, think again. Don't take this personally, but when Kara, the graduate assistant, finds our magazine name misspelled (one "l," not two) in your sloppy handwriting, she arranges a conference call among editors. "Are your wills in order?" she queries, "Because you will die laughing."

We do. We die laughing. That's a trope. A hyperbole. You might try using some in your writing. Because—and don't take this personally, but I tell you this because the creative writing instructor in me can't stand someone suffering from a total lack of creativity—your manuscript contains not one memorable phrase, not one original idea, not one stylistic innovation.

In fact, as long as I have your attention (assuming you know how to read), I want to ask you something: Do you own any contemporary fiction, poetry, or nonfiction books? Have you ever opened anything other than *Where's Waldo?* When did you decide on Spark Notes over the texts? Are you aware the *New Yorker* is something more than a Big Apple resident? Do you skim even the cartoon captions? Take my advice: Study them, if for no other reason than to learn to write realistic dialogue, using the vernacular, contractions, and sentence fragments.

Again, don't take this personally, but your plot couldn't keep a vampire awake at a necking party. Deus ex machina went out with Dickens, and your happy ending reflects your fantasies. We look for the crafted manipulation of mimetic particulars to superimpose an aesthetic reality upon subjective and objective perception.

But why are we wasting time telling you all this when you couldn't write anything more convincing than a grocery list? We don't know, especially because you probably stopped reading our rejection letter at "Unfortunately." We inform you of these matters for the same reason we publish our magazine, because we hope someday we'll be read.

So now it's on to the next slush-pile submission. Don't take this personally, but I look forward to whatever crosses my lap after yours because I know more surely than my wife will want to eat out tonight that it will be an improvement.

Sincerely yours,

Malcolm Joy Goodfellow

BTW, don't take this personally, but if you really want our advice, here it is: Stop writing or kill yourself. At the very least, don't send anything else. Anywhere. To anyone. Save postage, paper or, if e-mailing your work, time.

Also, your manuscript arrived without an SASE, so this letter will not be mailed. Naturally, you thought we would accept your work and would call with good news. Don't take this personally, but you're delusional. Seek help. But not here.

One last thing: The editorial staff pooled our resources and came up with the postage to send your submission back to you, as we didn't want it in our shredder. That's hyperbole again, but you will fail to find it funny, much less offensive, because you think so highly of your writing you will think we are in the wrong, which clearly we are not, as we edit a literary magazine and you are dependent upon our judgment for your self-esteem. It's also ironic, but you wouldn't know irony if it swallowed your tongue. You wouldn't know ambiguity if it pole-danced for you.

Hey, look, AUTHOR, just kidding about all the above. We really loved your submission and would like your permission to publish it in our next issue. We just wanted to know if anyone appreciated the work that goes into writing a sympathetic rejection letter enough to read it. Congratulations! Proofs will arrive in about a month for your revision/approval. Thanks again for thinking of us. We invite you to send more work in the future. By the way, your name has been bandied about as an "Advisory Editor." Let us know what you think.

Best wishes,

Mal ©

About the Authors

Eric Cline has sold two stories to *Ellery Queen's Mystery Magazine*. The first, "Two Dwarves and Eight Chained Ourang-Outangs," appeared in the June 2011 issue. He has published three stories in *Every Day Fiction*.

Corey Mertes is an attorney and a former craps dealer and ballroom dance instructor living in North Kansas City, Missouri. This is his third published story.

M. Garrett Bauman's stories have been in *The New York Times, Sierra, Yankee, Utne Reader, Gettysburg Review,* and *Story,* and he won the Great Books fiction contest in 2010.

Joe Novara has written a number of humorous stories for *Mother Earth News, Horse and Rider,* and others. Other works include a young-adult title (*Wa-Tonka,* Pelican Publishing) and a collection of short stories (*From My Side of the Fence,* Syncopated Press). Read more at smashwords.com/profile/view/Joenovara.

Sally Bellerose is the author of *The Girls Club* (Bywater Books, 2011) and was awarded an NEA Fellowship based on an excerpt from it. The manuscript was a finalist for the James Jones Fellowship, the Thomas Wolfe Fiction Prize, and the Bellwether Endowment. Visit sallybellerose.wordpress.com. "Dead Man's Float" was also published in *Boston Literary Magazine* (Winter 2006) and *Sniplits* (Summer 2008).

Andrew S. Williams is a science-fiction writer living in Seattle. His work has appeared in *Jersey Devil Press* and *Every Day Fiction*. His website is offthewrittenpath.com, where he writes about life, writing, travel, and body-painted bike riding.

Merrie Haskell works in a library with over seven million books and finds this to be just about the right number. Her first novel, *The Princess Curse* was published by HarperCollins Children's Books in 2011. "One Million Years B.F.E." first appeared in *Escape Pod* (2006).

Florence Bruce attended Drury College in Springfield, Missouri, and later the University of Memphis. She is a constant reader, especially of American history, and has worked at learning to be a writer all her life.

Christina Delia's writing is featured in the anthologies *Random Acts of Malice: The Best of Happy Woman Magazine*, *In One Year and Out the Other* (Pocket Books), and *Best of Philadelphia Stories: Volume 2*. She resides in New Jersey with her husband, Rob.

Katherine Tomlinson used to be a reporter but discovered she preferred making things up. Her work has appeared in *Astonishing Adventures*, *A Twist of Noir*, *Dark Valentine*, *Eaten Alive*, *Powder Burn Flash*, *ThugLit*, and *Alt-Dead*. Read more at katherinetomlinson.com.

Skye Hillgartner attends Smith College where she studies English literature and costume design. She plays the ukulele, has attended Elf School in Iceland, and calls Ashland, Oregon, home.

Jess Del Balzo's work has been published in various journals and anthologies, most recently *Knocking at the Door: Poems About Approaching the Other*. In 2007 she released an album of spoken word and music called *Lampshade Girls & Other Renegades*. She lives in New York City. "The Newest Edition of Richard Phlattwaire" appeared in *Thieves Jargon* in 2003.

James Sabata obtained an M.A. in creative writing from the University of South Dakota. His short story "The Gossip Hounds of Sherry Town" was published in the Library of the Living Dead's anthology *Malicious Deviance*. His short story "The Hole" is available in Static Motion's *Like Frozen Statues of Flesh*.

Johnny Gunn's story collection *Out of the West: Tales of the American Frontier* (Bottom of the Hill Publishing) was released in December 2010. He recently published a story in *The Storyteller*. He lives with his wife, Patty, two horses, and many chickens about twenty miles south of Reno, Nevada.

Phil Richardson lives in Athens, Ohio. He is married and has two sons; one of them is a clown and one isn't. Two of his stories, "The Joker is Wild" and "Garden Ornamentals," were nominated for the Puschcart Prize. More stories can be found at web.me.com/philrichardson.

Adrian Dorris's short fiction has appeared in *Blackbird*, *Portland Review*, *Slush Pile*, and *subTerrain*. "Precision Forged" was published in *Pindeldyboz* in September 2009.

Siobhan Gallagher graduated from Arizona State University. She lives in the Tucson area.

Charles N. Beecham spent the first half of his life in the Air Force, earning the distinguished Flying Cross in World War II and retiring as a lieutenant colonel. He became an artist, sculptor, and actor, appearing in movies and TV shows such as *D.O.A.*, *Dallas*, and *Walker, Texas Ranger*. His paintings are displayed in museums in Ohio, Oklahoma, and Oregon. He was inducted into the Oklahoma Military Hall of Fame in 2007. "Jiggs and Bob" appears in *Grandpa Remembers*, written for his grandchildren.

Desmond Warzel is the author of two dozen science fiction, fantasy, and horror short stories. He lives in Pennsylvania, and has been a wrestling fan since 1986 and doesn't care who knows it. "Wrestling With Alienation" appeared in *Redstone Science Fiction* (Nov. 2010).

Courtney Walsh's longer, more serious stories have appeared in *Hunger Mountain*, *New Orphic Review*, *The Long Story*, and *Callaloo*. He is a retired English teacher.

William R.D. Wood lives in the Shenandoah Valley. He grew up in the U.S. Navy and now spends his days troubleshooting other people's problems. His fiction is spreading, but his truth will always be found at home: writebrane.blogspot.com. "Headhunter" originally appeared in the October 2009 issue of *Flash Me*.

Robert Perchan's poems, stories, and essays have appeared in scores of literary journals, and in anthologies published by Dell, Black Sparrow, City Lights, and Global City Press. His prose poem novella *Perchan's Chorea: Eros and Exile* (Watermark Press, 1991) was translated into French and published by Quidam Editeur in 2002. His poetry chapbooks *Mythic Instinct Afternoon* and *Overdressed to Kill* won the 2005 Poetry West Chapbook Prize and the 2005 Weldon Kees Award, respectively. "My First Foreign Woman and the Sea" was first published in *Furious Fictions*.

Edward Palumbo holds a B.A. in English from the University of Rhode Island. His fiction, poetry, and comic shorts have appeared in periodicals and anthologies including *The Poet's Page, Rough Places Plain, Tertulia Magazine, Reader's Digest*, and *Ancient Paths*.

Tom J. Lynch is a web developer in Washington, D.C., a graduate student in Illinois, and a father in central Virginia, where he lives because it's hard to parent over the Internet. His previous credits include a poem scrawled on the wall of a bathroom stall, and some flash fiction scribbled on a piece of paper that was later folded into a toy boat, set adrift in storm runoff, and sucked into a sewer.

Kenton K. Yee has placed stories in *Brain Harvest, Word Riot*, and *Bartleby Snopes*. A Ph.D physicist, Ken adores irrealism, quantum mechanics, and orange sorbet. "Irreverisble Dad" previously appeared in *Brain Harvest*, August 2011.

A.J. Sweeney is a freelance writer in Brooklyn. She lives with her husband across the street from a cemetery and a high-voltage ConEd substation and hopes that one day, maybe during a thunderstorm, this combination will result in some really cool zombie action.

Beth Cato is an associate member of the Science Fiction & Fantasy Writers of America. Her recent publications include *Daily Science Fiction, The Pedestal,* and a story in *Mountain Magic: Spellbinding Tales of Appalachia* (Woodland Press). "Brains for Breakfast" was published online as an honorable mention in the 2009 Ligonier Valley Writers' Zombie Flash Fiction Contest.

Eric Pinder is the author of *North to Katahdin, Cat in the Clouds,* and other books about animals and nature. He lives in the middle of moose country in northern New Hampshire. "Clueless" first appeared in the literary journal *Happy* in 1996.

Kirk Nesset is the author of two books of short stories, *Paradise Road* (University of Pittsburgh Press) and *Mr. Agreeable* (Mammoth Books); as well as a book of translations, *Alphabet of the World: Selected Works by Eugenio Montejo* (University of Oklahoma Press); and a nonfiction study, *The Stories of Raymond Carver* (Ohio University Press). He was awarded the Drue Heinz Literature Prize in 2007 and has received a Pushcart Prize and grants from the Pennsylvania Council on the Arts. He teaches creative writing and literature at Allegheny College. "Mr. Agreeable" previously appeared in Nesset's book *Fiction.*

Rebecca Roland's work has appeared in *The Absent Willow Review, Everyday Weirdness,* and in the anthology *Shelter of Daylight.* She lives in New Mexico with her family and works as a physical therapist when she's not writing. "The Secret Ingredient" appeared in the anthology *Shelter of Daylight* in October 2007.

David O'Neal's work has been published in *Sensations, Writers' Forum, The New York Times, The Marin Poets Anthology, Vision, The Eclectic Muse, The Lyric, Red Heart/Black Heart* (anthology), and *The Poetry of Science.*

Over thirty years, **Gail Denham** has had short stories, poetry, essays, news articles, and photos published in many national and international publications.

Marsh Cassady is a former professor of both creative writing and theater. He is the author of 52 published books—fiction, nonfiction, drama, and haiku—and many short pieces. His play *To Ride a Wild Pony* appeared Off-Broadway.

Corey Mesler has been published in numerous journals and anthologies. He has published four novels, two books of short stories, numerous chapbooks, and two full-length poetry collections. He has been nominated for a Pushcart Prize numerous times, and two of his poems have been chosen for Garrison Keillor's Writer's Almanac podcast. He runs a bookstore in Memphis. "Aftermath" appeared originally in *Notes Toward the Story and Other Stories* (Aqueous Books, 2011).

R.W. Morris is a twice-retired (once from the army and once from the post office) senior citizen and sporadic writer with some success at being published over the years. His biggest coup with to CBC Radio in 1980 for "just under a thousand bucks."

Daniel Chacon is the author of three books and is a winner of the American Book Award, the Hudson Prize, and a Christopher Isherwood Foundation Grant.

Nathaniel Lee's fiction has appeared in *Podcastle, Pseudopod,* and *Abyss & Apex*. He lives in North Carolina with his wife and obligatory cats, and he works as a phone monkey to keep them all fed.

Robert Taylor is a freelance writer and novelist with a special interest in the humor and fantasy genres. **Lindsay Gillingham Taylor** is a freelance writer, poet, and musician. The couple resides in Oregon with their kids, dogs, cat, and, yes, goldfish. More at smashwords.com.profile/view/rjt.

Darren Sant is a writer who lives in Hull, U.K. His stories have been published both in print and online. Find him on Twitter @groovydaz39. "Duel" was first published at Flash Fiction Offensive (June 2011) It was also included in Sant's collection *Flashes of Revenge* (Trestle Press, 2011).

Sonia Orin Lyris's stories have been published in *Asimov's SF, Pulphouse, and Expanse,* as well as anthologies *New Legends* (Bear), *Infinite Loop* (Constantine), *Cyberdrams* (Dozois and Williams), *Tapestries and Distant Planes* (HarperPrism), and *The Tomorrow Project* (Intel).

Robert Pepper specializes in bringing dark humor and irony to stories from his own life and his own imagination.

Douglas Hutcheson (twitter.com/DouglasHutch) co-edited *Harvest Hill: 31 Tales of Halloween Horror.* His stories include "The Travellin' Show" in *History Is Dead*, "An Uncloudy Day" in *Groanology 2*, "Do Us Part" in *Ghostology*, "No Brother to Hold Me" in *Hellology*, and "As the Worm Turns" in *Zombies Without Borders*.

Katherine A. Turski lives in North Texas with her husband and clerks by day for a local library. When she has time, she enjoys reading, baking, and watching corny B-movies from the '30s and '40s.

S. Michael Wilson is an author and screenwriter in New Jersey. He is the author of *Performed by Lugosi,* the editor of *Monster Rally*, and a regular contributor to the film review podcast Moviesucktastic. For more, go to smichaelwilson.com.

Daniel Kason graduated from Union College with a B.A. in English. His short story "Dark Creation" appeared in *Indigo Rising*, and he is currently seeking an agent for his science-fiction novel. He is pursuing a Ph.D. in English at the University of Maryland.

S.G. Rogers's short fiction has been published by *Absent Willow Review, ReadShortFiction, Aurora Wolf,* and *Luna Station Quarterly.* Her novel, *The Last Great Wizard of Yden,* was published in 2011 by Astraea Press.

Jason Schossler's first book of poetry, *Mud Cakes,* is available from Bona Fide Books. He is the inaugural recipient of Bona Fide's Melissa Lanitis Gregory Poetry Prize, and the recipient of Reed's Edwin Markham Poetry Prize, two Pushcart Prize nominations, and the 2010 Emerging Writer award from *Grist: The Journal for Writers.* "For Wile E. Coyote, *Apetitius giganticus*" appeared in a slightly different form in *Green Mountains Review.*

Colleen Shea Skaggs loves to write and read good fiction. Her short fiction has appeared in various literary journals. She is an active member of the Idaho Writers League.

Douglas Smith's stories have appeared in over 100 magazines, including *InterZone, Amazing Stories, The Third Alternative, The Mammoth Book of Best New Horror,* and *On Spec,* as well as in anthologies from Penguin/Roc, DAW, and others. He was a John W. Campbell Award finalist for best new writer and has twice won the Aurora Award for best speculative short fiction by a Canadian. "Nothing" appeared in Smith's collection *Chimerascope* (ChiZine Publications, 2010).

K.G. Jewell lives in Austin, Texas. He once rode his bicycle across the country. He stopped counting the flat tires somewhere in Nebraska. His website, which is never updated, is lit.kgjewell.com

Steve Cushman has published a short-story collection, *Fracture City,* and two novels, *Portisville* and *Heart with Joy.* Visit stevecushman.net. "The Boat" previously appeared in *Fracture City.*

Celeste Leibowitz writes articles, short stories, and grant proposals. She lives in Brooklyn with her husband, Bruce, and son, Jason. She works as a development associate with Big Apple Performing Arts. A longer version of "Grandma's Pillbox" appeared in *The Electric Dragon Café*.

Janel Gradowski's work has appeared in *Litsnack, Luna Station Quarterly, Yellow Mama, Long Story Short* and *Every Day Fiction*. Visit her blog: janelsjumble.blogspot.com

Sealey Andrews writes horror and dark fantasy from her home in Seattle. When she's not writing, she can be found reading slush at *Every Day Fiction*, or at the sushi bar down the street from her house. "Kitchen Basics" was originally published online at *Everyday Weirdness* in early 2010.

Sean Flanders received an English/creative writing degree from Minnesota State University, Mankato, and currently lives in Rochester, Minnesota.

Deirdre M. Murphy is a writer of speculative fiction, as well as an artist and musician. You can find her work a number of places online, including tornworld.net and her blog, wyld_dandelyon.livejournal.com

Noel Sloboda lives in Pennsylvania with his wife and several German Shepherd rescues. "Detached" originally appeared in *The Angler*.

Cindy Tomamichel has worked as a geologist and is currently an environmental scientist. She has three finished action-packed novels, one science-fiction, one romance, and one fantasy.

Thomas Pluck lives in New Jersey with his wife, Sarah, and their two feuding cats. He is a systems administrator and trains in mixed martial arts. He is working on his first novel. Find him online at pluckyoutoo.com

Peggy McFarland has worked in radio and restaurants, sometimes simultaneously. Her many years behind a bar have helped her write interesting characters. (If anyone asks, they are all fictional.) She lives in New Hampshire with her family and a neurotic dog. "Charlie Makes His Way" was published as an honorable mention in a content by Silverthought Online.

Sally Clark lives in Fredericksburg, Texas, where she does not garden or eat vegetables. Her poetry and stories have been published in numerous magazines, journals, and anthologies. Find her at sallyclark.info. "Milk Jug Garden" has previously been published in *Green Prints: The Weeder's Digest* (Green Prints, Spring 2006) and under the title "Tomato Libations" in *The Ultimate Gardener* (HCI Publishers, 2009

Brent Knowles is a game designer and author. He has been published in *Neo-Opsis, On Spec,* and *Writers of the Future (Volume 26)*. He can be found at brentknowles.com.

Elizabeth Creith writes fiction and poetry, primarily fantasy. Her work has appeared in *Thema, Odyssey,* and *Silver Blade,* among other publications. Elizabth writes in Northern Ontario, distracted occasionally by her husband, dog, and cat. She blogs at ecreith.wordpress.com.

Cathy C. Hall is a humor writer from the metro Atlanta area. Her essays, articles, and (very) short stories have been published in both adult and children's markets. She's currently working on a (very) funny middle-grade novel or two while planning her takeover of the (writing) world.

Kathy Allen attends high school in Bakersfield, California. Kathy enjoys working with special-needs youth as a peer counselor. She is a voracious reader and also loves writing short stories and creating original pieces of art.

Michael Penkas's short stories have most recently been published in *Shock Totem* and *One Buck Horror.* He also has stories slated to be published in *Lady Churchill's Rosebud Wristlet* and *Black Gate*. "Return of the Zombie" was published online at *Everyday Weirdness* in May 2009.

Cynthia Rogan has seen three of her one-act plays produced and seven of her short works included in various anthologies and periodicals. Her novels *The Courier, Symphony of Dreams,* and *Switch* are forthcoming.

Ginny Swart is a South African writer, living in Cape Town. She's had nearly 300 stories accepted by magazines around the world and four romance novels published by Ulverscroft UK. She'd love to write a serious, meaningful book one day, but every time she sits down to her keyboard, short stories come jumping out. "Coffee With Anna" appeared in *That's Life* (2009).

In addition to writing TV animation on shows such as *Pinky and the Brain* and *Freakazoid!*, **John P. McCann** has penned short stories for various publications, including *Journal of Microliterature* and *Necrotic Tissue*. He is working on his first novel and keeps a modest, cleanly run website at writeenough.blogspot.com. "Fresh Ideas" has been published online at *Every Day Fiction* in May 2010, and in the print anthology *The Best of Every Day Fiction Three* in May 2011.

David Steffen has published short fiction in *Bull Spec, Pseudopod,* and *Brain Harvest,* among others.

David W. Goldman paid off his loans from a well-known Boston trade school by moving to the Pacific Northwest, abandoning his trade, and becoming a software company. He now lives in Portland, Oregon. More of his stories can be found at DavidWGoldman.com. "Health Tips for Traveler" was originally published in *Nature* (Vol. 467 Sept. 2, 2010).

Barry Ergang is the winner of a Derringer Award from the Short Mystery Fiction Society for the best flash-fiction story of 2006. He is a former managing editor of *Futures Mystery Anthology Magazine* and first senior editor at *Mysterical-E*. His fiction, poetry, and nonfiction have appeared in numerous publications, print and electronic. Visit writetrack.yolasite.com. "The Loom of Doom Galls Mainly in the Tomb" was first published in *Crime and Suspense* (November 2006).

Sue Burke was born in Wisconsin and lived briefly in Texas, y'all, before moving to Madrid, Spain. More information at www.sue.burke.name. "The Souvenir You Most Want" won second place in the 2002 PARSEC Science Fiction and Fantasy Short Story Contest and was published in a booklet of winners.

Elaine Isaak is the author of *The Singer's Crown* and sequels *The Eunuch's Heir* and *The Bastard Queen*. A mother of two, Elaine also enjoys rock climbing, weaving, and taiko drumming. Visit elaineisaak.com to read sample chapters and find out why you do not want to be her hero.

Megan Todd Boone is a writer and photographer who lives in Southern Oregon. She cheats at Monopoly.

Steve Koppman has contributed to literary and regional magazines and stories and essays to anthologies. His short plays have been produced Off-Off-Broadway and in California, Chicago, Michigan, and Pennsylvania. His satire, commentary, and journalism have appeared in *The Nation, San Francisco Chronicle, Chicago Tribune*, and *Village Voice*. He lives in Oakland, California. "My Wife" originally appeared in the Spring 1996 issue of *ZYZZYVA*.

Tara Laskowski is from Wilkes-Barre, Pennsylvania, and now lives outside of Washington, D.C. Her short-story manuscript "Black Diamond City" won the Santa Fe Writers Project 2010 Literary Awards Series, and she has stories forthcoming in three anthologies. Visit taralaskowski.com. "The Hamster" was published in the online journal *SmokeLong Quarterly* in March 2009.

Jason Sanford has published a number of stories in the science-fiction magazine *Interzone*, and has won their last three Readers' Polls. *Interzone* recently released a special issue focused on his fiction. His other credits include *Year's Best SF 14, Analog, Intergalactic Medicine Show, Tales of the Unanticipated, Mississippi Review, Pindeldyboz,* and *Diagram*. His short-story collection *Never Never Stories* has been published by a small press. He was a finalist for the 2010 Nebula Award for Best Novella.

John M. Solensten has published four novels, two short story collections, and more than thirty short stories as well as poems and chapbooks. He's a retired university literature teacher. He lives in Burnsville, Minnesota, with his wife, Brenda.

Andrea Brill has spent the last four decades either reading about or thinking about humorous topics. Andrea is also an artist, a philatelist, and an avid photographer. She lives in North Carolina with her husband, son, and lemon beagle, Skip.

John Haggerty is a writer living in San Mateo, California. His work has appeared in *Confrontation, High Desert Journal, Los Angeles Review, Opium Magazine, Santa Monica Review,* and *War, Literature & the Arts*. His short story "Ghost Lights" was a runner-up for the 2007 Bridport Prize, and his story collection was short-listed for the 2011 Scott Prize. "Outside the Box" was first published in *Opium*.

Scott W. Baker's works have appeared in numerous publications, including *Writers of the Future, Volume 26,* and on the podcast Escape Pod. His flash fiction has also been featured in *Every Day Fiction* and *Daily Science Fiction*. A full list of publications is available at scottwbaker.net. A longer version of "Excuse Me" appeared in *The Rejected Quarterly* in 2009.

Joe Ponepinto is the book-review editor for the *Los Angeles Review*. He is the winner of the 2011 Springfed Arts Writers Contest in fiction. His work has been published in a variety of journals. He lives in Michigan with his wife, Dona, and Henry, the coffee-drinking dog.

Jamie Lackey attended James Gunn's Science Fiction Writers Workshop at the Center for the Study of Science Fiction in 2010. His work has appeared in *The Living Dead 2, Bards and Sages Quarterly,* and *The Drabblecat.* He works as an assistant editor on *The Triangulation Annual Anthology Series* and he reads slush for *Clarkesworld.*

Jay Werkheiser lives in eastern Pennsylvania, where he is a mild-mannered chemistry teacher by day and an equally mild-mannered science-fiction writer by night. His stories have appeared in *Analog Science Fiction and Fact* and in *Daily Science Fiction.* "The Plum Pudding Paradox" was previously published by *Daily Science Fiction* (December 2010).

Lisbeth Mizula has been chosen for the Rice University Susanne M. Glasscock School of Continuing Studies, placed in writing contests with The Write Ingredients (The Woodlands, Texas), performed standup in local comedy clubs, and published nonfiction articles in the *Humble Tribune.*

Richard Holinger's work has been nominated for a Pushcart Prize three times. His fiction has appeared in *Witness, Iowa Review, WHR, Other Voices, ACM, Cream City Review, Flyway, Madison Review, Flashquake,* and *Downstate Story.* His creative nonfiction and book reviews have been accepted by *North American Review, Southern Review, Midwest Quarterly, Cimarron Review, Crazyhorse,* and *Northwest Review.* He has a Ph.D in English with a creative writing emphasis and was awarded an Illinois Arts Council Artists Grant for poetry.

Uncle John's Bathroom Reader Classic Series

Find these and other great titles from the Uncle John's Bathroom Reader Classic Series online at www.bathroomreader.com.

Or contact us at:
Bathroom Readers' Institute
P.O. Box 1117
Ashland, OR 97520
(888) 488-4642

The Last Page

FELLOW BATHROOM READERS:
The fight for good bathroom reading should never be taken loosely—
we must do our duty and sit firmly for what we believe in,
even while the rest of the world is taking potshots at us.

We'll be brief. Now that we've proven we're not simply a
flush-in-the-pan, we invite you to take the plunge:
Sit Down and Be Counted! Log on to *www.bathroomreader.com*
and earn a permanent spot on the BRI honor roll!

If you like reading our books...
VISIT THE BRI'S WEBSITE!
www.bathroomreader.com

• VISIT "THE THRONE ROOM"—A GREAT PLACE TO READ!
• RECEIVE OUR IRREGULAR NEWSLETTERS VIA E-MAIL
• ORDER ADDITIONAL *Bathroom Readers*
• FACE US ON FACEBOOK
• TWEET US ON TWITTER
• BLOG US ON OUR BLOG

Go with the Flow...

Well, we're out of space, and when you've gotta go, you've gotta go.
Tanks for all your support. Hope to hear from you soon.
Meanwhile, remember...
Keep on flushin'!